A VISION FROM THE PAST . . .
HOPE FOR THE FUTURE

As the sky burst with shattering explosions and the battlefield in front of him was a wall of flames, Ben Barron suddenly saw a strange, fleeting vision of a bright country morning in his boyhood. A little girl in a blue calico dress that matched her eyes was swinging on a gate as he passed her house. She smiled sweetly.

Strange that such a vision should come to him in the midst of this scene of carnage, with the scorching smell of fire on his garments. Such fantastic thoughts!

"If I ever get through this, I'll find her—even if I must search the world!" he promised himself.

Bantam Books by Grace Livingston Hill
Ask your bookseller for the books you have missed

Grace Livingston Hill

THROUGH
THESE FIRES

*This low-priced Bantam Book
has been completely reset in a type face
designed for easy reading, and was printed
from new plates. It contains the complete
text of the original hard-cover edition.*
NOT ONE WORD HAS BEEN OMITTED.

THROUGH THESE FIRES

*A Bantam Book | published by arrangement with
J. B. Lippincott Company*

*PRINTING HISTORY
Originally published 1943
Bantam edition | October 1976*

ISBN 0-553-02756-5

Published simultaneously in the United States and Canada.

*Bantam Books are published by Bantam Books, Inc. Its trade-
mark, consisting of the words "Bantam Books" and the por-
trayal of a bantam, is registered in the United States Patent
Office and in other countries. Marca Registrada. Bantam
Books, Inc., 666 Fifth Avenue, New York, New York 10019.*

PRINTED IN THE UNITED STATES OF AMERICA

1

THE SUNSET WAS startling that night, bursting angrily
through ominous clouds that had seemed impenetrable
all day, and fairly tearing them to inky tatters, letting
the fire of evening blaze into a terror-stricken world
sodden with grief and bewilderment. Like an indomita-
ble flag of mingled vengeance and hope it pierced the
dome of heaven and waved courageously, a call, a sum-
mons across the thunderous sky and above a drab
discouraged world. It broke the leaden bars and threw
down a challenge to disheartened, straggling fighters
who had been brave that morning when the battle
began, and who had gone on through a day of horror,
seeing their comrades fall about them, facing a cruel
foe, fighting on with failing strength, and in the face of
what seemed hopeless odds.

And then that fire of glory burst through and flung
its challenge, and the leaders seemed to gather courage
from the flaming banner in the sky. Herding their scattered comrades together, they took new heart of hope,
and turning, renewed the warfare more fiercely than
before.

Benedict Barron was one of those discouraged, faint-
ing soldiers who had fought all day, on very little food,
and who more and more was feeling the hopelessness of
what he was doing. What useless wasting of life and
blood for a mere bare strip of land that didn't seem
worth fighting for. And yet he had fought, and would
continue to fight, he knew, as long as there was any
strength left in him.

Mackenzie, their haggard-faced captain, drew them
into a brief huddle and spoke a few low desperate
words, pointing toward that gray distance before them
that looked so barren and worthless, so unworthy of
struggle.

"Do you see that land ahead?" he asked his men, a fierce huskiness in his vibrant voice. "It looks gray and empty to us now, but it is the way to a great wealth of oil wells! It is the way to victory, for one side or the other. Which shall it be? Victory for us, or for our enemies? If the Jerries get those oil wells they undoubtedly will win! We are trying to head them off. Are you game?"

There was a moment of dead silence while his words sank into the tired hearts of the exhausted men, as they looked at their captain's grim determined face, and thrilled with the words he had spoken. Then those tired soldiers took a deep breath and brought forth a cheer, in which Victory echoed down the gray slopes toward the enemy, Victory for freedom! Not for the enemy! And it was Benedict Barron whose voice led the cheer, and beside him his comrade Sam Newlin took it up.

Oil wells down there in the gray darkness, banner of fire in the sky, lighting the way to victory. Yes, they would go, every one of those tired soldiers, even if it meant giving their lives in the effort. It was worth it. Never would they let the enemy have free access to all that oil. This was what they had left their homes and their dear ones to do, and they would do it, even unto death. Victory! On to Victory!

They plunged down toward the dim gray twilight ahead, Ben Barron's face alight from the brightness above him, his lips set, his gaze ahead, new strength pouring through his veins. The weariness of the day was forgotten. A new impetus had come, a reason for winning the victory. Something to be greatly desired, symbolized by that bright arrogant banner of fire above them.

Into the dusk Ben Barron plunged with the flaming banner above, looking toward the land they must take, and hold at all costs. The dying sun in its downward course shot vividly out with its great red eye, bloodshot, daring the men not to falter. Then suddenly it dropped into its deep blue shroud leaving only shreds of ragged gold as a hint of the glory that might be won. Afterward darkness! For even the edges of glory-gold were blotted out in the darkest night those men had ever known.

A great droning arose in the sky behind and it seemed to Ben Barron that he was alone, with all the responsibility resting on him. There were oncoming planes, an ominous determined sound, their twinkling lights starring the heavens as if they had a right to be there, reminding one of Satanic entrances: "I will be like the Most High"—the arrogance of Lucifer.

The men groaned in spirit, and thrust forward. But suddenly came a sound of menace, and like bright wicked stars, fire dropped from the skies, blazing up in wide fierce waves of flame sweeping before them, filling all the place through which they were supposed to pass.

Bewildered, they looked to their captain, hesitated an instant, till they heard his determined husky voice ring out definitely:

"Press on!"

"Fire!" they breathed in a united voice of anguish.

"Press on!" came Captain Mackenzie's answer swiftly. "You *must* go through these fires! This land must be held *at all costs!"*

Afterwards it came to Ben to wonder why? Oh, he knew the answer, the oil wells must be held. The enemy must not take them. But why did fires have to come and obstruct the way? It was hard enough before the fires came. How were they to go. through fire? Where was God? Had He forgotten them? Why did He allow this fire to come? It seemed a strange thought to come to Ben Barron as he crept stealthily through the shadows into the realm of light where the enemies' guns could so easily be trained upon them. But at the time he was occupied with accomplishing this journey toward the fire, with the firm intention of going through it. There was a job to be done on the other side of this wall of fire and he must do it!

And then there was the wall of fire, just ahead!

"Here she comes!" yelled Sam. "Let's go!"

Great tongues of flame, roaring and hissing, and overhead falling flames! It seemed the end. And yet

Ben knew he must go through. Even if he died doing it, he must go. Those oil wells must be held. The Jerries must not get them. Perhaps just his effort was needed for the victory. Perhaps if he failed others would fail also. The circle of defenders must not be broken! The strength of a chain was in its weakest link. He must not be that weakest link. His place in the formation must be steady, held to the end!

How hot the flames! How far that heat reached! He had to turn his face away from the scorch to rest his eyes, or they would not be able to see to go on. And the flaming fields ahead would soon burn over. He must creep through as soon as they were bearable. He must not be turned back nor halted by mere hot earth. It was night, and the wind was cold. They would soon cool off enough for him to go on.

These thoughts raced through his fevered brain, as he crept forward, seeing ahead now beyond those dancing fires, the dark forms of other enemies their guns surely aimed! He could hear the reverberations of their shots as they whistled past him. He had to creep along close to the ground to dodge those bullets.

It seemed an eternity that he was creeping on in the firelit darkness, pausing when more fire came down from above, to hide behind a chance rock, or a group of stark trees that had not been consumed, gasping in the interval to catch a breath that seemed to escape from his control.

At times there came the captain's voice, in odd places, at tense intervals, almost like the voice of God, and Ben's overweary mind sometimes confused the two, so that he became convinced that it was God who was leading them on, speaking to them out of the fire.

Perhaps it was hunger that made his head feel so light, but he had not thought of food. There were pellets in his wallet that he could take for this, but he was too tired to make the effort to reach them. If only he might close his eyes and sleep for a moment! But there was the fire, and the order was heard again, "Forward!"

They must all pass through. There was no time to wait for the blistering ground to cool. They must pass through quickly. They had been taught their manner of procedure. Through this fire—and then the enemy beyond! There would be bullets. He could hear one singing close now! There would be another close behind that. Their spacing was easy to judge.

There! There it came. A stinging pain pierced his shoulder, and burned down his left arm like liquid fire. But he must not notice it. He was one of a unit. If any in their battalion failed, then others might fail. They *must not* fail! That rich oil country must be held at any cost. The captain's words seemed to be still on the air, close to his ear, though it was a long time since they had been spoken. But they rang in his heart clearly as at first. "Forward! *Through these fires*."

There came a moment with a clear ringing word of command when they struggled up to their feet and actually plunged through. The scorching heat! The roaring of the flames! The noise of planes overhead! The falling of more fire! All was confusion! Could they win through?

Afterward there was fierce fighting. No time to think of wounds and the pain stinging down his arm. It was only a part of his job. He had to hold those oil wells!

The night was long and there were more fires to cross. More fighting, the ground strewed with wounded and dying, nothing that one would want to remember if one ever got home. Home! Peace! Was there still such a place as home? Was there any peace *any*where?

A strange fleeting vision of a quiet morning, he on his way somewhere importantly, a young school boy in a world that still held joy. A little girl in a blue calico dress that matched her eyes, swinging on a gate as he passed. Just a little *little* girl, swinging on a gate, and giving him a shy smile as he passed. He didn't know the little girl. The family were newcomers in the neighborhood, but he smiled back and said, "Hello! Who are you?" And she had answered sweetly, "I'm Lexie." And he had laughed and said, "That's a cute name! Is it short for Lexicon?" But she had shaken her head and answered, "No. It's Alexia. Alexia Kendall." In quite a reproving tone.

Strange that he should think of this now, so many years ago, a brief detached picture of a child on a gate smiling, a cool morning with sunshine and birds, and a syringa bush near the little house that belonged to the gate. Strange that such a vision should come into the midst of this scene of carnage, with the scorching smell of fire on his garments, and in his hair and eyebrows. Just a sweet little stranger in a quiet bright morning with dew on the grass by the roadside, peace on the hills, and no walls of fire to cross! Strange! Ah! If he might just pause to think of that morning so long ago it would rest him! But there were those wells, and more fire ahead, and the enemy, overhead more planes! There came a flock of shells! The enemy again! Was he out of his head? This didn't seem real. Oh, why did these fires have to come? It was bad enough without them!

But now he was in the thick of the fight again, and his vision cleared. Strange how you could always go on when there was a need and you realized what it meant if you lost the fight! He must go on! Could he weather this awful heat again, with the pain in his shoulder to bear? Back there on that dewy morning going from his home to school, what would he have said if anyone had told him that this was what he had to do to prove his part in the righteousness of the world? Would he have dared to grow up and go on toward this?

But yes! He *had* to. A boy had to grow into a man. Did everyone have to go through fire of some kind?

That little girl in the blue dress? Where was she? He had never seen her again since that morning. His parents had moved away from that town, and he had never gone back. Strange that he should remember her, a child. Even remember her name. Alexia Kendall! Would he ever see her again? And if he did would he know her? Probably not. But if he ever came through this inferno and went back to his own land he would try to find her, and thank her for having come with that cool happy memory of a little girl swinging on a gate, carefree and smiling. No wall of fire engulfing her! Oh no! God wouldn't ever let that happen to a pretty little thing like that. Little Alexia! She must be safe and happy. Why, that was why he had to win this war, to make the world safe for such little happy girls as that one! Of course! The very thought of it cooled and steadied his brain, kept his mind sane.

There! There came another shower of fire! Fire and dew side by side in his mind. Oh, these were fantastic thoughts! Was he going out of his head again? Oh, for a drop of that dew on the grass, that morning so long ago!

"If I ever get through I'll thank her, if I can find her!" he promised himself. "I'll pay tribute to her for helping me think this thing through."

Halfway round the earth Alexia stood in a doorway, holding a telegram in her trembling hand, a cold tremor running over her as she read.

In the house, the same little house with the white fence where she had swung on the gate so many years ago, her bags were all packed to go back to college for her final term, with a delightful important defense job promised her as soon as she was graduated.

And now here came this telegram right out of the blue as it were, to hinder all her plans and tie her down to an intolerable existence, with no outlook of relief ahead! This message might be laying the burden of a lifetime job on her slender shoulders. It was unthinkable! This couldn't be happening to her after she had worked so hard to get to the place she had reached.

Alexia's father had died a year after she had swung joyously on the gate that spring morning when Benedict Barron had passed by and seen her. But Alexia's mother had worked hard, a little sewing, a little catering, an occasional story or article written in the small hours of the night when her body was weary, but which brought in a small pittance, and she had kept her little family together.

The family consisted of the two little girls. One a young step-daughter a couple of years older than Lexie, and very badly spoiled by an old aunt who had had charge of her since her own mother had died, until her father married again.

It would have been easier for the mother after her

husband's death, if this step-daughter could have gone back to the aunt who had spoiled her and set her young feet in the wrong selfish way. But the old aunt had died before the father, and there was no one else to care or to come to the rescue, so Alexia's mother did her brave best to teach the other girl to love her, to love her little sister, and to be less self-centered. She worked on, keeping a happy home behind the white gate, and putting away a little here, a little there, for the education she meant both girls should have, Elaine as well as her own little girl.

But Elaine was not on study bent. She skimmed through three years of high school carrying on a gay flirtation with every boy in the grade, and cutting the rules of the institution right and left. Mrs. Kendall often had to go up to the school to interview the principal, and promise to do her best to make Elaine see the world as it was, and not as she wished it to be. And so with many a heartbreak and sigh, with tears of discouragement, and prayers for patience, she dragged Elaine through high school by main force as it were, and landed her in a respectable college for young women, where the mother hoped she would do better. But Elaine, during the latter half of her first year in college, ran away with a handsome boy from a boys' college not many miles away, and got married, and so for a time the mother had only one girl to look after, and the way seemed a little easier. For the boy who had married Elaine was the son of wealthy parents, and Mrs. Kendall hoped that at last Elaine would settle down and be happy under ideal circumstances where she could have all the luxury that her lazy little soul desired, and the way would be open for herself to have a little peace.

But they soon found out that they were by no means rid of Elaine. Again and again there would be trouble and Elaine would come back plaintively to her long-suffering stepmother for help to settle her difficulties. For the wealthy parents had not taken a liking to Elaine, in spite of her beauty and grace, and they soon discovered her tricky ways of procuring money from them which they would not have chosen to give. Again and again the stepmother would have to sacrifice something she needed, or something she had hoped to get for Alexia, in order to cover some of the other girl's indiscretions. It ended finally in a sharp quarrel and a quick divorce, which not only failed to teach the selfish girl a lesson, but left her bitter and exceedingly hard to live with.

She had come back to her stepmother, of course, utterly refusing to return to her studies. She spent her time bewailing her fate, and sulking in bitterness, unable to see that it was all her own fault.

All this had made a great part of Alexia's school days most unhappy. Elaine would sulk and weep and blame them all, and there would be periods of deep gloom in the little house behind the white gate where Lexie used to swing so gaily. So, amid battle after battle life went on till Lexie was in high school. Then, wonder of wonders, Elaine fell in love with a poor young man, and in spite of all the worldly wisdom they offered her, to show her how this time she would not have money to ease the burdens of life, she married him. She wouldn't believe that they would be poor. She said Richard Carnell was brilliant and would soon be making money enough, and anyway she loved him, and off she went to the far west.

So Lexie went on in high school in peace, with sometimes a really new dress all her own, and not one made over from one of Elaine's. Mrs. Kendall settled down to work harder than ever to save to put her girl through college.

It was about the time that Elaine's first baby arrived, when Lexie was still in her second year at high school that she took to writing her stepmother again, high scrawling letters asking to borrow money. There was always a plausible tale of ill-luck, and a plea of ill-health on her part which made it necessary for her to hire a servant, sometimes two, and she didn't like to ask Dick for the extra money, he was so sweet and generous to her. "And mother," she added naively, "wasn't there some money my father left which rightly belongs to me, anyway?"

There wasn't, but the stepmother sent her a small amount of money to help out a little, realizing that it would not be the last time this request would be made. She also told her plainly that her father had left no money at all. That his business had failed just before his last illness, and she herself had had to get a job and work hard to make both ends meet ever since.

The next time Elaine wrote she said that she distinctly remembered her father telling her own mother before she died that their child would never be in need, that he had taken care of that and put away a sufficient sum to keep her in comfort for years.

As Elaine was between two and a half and three years old when her own mother died that seemed a rather fantastic story, but Mrs. Kendall had learned long ago not to expect sane logic nor absolute accuracy from Elaine in her statements, and she had patiently let it go.

Lexie, as she grew older and came to know the state of things fully, was very indignant at the stepsister who had darkened the sunshine in her young life time after time, and one day when she was in her second year of college she brought the subject out in the open, telling her mother that she thought the time had come to let Elaine understand all that she had done for her all the years. How she had actually gone without necessities to please the girl's whims. Elaine had a husband now, and a home of her own. Perhaps it was only a rented house, but her husband was making enough money to enable her to live comfortably, and Elaine had no right to try and get money out of them any longer. Suppose Elaine did have three children, she had two servants to help her now, didn't she? Elaine would complain of course, she had always done that, and say she was sick and miserable, but she went out a great deal, belonged to bridge clubs and things that cost money and took time and strength. Why should her stepmother have to sacrifice to help out every time Elaine wanted to give a party or buy a new dress? Oh, Lexie was beginning to see things very straight then, and though she was born with a sweet generous nature she couldn't bear to see her dear mother put upon by a selfish girl who was never grateful for anything that was done for her.

But Mrs. Kendall, though she acknowledged that

there was a great deal of truth in what her daughter said, told Lexie that she felt an obligation toward Elaine because of a promise she had made Elaine's father before he died. He had been greatly troubled about Elaine, convinced that he had been to blame for leaving her so long with the old aunt who had spoiled her, and he implored his wife to look after her as if she were her own, and she had promised she would. Furthermore she had begged Lexie to try to feel toward Elaine as if she were her own sister, and to be kind and considerate of her needs, even if she, the mother, should be taken away. So with tears Lexie had kissed her mother, and promised, "Of course, mother dear. I'll do everything I can for her. If she would only let you alone, though, and not be continually implying that you were using or hiding money of hers."

Lexie's mother died during Lexie's third year of college, and Elaine sent a telegram of condolence, and regretted that she could not come east for the funeral because of ill health and lack of funds for the journey.

This ended the pleas for money for the time being, and poor Lexie had to bear her sorrow, and the heavy burdens that fell upon her young shoulders, alone. Though there was no heartbreak for her in the fact of Elaine's absence. Elaine had never been a comfortable member of the family to have around.

Elaine sent brief scant letters that harped continually on her own ill-health, as well as what a lot of work there was connected with a family of children, especially for a sick mother, and one whose social duties were essential for her husband's business success.

Lexie had been more than usually busy of course, since her mother's death, and she had taken very little time to reply at length to these scattered letters. Her attention was more than full with her examinations, and arranging for a war job after graduation. If she thought of Elaine at all it was to be thankful that she seemed to have a good husband, and was fully occupied in a far corner of the country where she was not likely to appear on the scene.

Lexie had come back during vacation to attend to some business connected with the little home that her mother had left free from debt. She had felt it should be rented, or perhaps sold, though she shrank from giving it up. But she had put away a great many of her small treasures, and arranged everything so that the house could be rented if a tenant appeared, and now she was about to return to her college for the final term. Her train would leave that evening, and her bags were packed and ready. She was about to eat the simple lunch of scrambled eggs, bread and butter and milk which she had but just prepared and set on the corner of the kitchen table, when the doorbell rang and the telegram arrived. The telegram was from Elaine!

Lexie stood in the open doorway shivering in the cold and read it, taking in the full import of each type-written word, and letting them beat in upon her heart like giant blows. Strangely it came to her as she read that so her mother before her must have felt whenever Elaine had launched one of her drives for help. Only her mother had never let it be known how she felt. For the sake of the love she bore her husband, and the promise she had made at his deathbed she had borne it all sweetly. And now it was her turn and her mother had expected her to do the same. But this was appalling! This was more than even mother would have anticipated.

Then she read the telegram again. It was a day letter:

Dick in the army fighting overseas. Reported missing in action. Probably dead. I am coming home with the children. Have been quite ill. Have rooms ready. Am bringing a nurse. Will reach the city five thirty p.m. Meet train with comfortable car.

Elaine

Lexie grew weak all over, and turning tottered into the house closing the door behind her. She went into the dining room and dropped down into a chair beside that lunch she had not eaten, laying her head down on her folded arms on the corner of the table, her heart crying out in discouragement. Now what was she to do? How like Elaine to spring a thing like this on her without warning. Giving orders as if she were a rich woman!

Sending her word at the last minute so that it would be impossible to stop her.

Lexie lifted her head and looked at her watch. Could she possibly send a telegram to the train and stop her? Turn her back? Tell her she was about to leave for college? Her own train left at two thirty. There was no other that night. What if she were to pay no attention to the telegram? Just let Elaine come on with her nurse and her three children and see what she had done! It was time she had a good lesson of course. She simply couldn't expect her sister to take over the burden of her life this way.

On the other hand, there was her promise to her mother, and in fact, what would Elaine do if she arrived and found no car waiting, no house open, no key to open it?

Well, she had a nurse with her, let them go to a hotel!

But suppose she had no money? Still she must have some money or she could not have bought her tickets and started. She couldn't have afforded a nurse. But then of course Elaine never bothered about affording anything. She always got what she wanted first and let somebody else worry about paying for it.

But how did Elaine happen to telegraph to her here? Ah! She had not told her sister that she was expecting to go back to college during the midyear vacation and do a little studying while things were quiet. Elaine expected her to be here in the home of course, during holidays, as she invariably had been heretofore. And if she had carried out her plans and that telegram had been a couple of hours later in arriving she would have been gone, and the telegram would not have found her. What then would have happened to Elaine? Well, why not *go* and let happen what would happen? Surely Elaine would find some way of taking care of her brood. She couldn't exactly come down upon her at college. She wouldn't know where she had gone either. Why not *go?*

It must have been five minutes that Lexie sat with her forehead down upon her folded hands trying to think this thing through. The same old fight that had shadowed all her life thus far! Was it going on to the

the end for her, as it had gone on for her mother? Or should she make a stand now, and stop it?

And then would come the thought that Elaine seemed to be in real trouble now, her husband probably dead, herself sick—and very likely she really was! It didn't take much to make Elaine sick when things didn't happen her way. And those three children! She couldn't do hard things to children. She *couldn't* let them suffer because they happened to have an insufferable mother! She had never seen those three children, but children were always pathetic if they were in trouble! Oh, what should she do?

Here she was ready to leave, just time to eat those cold scrambled eggs that had been so nice and hot when that telegram arrived. Her house was all ready either to close for the present, or to rent if a tenant came, her things packed away under lock and key in the attic, and all her arrangements for the rest of the college year made. There was still time to take a taxi to the North Station and get her train, before that western train arrived with the onslaught of the enemy, and yet she wasn't going to have the nerve to do it! She felt it in her heart behind all her indignation and bitter disappointment that she wasn't going to leave Elaine in the lurch. She had been brought up a lady, and she couldn't do it. She had been taught to give even a little more than was asked, and she was going to go on doing it the rest of her life, maybe.

But no! She *wouldn't!* She *mustn't!* She would just stay long enough to have a showdown with her sister. She would make her understand that there was no money anywhere, and the job she had secured was on condition that she had finished her college course. She must do that or her whole life would suffer. She would let Elaine understand that she could not shoulder the burden of her family. She would stay long enough for that. It was what her mother probably should have done, and now it was *her* duty. She would try to be kind and sympathetic with Elaine in her sorrow, and she would try to help her back to a degree of health, but then she would make her understand that it was right *she* should get a job herself and support her children. Yes, she would do that! She would not weaken. She had a right and a responsibility to think of herself and her own career too, and of course even if she had to help Elaine financially, it was essential that she finish her course and get ready to earn as much as possible for them all. Yes, that was what she would do!

And now, just how should she go about all this? Shouldn't she begin at once to be firm with Elaine? To let her understand that she couldn't afford taxis and cars? What ought she to do? Wire the train that Elaine must get a taxi, or just not make any reply at all? And how should she prepare for this unexpected invasion? For indeed it seemed to her as she lifted tear-filled eyes and looked about the room, like an invasion of an enemy.

She felt condemned as the thought framed itself into words in her mind, but she had to own that that was the way she felt about it. And thinking back over the years and her mother's words from time to time, she knew this was something her mother would have told her she must do as far as was possible. Perhaps it would not turn out to be as bad as it promised. Perhaps it was only for a brief space while Elaine adjusted herself to her circumstances, but whatever it was it was something that her mother would have expected her to do, something that perhaps God expected her to do.

Not that Lexie had ever thought much about God except in a faraway general way, but somewhere there was a Power that was commanding her. It was as if there was an ordeal ahead which challenged her. Why? Was it right she should go? It was like a wall of fire before her, through which she must pass, and there was now no longer a question whether she would go. She knew she would. The only thing was to work out just what was the wisest way to do it.

With her eyes shut tight to force back the two tears that persisted in coming into them, Lexie kept her face down and pressed her temples to try and think. Whatever she was going to do for the winter, it was *now, today,* that she had to settle. She wasn't going to run away from the message that had come at this last minute. If this was an emergency, and a time of grief—and ob-

viously it was—just common decency required that she
do something about it. Therefore she *must* stay here in
the house until Elaine came and they could talk it out.
She must see if her sister was really sick, sicker than
she used to be sometimes when she just didn't want to
go places and do things that seemed to be her duty. If
she was really sick, of course she, Lexie, must stay and
do something about it until some other arrangement
could be made, sometime, somewhere. That could be
held in abeyance until Elaine was here.

Next, the house must be put in order to accommodate the oncoming guests, or else there must be some
room or rooms hired somewhere to accommodate them.
Undoubtedly the home would be the cheapest arrangement, unless it might open the way for Elaine to take
too much for granted. But there again she must wait
till she knew the exact situation. And last, but by no
means the least important, was the matter of transportation from the city for an invalid, or a supposed invalid. But that too would have to be accepted as a fact
until the contrary was proved. And now she began to
see how hard her mother's way must have been. Must
she go to the expense of going down to the city after
them? There was much to be done in the house to make
it habitable if they were coming here. She would have
no time to do it if she went to the city.

What she finally did was to run out to a public telephone and call up the Traveler's Aid at the city station,
asking the representative to meet the train, and arrange for whatever way of conveyance she felt was
necessary, giving a message that she was unable to meet
the train herself. She made it plain that none of them
had much money to spend for anything that was not a
necessity, and unless the invalid felt she could afford
taxis, and was utterly unable to travel otherwise, please
make some other arrangement.

The woman who answered her call was a sensible
person with a voice of understanding, and seemed to
take in the situation thoroughly, and when Lexie came
out of the telephone booth there was a relieved feeling
in her mind and less trouble in her eyes. At least she
had provided a way of transportation, and that matter

was disposed of without her having to go into the city. Now she would be able to get a bed ready for Elaine. Even if she wasn't going to stay in the house all night there would have to be a suitable bed for her to lie down on as soon as she arrived—if she *really* was sick. Somehow Lexie was more and more uncertain about that. She had known Elaine so long, and so well. But she climbed to the well-ordered attic, where everything was put away carefully, and searched out blankets, pillows, sheets and pillow cases, a few towels and some soap. These would be necessities at once of course.

As she worked her mind was busy thinking about a most uncertain future. Trying to plan for a way ahead in which her most unwilling feet must go. Some urge within her soul forbade that she shrink back and shirk the necessity.

Yet of course she was not the only one in the world who had trouble.

2

THEY WERE FIGHTING a war, out across the ocean. Well, she was fighting a war with herself at home. With herself? No, maybe it wasn't with herself. Maybe it was something that affected the world, that is a little piece of it. It might even be important to the world how she took this added burden that had come upon her. Could that be possible? From God's standpoint perhaps.

So Lexie thought to herself as she went about swiftly putting Elaine's old room to rights, enough to rights to make a place for her to lie down when she arrived. Of course she would do her best to make her see how impossible it would be for her to stay, but there had to be a place for her to lie down.

Hastily she made up the bed with such things as she had been able to find in the attic without unpacking too many boxes. She wanted Elaine to realize how inconvenient her coming in this sudden way had been for her. And yet all the time as she thought it she knew Elaine *wouldn't* realize. Elaine would just take it for granted that it was her due to be served, and would probably growl at the service, too, and consider it inadequate.

She drew a deep sigh and wished with all her heart that the telegram had not arrived until she had left for college. Perhaps Elaine would have been discouraged then, and gone back west. Still, of course she wouldn't. Elaine wasn't made that way. Elaine demanded service, and if it wasn't on hand where she chose to be she turned heaven and earth till it came. Oh, why did this have to come to her after all the other hard things she had been through? Other girls had normal lives with pleasant families and nobody much to torment them, and here she was saddled not only with her unpleasant sister, but also her three unknown children, who would probably be as unpleasant as their parent, poor little things! And she couldn't stand it! No, she *couldn't!* How could a young girl only twenty, with her own way to make, and her college finals just at hand, be expected to take over and bring up a family of three children, to say nothing of their mother, who probably by this time was posing as a hopeless invalid, and doing it so prettily that everybody else would pity her?

But there was no use thinking such bitter thoughts. Whatever else her sister was not, she certainly was in trouble enough now, with her husband as good as dead, for that was what "missing in action" usually meant. And if she really loved him, as she *said* she did, it was hard of course. Although it was hard for Lexie to believe that Elaine really loved anybody but herself.

It was perhaps fortunate for Lexie's firm resolves to be frank with Elaine and make her understand how hard she was making things, that there was very little time to relent. For Lexie's sweet temper and natural generosity were apt to make her soft-hearted, and if there had been a great deal of time to prepare for her unwelcome guest, she might in spite of herself have done much to make the house look homelike and livable again. But there was not much time, and there were limitations, due to the fact that most of the pleasant furnishings and treasured things of the family were securely packed and locked away so that it would take time to unpack, air and put them about in their places again. That would hardly be worth while if Elaine was only to be there a few hours, or at most a few days. Perhaps if she were really sick she ought to go to a hospital. Although Elaine always hated the very name of hospital and refused to be sent to one ever. But of course she might have changed. She must have been there when her children were born, and perhaps had got over her foolish ideas of prejudice against it. But if she went to the hospital, what would become of the three children? Because of course no hospital would allow them to come when they were not sick. And there was no one, no relative, who could be called in to look after them. It would just mean that she, Lexie, would have to stay with them, and she *couldn't* do that. She *must* go back to college! For economy's sake if for nothing else, she must finish her course and get her job!

And there she would pause and sit down in despair. Oh, why, *why* did this thing have to come to her just at this time when she was putting every bit of nerve and energy into an attempt to finish her course with honor and at least a degree of excellence?

This question was still beating itself back and forth in Lexie's heart when at last she realized that it was time for the travelers to arrive, and there was nothing she could do about it but wait.

But as time went on and nothing happened, Lexie was frantic. She decided to run down to the drug store and telephone to that Traveler's Aid again. If she didn't get her now she would be gone, relieved by the night operator, and they might not be able to tell her anything. So closing the door and slipping the key under the old cocoa mat where they used to hide it when they were children, she hurried down the street and telephoned.

It was some time before she succeeded in getting the Traveler's Aid and discovered that the shift had already changed and another woman was on duty. The other woman however could give her a little information from their record. Yes, the train had been met, the family was on board, and their representative had put them in a very good taxi. The lady had insisted on a comfortable one. It cost a little more, but she said she didn't care, and they were started off soon after arriving. "The nurse who was with them," added the woman, "seemed unwilling to remain with the case. She said she felt she had made a mistake in coming, was homesick and wanted to return west on the next train. We finally persuaded her to stay with the lady until she reached her destination, but she said she wanted you notified to get another nurse at once, as she was returning to the city with the taxi. She never expected to have to look after three children as well as a helpless patient. If we had known how to reach you we would have phoned, but they said you had no telephone. We thought you ought to know. Somebody will have to look after the lady. She seemed quite helpless."

Lexie's heart sank as she thanked the woman and hung up the receiver. So! The atmosphere was growing blacker and blacker. Now what was she to do? Would she have to look after Elaine herself? She groaned in spirit and hurried back to the house, but as she opened the white gate she sighted a taxi coming down the road. They had *come,* and the fight was on! It was going to be bad, but she had to go through it somehow.

And then the taxi stopped before the door and three children descended in a body and stared at her and the house.

"Is that the house?" asked a supercilious girl of seven, with a sneer on her lips and a frown on her brow. "Good night! That's not a house, that's a dump! What did you bring us here for, Elaine? We can't live in a tiny little place like that!"

Then a boy of five blared out hatefully:

"It's not a house, it's a dump! I ain't a-gonta live in a dump like that! Jeepers! You can't do that to me!"

And a little girl of three began to cry and bawl out, "I wantta go home! I *won't* stay here! You're mean to bring us here!"

"Shut up!" said the woman Lexie supposed was the nurse. "Don't you know your mother's sick?"

"I don't care 'f she is," roared the boy. "She hadn't ought to uv brought us here, an' I ain't a-gonta stay, *so there!"*

Two of the neighbors who lived in houses across the street came curiously out to their doors and looked at the arrivals in amazement. Then seeing Lexie coming out to the gate hurriedly, they decided that these must be her new tenants and beat a hasty retreat indoors again, probably with sinking hearts at the prospect of such loud-mouthed children for neighbors.

But Lexie went quickly to the side of the taxi where her sister still lay back among pillows, wanly, and tried to manage a welcoming smile for her.

"My *dear!"* she said, hoping her voice sounded cordial, at least to the nurse. "I was so sorry that I couldn't manage to meet you in the city—"

"Yes?" said Elaine in her coldest, haughtiest tone. "I was too. Such a jaunt as I've had coming out! I should think you might at least have managed to send some neighbor. Mr. Brotherton I'm sure would have been glad to come after me if you had asked him, but I know you never did like him. I couldn't understand why—" complained the sweet drawling voice.

"Sorry, Elaine, but Mr. Brotherton has moved away. Gone to Washington, doing something in a war job."

"The very idea!" said Elaine, as if this was somehow her sister's fault. "Well, then, why didn't you ask Mr. Wilson, or Mr. Jackson? Their cars are old and shabby I suppose, but they would have done in a pinch."

"Mr. Wilson's car has been sold," said Lexie coldly. "They couldn't afford to run it any longer in the present state of gas and tires, and Mr. Jackson works in a defense plant in the city and takes a lot of other workers with him to the plant in his car every morning. He doesn't return till six o'clock. And there isn't any other available car in the neighborhood. I'm sorry you had an uncomfortable ride, but now, I guess we should make some arrangements before you get out. You know your telegram just caught me as I was about to leave for college, and I have the house all ready for renting, in case a tenant comes while I am gone. Things aren't very livable here, and I thought you might not care to stay. A great deal of the furniture is stored in the attic. I didn't know but you would want to go to a hotel in the city till you could make further arrangements."

Lexie was talking fast, trying to get her ideas across before Elaine could interrupt. There was a shadow in her troubled eyes as she studied Elaine's face. Elaine did look white and drawn. There were dark circles under her eyes, too, and the old petulant pout to her lips grew into a decided sneer as she looked her sister down.

"But you can't do that!" she said in her high angry voice. "*Rent* the house! What *an idea!* It's *my* home as well as yours, isn't it? You didn't ask my permission to rent it. Of course you couldn't get enough rent for this little dump away out here in the country anyway, to make it pay. Not enough for me to consent. After it was divided between us it would be nothing. And it will shelter us anyway. No, certainly not! I won't consent to renting! I'm going to stay right here and look into my father's affairs. I'm quite sure there was some money left to me, if your mother didn't use it up sending you in luxury to an expensive college! It's high time I looked after things!"

Lexie's lips set firmly in a thin line, and two spots of angry color flew into her pale cheeks. But she couldn't stand here and fight, with this strange nurse and the taxi driver looking on. Besides the neighbors were coming back to their front doors to see what it was all about. Lexie took a deep breath and summoned her courage.

"Very well," she said quietly, "suppose we get you into the house then. I fixed a bed for you to lie down on in your old room. Can we get you upstairs?"

"No," said Elaine crossly, "I'm not able to walk upstairs. Not unless the driver would carry me up."

"No *ma'am*," spoke up the driver sharply. "I'm not allowed to stop long enough to do anything like that. Not unless you wantta pay me five dollars extra."

"Oh, dear! The idea! Well, what's the matter with the downstairs sitting room, Lexie? That was always a pleasant room anyway, and handier for carrying my meals, too."

"Oh," gasped Lexie, "why, there isn't anything in it. No bed. No furniture at all! It would take some time to get a bed downstairs and set it up. I don't believe I would be able to do that by myself either."

"No furniture! How ridiculous! What have you done with the furniture? I hope you didn't have the temerity to sell any of it. I intend to pick out what I want of it first before that happens. You know it was *all my* father's anyway."

"Oh no," said Lexie. "Some of it was mother's. She used to tell me about the old rocking chair and bureau that were her grandmother's, and there were several things that I bought myself with the first money I earned. But I guess we won't fight over that." Lexie ended with a fleeting smile. "We must get you in and comfortable first, and then perhaps you would like me to send for a doctor, would you?"

"Certainly not! I don't want any little one-horse doctor from this dinky town. I'm under a noted specialist, you know, and I'll have to contact someone in the city whom my doctor recommends. But I suppose if you have let things get into this barren state I'll have to do the best I can for tonight. I suppose I'll have to try to get up the stairs with the help of the driver and the nurse. Nurse, you carry my wraps and pillows up first and make it comfortable for me, and then when you come down we'll go up slowly. Perhaps it won't be so impossible."

"Well, if you hurry I'll help you up," said the nurse grimly, "but then I'm done. And I'll thank you to pay me what you promised for bringing you over."

"Oh, dear me! How tiresome! What kind of a nurse are you anyway, talking that way to an invalid? Of course you'll get paid. My sister will look after all that. I've spent every cent I had when I started. Lexie, will you attend to this, and get enough for the driver too. How much was it, driver? Five dollars, did you say?"

"No, lady, it was seven dollars and a half."

"But I'm sure you said five. I distinctly remember you said five."

"Look here, lady. My car registers the miles, see? And I haveta go by the meter. I gave you the slip. It's seven dollars and a half. I told ya before we started I couldn't say just how much it would be till I saw how many miles it was, and you, lady, you didn't know! You just said it wasn't far."

"Oh, dear! How tiresome you are! Lexie, get five dollars for him. He'll have to be satisfied with that or nothing. And Lexie, get about twenty more. I'll have to pay the nurse for some things she bought for me on the way, and the meals we had on the train. How much was it in all? I have the memorandum here somewhere. Hurry, Lexie, and let's get this thing over and get me to bed as quickly as possible. I feel as if I might be going to faint again. All this discussion is bad for me. Won't you get the money, quickly?"

Lexie was looking aghast.

"I'm sorry, Elaine. I just haven't got that much money. I had only about three or four dollars left when I got my ticket paid for."

"Oh, that's all right, Lexie, run in the house and make out a check. Make two, one for the driver and one for the nurse. Here! Here's the nurse's bill. Add ten to it for her trouble on the way."

Great trouble descended upon Lexie.

"I'm sorry, Elaine, but I haven't got my check book here. I left it at college. You know I only came up for a couple of days to get the house in order to rent. The agent wrote me that he thought he had a tenant, and I knew this was the only time I could get away from my classes to do this work, so I came in a great rush, and brought very little baggage. Just an overnight bag. So I have no check book."

"Well, but surely you can find an old check book around the house somewhere. Go look in your old desk. Or go borrow a blank check from the neighbors."

"No," said Lexie positively. "I have no money in our local bank here. My account is in the bank at the college town. I'm sorry, but remember I didn't know you were even coming. In fact, Elaine, I haven't very much money left, not even in the bank. It has cost a good deal for the last days of college."

"Oh, yes?" said the sister with a hateful inflection in her tone. "Of course you'll say that. Well, what has become of the money? I know there was a whole lot saved up for *our* college courses, and *half* of that was *mine*, you know. Suppose you hand that over. That ought to be plenty to pay these two, and get rid of them.

"I'm sorry, Elaine, but the money that was for our college courses was only what my mother had saved from her own salary in the job where she worked as long as her health allowed, and there was only enough left to bury her."

"Oh, *really!* You must have had *some funeral!* I suppose you bought a lot in the most expensive part of the cemetery, and ordered the handsomest casket on the list!"

Sudden tears sprang into Lexie's eyes as she remembered the plain simple casket, the cheapest thing that could be had, that had been her mother's choice in the few words of direction she had left behind her.

"No!" she said choking down a sob and shaking her head with a quick gasping motion. "It wasn't like that! Oh, please *don't,* Elaine! She loved you and did her best for you. She had no show nor expense at her going. If you had chosen to come you would have seen. You would have been ashamed to say what you have just said."

"There! I thought you would find fault with me for not coming to her funeral! But I tell you I was too sick to travel, and it happened that I had no one to leave my children with. My husband was gone to war, and I was alone. You don't seem to care what my situation was."

"Don't, Elaine, please. I'm not finding fault with you, and of course I know you were sick. Now let's end this useless talk and get you into the house and try to make you as comfortable as possible. Remember you hired these people and if a check will satisfy them it's you who will have to give it."

Lexie turned and ran up the walk into the house, thankful to have her sudden rush of tears hidden for the moment. But she found to her dismay that she was not alone in the house. The children, unobserved for the time, had taken full possession. The oldest girl was ransacking the bookcase, pulling out armful after armful of Lexie's cherished books and casting them hit-or-miss about the floor, some halfway open, some tumbled in a heap with their pages turned in messily, some piled crookedly.

The little boy had placed a stool before a table which he had shoved against the fireplace. Then he had climbed to the top of the table to investigate the clock which stood on the mantel. As Lexie arrived in the room he was about to pull off the hands of the clock, and crowing as he did it.

The youngest girl was seated in the dining room calmly eating up the cold scrambled eggs and bread and butter that Lexie had arranged for her own hurried lunch. She could see her through the doorway, and was only thankful that she was harmlessly occupied for the moment. She made a dash for the boy on the table, put firm hands about his tough young wrists, holding them so tightly that he was forced to let go of the frail clock hands, and then as she swept him from the table and swung him around to plant his feet on the floor he set up the most unearthly howl she had ever heard from the lips of a child, and promptly started his stubby young toes to kicking her shins most unmercifully.

For answer she reached down and enfolded him in a grip such as he had seldom encountered. Lexie was indignant enough to hold even that fierce young animal quiet for the moment.

"You lemme alone!" he shrieked, and his voice rang out to the mother and nurse and driver in the taxi; and beyond, to the whole neighborhood.

"*Stop!*" said Lexie in a low tense voice. "Stop, do you hear me! If you don't stop this instant I shall spank you."

"You shan't spank me. You ain't my mother. She never spanks me! You *couldn't* spank me. I dare y' to!"

Lexie bore down upon him again, taking him by surprise, turned him firmly around and laid several smart spanks on the young bare legs below the abbreviated trousers. Sharp stinging slaps they were, cutting into the soft young flesh and bringing the quick color to the surface.

The older girl suddenly arose from her literary pursuits and went over to her brother. She lifted her skinny little fists and struck at Lexie's face, an ineffectual blow.

"You stop that! You just let my brother alone!" she shrieked. "Don't you dare touch my brother. My mother'll kill you if you lay a hand on my brother. My mother don't believe in spankings. You stop or I'll *bite* you!" and she sprang at Lexie's wrist. But Lexie drew back just in time and administered a sharp slap on the little girl's open mouth, which sent the child roaring out to her mother, with great angry tears rolling heavily down her thin little face.

This was a bad beginning, but Lexie knew that she must take her stand, right at the start, if she had to live with children like this, and she couldn't have them wrecking everything in the house just in the first few minutes, whether they stayed or not.

"Now," she said as she drew a deep breath and tried to stop trembling, and to talk gently but firmly. "You can sit there and think what you have done. You're not going to be allowed to break things here! You've got to act like a little gentleman if you want to be treated like one. Otherwise I shall spank you. I won't have this kind of thing going on. If you behave yourself we can have a pleasant time together, and there will be things you will enjoy, but if you act like a naughty boy you'll have to be treated like one."

She turned and swept the table back into its place, took the clock from the mantel and locked it inside the bookcase out of reach. Then catching up her purse she hurried out to the group at the gate.

The little girl was engaged in giving an account of the altercation in the house:

"That lady in the house is spanking Gerald. She took him up in her arms and held him tight and slapped him awful hard on his bare legs! She's a hateful old thing! Don't let's stay here in this dump, Elaine. Let's go back to our home! She's a wicked old woman!"

And from the house there issued such young masculine roars of rage as made the whole neighborhood ring and echo, and brought every householder to the doors and windows to see what had happened to their usually peaceful community.

To this accompaniment Lexie hurried out, counting out her money as she came.

"I have five seventy-five," she said as she handed out the money, distress in her face.

"Shut up, Angelica!" said the mother fretfully. "Why bring that up now? Wait until I get into the house and I'll settle with your aunt. And you, Lexie, go on back into the house with your stingy pocketbook. I've settled with these two. They are getting me to bed and then they're going. I found I had a little change left in my purse, and I was tired of waiting on you. Now, nurse, lift me up and help me get on my feet. Then I can manage to walk between you and the driver. Lexie, suppose you go into the house and get me a cup of coffee. I'll need it after walking so far. Perhaps you can make yourself that useful. And for heaven's sake keep your hands off my children. If you can't control your temper, I don't see how we are going to stand having you around."

Lexie wanted to tell her sister that she wouldn't have to stand having her there, that she was going back to college, but she shut her gentle lips firmly and hurried into the house.

A moment later she met her sister at the door with a good cold glass of water.

"I'm sorry, Elaine, there isn't a bit of coffee in the house. I thought perhaps this glass of water would help."

Elaine looked at the water with disdain.

"Water!" she said with contempt. "How does it happen there is no coffee in the house?"

"I found a little box of tea in the pantry," said Lexie. "Would you like a cup of tea? I put the kettle on. It will be ready very soon."

"Tea!" said Elaine contemptuously. "You know I never could abide tea. You certainly are about as little help as anybody I ever saw. Get out of my way. I can't stand here forever!" and she edged her way slowly and ostentatiously into the house. Then with many sighs and groanings she was helped up the stairs to the bed Lexie had prepared for her. Even then it was some minutes before the unhappy invalid was settled on the bed, her hat off, her shoes unfastened, and the two assistants departed; thanking their stars that they did not have to stay around that unpleasant woman any longer.

Lexie came hastily up the stairs after watching them depart, and felt that her war had begun.

"You'll simply *have* to help me get into bed!" said her sister sharply. "I'm not able to sit up here another minute."

"Of course," said Lexie gently, bringing skillful hands to the task. "I'm sorry you're feeling so miserable. Would you like me to go out and try to find a doctor?"

"Mercy no, not out here. You'll have to telephone to

the city for a doctor. I don't let every Tom, Dick and Harry doctor me. I've been under a specialist, you know. Can't you find me a nurse before dark? I've simply *got* to have a nurse. I'm scarcely able to lift my hand to my head. The journey has been so hard on me —and the anxiety about Dick. It's been awful! I'm sure I thought my own sister would be sympathetic enough to provide a nurse for me and have a heartening meal ready."

"I'm sorry, Elaine," said Lexie sadly. "I did all I could in the time you gave me. But you said you were bringing a nurse. I didn't know you would need one, you know. But wait until we get you comfortable in bed and then we can talk over what to do."

"Talk over!" said Elaine with rising voice, "what is there to talk over, I'd like to know? I should think you'd have all you could do to get us some supper and fix beds for the children, and find a nurse for me. You'll have to call up and get a servant, too, I should think. With three children we can't get on without at least one servant."

"Elaine, we'll have to consider how we can do all that," said Lexie firmly but sorrowfully. "As I told you I have only enough money to barely exist until I get my job, and even that isn't here. I'll have to go back to college and graduate first. Have you money to hire a nurse and a servant and let me go to my work?"

"Well, I should say not," said Elaine. "I'm down very nearly to the last cent as I told you. I expected you to finance that nurse and driver, but since you shirked out of that you'll certainly have to get the nurse and servant."

"That I can't do," said Lexie. "I simply haven't got the money!"

"Oh, very well," said the older sister coldly, "have it your own way. We'll send for my lawyer in the morning and get hold of that money that belongs to me, that your mother hoarded away, or I'll know the reason why. Just suppose you go out and get some supper ready." Elaine dropped down with a sigh on the pillows and closed her eyes, and Lexie, with a hopeless look at her sister turned and went downstairs wondering how she was going to work out this problem in a good and righteous way. How could she ever go through all this future that had suddenly spread itself out before her shrinking feet? This torture! Why did it have to come to her? Wasn't it hard enough without all this?

3

LEXIE CAST A helpless look around the neat little kitchen and began rummaging in the pantry. Obviously the first need of the invalid was something to eat. Could she find anything?

There was half a loaf of bread left, and a little butter. She could make some toast. If she could only find some coffee! Then suddenly she remembered a canister up on the top shelf where her mother used to keep coffee. Maybe there would be a little in it. She climbed up and took it down, rejoiced to find two or three teaspoonfuls of coffee left. It must have been there some time, and probably wouldn't be as good as freshly ground coffee, but at least it was something. Hurriedly she went about making it, and soon had a little tray ready. Toast and coffee and a bit of jam from a jar in the preserve closet. There was not much of anything left since her mother was gone, but she was glad to find even a little that was eatable.

As she started up the stairs she sent a glance out of doors. The three children were out on the sidewalk watching the neighbors' children who had come home from school and were playing hopscotch. Thankful that for the time being they were occupied she hurried up with the tray.

"I found a little coffee in mother's old canister," she announced cheerfully as she came into Elaine's room. "I made you a little toast too. There isn't much butter, but it's better than nothing."

Elaine turned over and scanned the tray scornfully.

"That the best you can do?" she said hatefully. But she reached for the cup and drank the coffee thirstily.

"I despise coffee without cream," she announced when she put down the cup.

"Well, there wasn't any cream," smiled Lexie. "Of

course there was nothing to do but bring what I had. And now, Elaine, if you're going to stay here for the night I'll have to go down to the store and get a few things. There isn't even an egg in the house, and there are only three slices of bread left."

"Well, for mercy sake! Why don't you telephone for supplies? You can't be spared to go down to the store. Somebody needs to look after those children! And they'll be howling for food pretty soon. Be sure you get a lot of sweet things or Gerald won't eat a thing. Get cookies. And that butter wasn't so good. Get a better quality, even if you have to pay more. I can't eat strong butter."

"Well, I'm sorry, Elaine, but that butter was some Mrs. Spicer gave me when I came yesterday, and I'm not sure I can get butter. You know we haven't any ration cards here, and you can't get butter without points. This war is upsetting a good many old habits, but I suppose we have to be patient till things right themselves."

"The perfect idea!" said Elaine. "Of course I brought my ration books along, but they are in the trunks. They won't come till tomorrow. But meantime you ought to have one with you. It's outrageous! Can't you tell the store keeper we have just arrived and I am sick?"

"I can *tell* him, yes," laughed Lexie, "but I'm sure from what Mrs. Wilson told me the other day that it won't do any good. He is not *allowed* to sell butter without coupons. However, I'll find something somehow. Now lie still and take a little nap. Will the children be all right playing by themselves?"

"Well, I'm sure I don't know. I certainly can't look after them," said the indifferent mother. "For pity's sake don't stay long! And Lexie, while you're out telephone my lawyer and ask him to come over right away, this evening if possible; if not, early in the morning. You'll find his address in my bag. I think I dropped it on the table in the living room as I came by. His name is Bettinger Thomas."

"Elaine! You don't mean Bett Thomas! The boy you used to go to high school with!"

"Why certainly!" said Elaine getting into her high

shrieking tone, prepared for an argument. "What's the matter with that?"

"But Elaine! My dear, perhaps you didn't know, but he's scarcely considered respectable. He's been connected with several shady cases the last few years. I don't suppose you'd heard."

"Oh, fiddlesticks! What difference does that make? He's a *friend,* and he's promised to see me through. I wrote to him. He was recommended to me out where I lived as being one who would carry his case no matter what, and that is what I want."

"But Elaine, he's unspeakable! You wouldn't want to talk to him. You can't ask him to come here!"

"Can't I? Watch me! If you won't telephone him I'll find somebody who can. Go hunt that nurse for me. She'll do what I ask her, and get her mighty quick, too!"

Lexie stood at the foot of the stairs for a moment speechless, too angry to dare to utter a sound. Then she turned silently and went out of the house and down the street. Wild thoughts were rushing through her mind. How was she going to endure this? How could she go on? Was there any reason why she should?

By the time she had reached the corner, and passed several smiling neighbors who greeted her cheerily, she had so far recovered her normal temper as to be able to smile, at least faintly. After all, why should she be so angry? Just because Elaine was determined to secure an unscrupulous lawyer to try to hunt out a flaw in her dear mother's dealings? Well, why should she be so upset? They certainly couldn't find any evidence. But a lawyer like Bett Thomas could *make* evidence, even if there wasn't any. He could get low-down people to swear to things that counted for evidence. She had heard of some of his dealings. Oh, what *should* she do? She couldn't have her dear dead mother's honorable name blackened by being dragged through a court trial. And yet—well, there was a God! Her mother believed that. And deep in her heart she did too, although she had never paid much heed to Him, except that she had always tried to order her life in a good and right way, as her mother had taught her. God, oh,

God, why did you let all this come to me? Didn't you want me to succeed, and graduate, and get that job, and take care of myself in a good respectable way? So, why did I have to go through this fire?

Lexie arrived at the store just before it closed for the evening. She hurried in and began to look around. What could she get without ration stamps? Of course Elaine had said her ration books were in her trunk, and would be there in the morning. Of course there were cereals, but Elaine never had liked them, and would her pestiferous children scorn them too? If she had the opportunity she would like to teach them to like them, but that really wasn't her present duty. She had hard problems to settle at once, and her immediate necessity was to get something they would all eat happily, and it wasn't going to be easy, either. Of course there were eggs, and she purchased a supply of those. They kept milk at the store and she got a couple of bottles. No butter nor meat because they were both rationed. No sugar either. How would Elaine stand that? Well, she would have to settle that difficulty with the government, although she would probably act as if it was all her sister's fault. Well, cookies and cakes! They would supply sweetness for the children. There were apples and pears and a few bananas, but there was no telling what the spoiled youngsters would condescend to eat.

She bought a few potatoes, some spinach and celery. There were oranges too. At the end Lexie struggled home with a towering paper bundle in her arms, and a heavy paper bag with a handle, in one hand, all full to overflowing. It was surprising how much she had been able to get with the little money she had. On her way home she was thinking how profoundly thankful she was that the nurse and the driver had not had to take *her* money. She wondered how much more Elaine had hidden in her purse. Well, there was no use thinking about that. They must have a talk that evening, or perhaps it would have to wait till morning if Elaine was not disposed to talk tonight.

When she got back to the little white house she found she was very tired, and would have liked nothing

better than just to sit down and cry. But that wouldn't
get anybody anywhere. There had to be some supper
got right away. It was after half past six. And she
heard Elaine calling her fretfully.

She hurried upstairs and found Elaine sitting up angrily in bed, arguing with a trio of naughty children.

"I know you are hungry," she was saying angrily,
as if the children were to blame for being hungry, "but
your aunt didn't have any supper ready for us, and
what can we do?"

"She's *bad! I hate* her!" roared Gerald glaring at her
from the foot of the bed.

"You certainly have been gone long enough to buy
out the store," Elaine snarled at her sister. "I hope you
got us a good hearty meal."

"I'm afraid not," said Lexie. "The store was just
about to close, and I had very little money, but I got
all I could without ration books."

"Fiddlesticks. Couldn't they trust you for the coupons? Didn't you tell them we would give them the
coupons tomorrow?"

"They are not allowed to sell things without the coupons."

"That's absurd, when they've known you for years.
They *know* you wouldn't cheat them."

"Well, they can't do that for anybody. Now, I'll go
down and get something for the children to eat, and
then you can tell me what you would like."

"Well, I can tell you now. I want a cup of decent
coffee, and a good tender juicy beefsteak."

"But my dear, we can't get beefsteak or coffee without coupons, or any more butter!"

The little boy began to howl.

"I want some butter!" he protested. "I want some
bread and a lot of butter!"

"There isn't any tonight Gerald. But maybe I can
find some jam down cellar. Won't that do?" asked
Lexie brightly.

"No it *won't!*" he roared. "I won't eat your old jam!
I want *butter!* A lot of it! You're a bad old aunt, you
are, and I don't like you."

In despair Lexie went downstairs and concocted the

nicest supper she could out of the stores she had bought.

The children came down presently, one at a time. Angelica first. Lexie, hurrying to get everything on the table, heard the child calling *"Hi,* Elaine! There's hardboiled-egg-wheels on the spinach, and the potatoes have their overcoats on."

And then she heard a howl from Gerald:

"I don't like old spinach! I won't eat it, even if it has got old egg-wheels on it. I hate spinach. I want *beef-steak!"*

Lexie took a deep breath. This was going to be an endurance test it seemed. Oh, why, why, *why?*

"Run up and call the other children, Angel," she said with a forced smile. "I'm just going to take the omelet up, and it needs to be eaten while it's piping hot."

The little girl gave one eager hungry look at her aunt's bright face, and hurried upstairs, calling the news about the omelet as she went.

But she presently came down again with a haughty imitation of her mother's tone.

"Elaine says it's no use for you to try to stuff spinach down us. We won't eat it. We *never* do! And she thinks that's pretty poor fare for the first meal when your relatives come home. She says we don't eat spinach nor omelet, and *you can't make us!"*

"Oh," said Lexie cheerfully, "that's too bad, isn't it, when we can't get anything else but what I've got here. But of course you don't *have* to eat it unless you like. I'm not going to try to stuff it down you. I only thought maybe you were hungry, and since these were the only things I could get for us tonight, you might be glad to have them. But if you don't want them, that's all right with me. As soon as I get the dishes washed and everything put away I'll try and fix a place for you to sleep. If you get to sleep soon I don't suppose you'll mind being hungry for tonight."

Angelica looked at her aunt aghast as she set the puffy brown omelet on the table, put the open dish of bright green spinach with its wheels of yellow and white egg beside it, and then sat down herself as if she were going to eat it all by herself. Deliberately she helped herself to some of each dish on the table and began to eat with slow small bites, smiling at the little girl pleasantly. Suddenly Angelica set up a howl.

"Come down here quick, Gerry! She's eating it all up! She's got a nice dinner all ready and she's *eating it up herself!* Hurry up and bring Bluebell down with you. Hurry, or it will all be gone!"

Lexie smiled to herself as she realized that she had conquered for once. Perhaps that was the way to manage them. Let them think you didn't care whether they ate or not. So she went steadily on eating slow mouthfuls while Angelica fairly danced up and down in a fury.

"Gerald! Ger-*a-l-d!* Come *quick!* She's eating it all up from us, and I'm *h-o-n-g-ry!*"

"Oh," said Lexie pleasantly. "Would you like to have some dinner? Suppose you sit down here beside me. What would you like to have?"

"I want some of that puffy om-let!" announced Angelica, slamming herself into the chair indicated. "And I want some of that nice green stuff with yellow wheels on it."

Lexie put a small amount of spinach on the child's plate, with a slice of lovely hardboiled egg on the top, and beside it a helping of beautifully browned omelet. The little girl lost no time in sampling the food.

"It's *good!*" she screamed. Gerald who suddenly had appeared in the doorway with Bluebell by the hand looked on jealously.

Lexie paid no attention to him until he came closer to the table.

"I *want* some!" he announced.

"Oh, do you?" said Lexie calmly. "Well, sit down on this other side, and I'll put a big book on a chair for the baby."

Amazingly they were finally seated, eating with zest.

"I want some *more,*" said Angelica, handing out her plate. "I want some milk, too. You've got milk."

"Why, of course. You can all have milk!" said Lexie, filling a glass for each one.

At last without any coaxing they ate, heartily, eagerly, and asked for more.

When the spinach and potatoes were all gone, except the small portion she had kept in the warming oven for Elaine in case she would deign to eat it, Lexie brought out a generous plate of cookies and a pear apiece, and the children by this time were almost appreciative.

"Say, these cookies are good," said Angelica, setting the pace for the others. "They've got good raisins in them."

"I don't like cookies," said Gerald. "I 'druther have chocolate cake."

"Well, that's too bad," said Lexie sympathetically. "Sorry we haven't any chocolate cake. You don't need to eat cookies if you don't like them," and she drew the plate back and did not pass it to him.

Gerald's reply was to rise up on his chair and reach out for the plate, knocking over Bluebell's glass of milk and sending a stream of milk over the table.

"I will so have some cookies! You can't keep me from having some!" declared the obstreperous child. "You just want to keep them all for yourself, but you shan't."

Lexie, rescuing the glass of milk before the entire contents was broadcast, said gently.

"Oh, I'm sorry. Did you want some? I understood you to say you didn't like them." She lifted the cooky plate just before Gerald succeeded in plunging a willful hand into its midst. "Sit down, Gerald, and I'll pass them to you."

Gerald settled back astonished, about to howl, but thought better of it, and presently had his mouth stuffed full of so much cooky he couldn't speak.

When that meal was concluded Lexie felt as if she had fought a battle, but she felt reasonably satisfied with the result. The children were still munching cookies and demanding more pears, and Bluebell was nodding with sleep in her chair. Lexie hadn't eaten much except those first few decoy mouthfuls, but she drank a little milk and hurried upstairs with the tray for Elaine. She was greeted as she entered the room by sounds of heart-rending sobs, and Elaine turned a woe-begone face to meet her.

"So you did decide to bring me something at last, did you? Of course I am only an uninteresting invalid, and it doesn't matter if I starve, but you certainly might have brought me a crust of bread."

"Well, I'm sorry Elaine," said Lexie with a sudden quick sigh. "I thought you would want the children fed first. And I'm not altogether sure you'll like what I've brought, but it was all I could get tonight. Toast and jam, a glass of milk. It isn't bad if you'd try it. I made a little new omelet for you, too, so it would come to you hot. Of course it isn't the beefsteak you wanted, but I'm afraid from all I hear, that you won't get much of that these days."

Elaine surveyed the tray with dissatisfaction, and was about to discount everything on it, but Lexie spoke first.

"Now I'll go and see if I can find some blankets and things to make up beds for the children. They are dropping over with weariness. If you need anything send Angelica up to the attic after me," and she quickly retired from the room before her sister had time to say anything more. But when she came down every crumb and drop was gone from the tray, and Elaine had retired to her pillow to prepare for another weeping spell.

"Did you contact my lawyer?" she asked sharply.

"Oh no, of course not. I hadn't time. I knew you all would have to have some supper. Now, do you want Bluebell to sleep with you?"

"Heavens, no! Do you think I could be bothered that way, me in my condition? She'll sleep all right by herself. She's not used to being petted, not since I've been sick, anyway. Not since the nurse left."

Lexie gazed in compassion at the poor baby, now asleep on the floor in the dining room, tears on her cheeks, and an intermittent hectic sob shaking her baby shoulders. Poor little mite, with nobody taking care of her, and already a hard belligerent set to her little lips! What could she do for her? Obviously she was the first one to be made comfortable. The rest could wait.

In quick thought she reviewed the possibilities of the house. There were two folding cots in the attic. She could easily bring those down for the two older children. There were plenty of blankets, now that she had opened the big old chest in which they were packed. But there was no crib for Bluebell. The last one in the family must have been her own, and only a very valuable piece of unneeded furniture would have survived so many years. But there was a wide couch in the room that used to be her mother's. She could make a bed for the baby up there, and herself sleep in her mother's bed, if she got any chance to sleep at all in this disorganized household.

Swiftly she went to work, and presently had a comfortable place for Bluebell, with chairs to guard the side so she couldn't roll off. Then she brought down the cots, an armful of sheets and blankets, and made up two beds for Angelica and Gerald.

"What in the world are you doing there in the next room?" called Elaine. "It seems to me you might keep a little still and give me a chance to sleep. And what is the matter with those two children? They've done nothing but wrangle since you brought the baby upstairs. I should think you might amuse them a few minutes and let me get a little rest before that lawyer comes. What time did he say he would be here?"

"There'll be no lawyer here tonight," said Lexie firmly. "And the best amusement those children can have is a little sleep. I've made up two cots here, and they'll soon be in bed. You better tell them what to do about nighties. I've got some things to attend to in the kitchen, and it's time we were all asleep. We're very tired. Angelica, go ask your mother where you can find your night things."

Lexie hurried away to find more blankets and left her petulant sister to deal with the two sleepy children. Returning a few minutes later she found all three in tears. Elaine crying heartbrokenly into her pillow like a wellbred invalid, Angelica struggling with a recalcitrant button in the back of her dress, which wasn't really a sewed-on button at all, but was only pinned on with a safety pin. Gerald was howling as usual.

"I won't sleep in that old cot. I just *won't, so there!* I want a real bed, not an old cot!"

Lexie, tired as she was, breezed into the room and spoke cheerfully.

"Well, come now, we're going to play the game of go-to-bed. Who wants to be *It?*"

The two young wailers stopped instantly, surveyed her for a moment and then changed face and put on eagerness.

"I would like to be *It*," said Angelica sedately, with a speculative attention that showed she was interested.

Then Gerald sounded his trumpet.

"That's not fair! *I* choose to be *It!* I'm the youngest, and you ought to let me be It. Isn't that so, Elaine? Mustn't they let me be It? I won't play if I can't be It!"

Then came Elaine's sharp voice:

"Certainly, Lexie. You must let Gerald have what he wants or he won't go to sleep tonight, and I shan't get any rest."

But Lexie chimed right over Elaine's voice, just as if she hadn't heard her at all. Lexie said cheerfully:

"Why yes, of course, you can be it *next*. You can't be first because you didn't choose to be as soon as I spoke. However, you can be It *second*, and that gives you a chance to watch the game and see if you can improve on the way Angel did it. That gives you quite an advantage you see. Besides, there's a prize! That is there are two prizes, and one is just as good as the other, because the winner of the second prize gets to choose whether he'll have one just like the first, or a new one. But there's one rule that makes them both alike. There positively won't be any prize at all if there is a *single squeal* or *yell* or *howl*. It's got to be all very quiet and gentle, because your mother is sick and needs being taken care of. Now, are you ready to hear the rules?"

"I am!" said Angelica. "I'm *very* quiet.

"Me too!" said the little boy in a subdued tone.

"Very well, then," said Lexie. "Rule number one, is that everything must proceed very quietly, no running nor pushing nor shoving. Rule number two, no dropping shoes noisily, nor fighting for hairbrushes. Rule number three. You must not leave your clothes on the floor. Lay them nicely on the chairs at the foot of the beds. You will find your night clothes each lying on your cots. Put them on smoothly and get quietly into bed. I will watch the clock and see which gets in first, and afterward if you are still quite quiet I will award the two prizes. Angelica gets the first chance to wash while Gerry takes off his shoes and stockings and puts them nicely by the chair. Then Gerry takes his turn washing, and the hands and faces must be clean, and I mean *CLEAN* you know. Now, are you ready? If you are, go stand on the edge of that board in the floor and watch my raised hand. When I drop it you may start. Ready?"

The two children scuttled across the room and toed the crack in the floor, watching her eagerly, silently. Lexie thrilled as she saw their interested faces. Then she dropped her hand.

"Go!" she said quietly.

Gerald dropped silently to the floor and went at the knot in his shoestring, while Angelica streaked it for the bathroom, silently, swiftly, earnestly they worked. Lexie was astonished that her game had interested them. From what she had seen of the children so far she had not dared to hope that it would.

Angelica was back in a trice, and Gerald gave a last yank to his shoestring and dashed to take her place at the washbowl.

In five minutes those two children were snuggled in their cots under the blankets awaiting the prizes with eagerness, and there hadn't been a single argument about which cot should be occupied by which child!

Lexie brought a large chocolate drop to Angelica, and gave the little boy his choice between another and a date. He chose the chocolate, and both lay happily licking their chocolates, while their tired young eyes blinked into quick sleepiness, and it wasn't many minutes before both were sound asleep.

"Well," said Elaine jealously, "what in the world did you do to them? I never saw them succumb so quickly. Did you give them a box of candy apiece, or administer a sleeping tablet?"

"Neither," whispered Lexie laughing. "We played a game of going to bed. I'll teach you how tomorrow. Now, do you want anything yourself before you go to sleep? Do you want something more to eat or drink, or are you going right to sleep?"

"No, I don't want anything more to eat. I want you to go out somewhere and telephone to that lawyer. That's the first thing on the docket. And next I want you to go wherever you keep such things, and bring me all mamma's private papers. I want to look them over before the lawyer gets here."

Lexie stood still a moment and faced her sister quietly. Then she said:

"Sorry! That's impossible! I will not ever telephone that man! I can't stop *your* trusting him, but I can refuse to have anything to do with the matter, and if you persist in it I shall simply have to go away and leave you. I cannot have anything to do with Bettinger Thomas."

"Oh, how silly and unkind and prejudiced you are! I didn't think you'd be unkind when I'm so ill! I can't see why you couldn't call him up and just say I wanted to see him. He'll understand. He knew I was going to call him. I sent him a telegram and told him I would call. You needn't let him know who you are. *Please*, Lex, do it *for me!*"

"No, Elaine, it's for your sake that I can't do it. I know him to be a bad, unprincipled man, and I'll save you from him if I can."

"You mean you'll do everything to save the money for yourself," sneered Elaine. "Well, if you won't do that, please go somewhere and telephone for a nurse. I've got to have one *tonight*."

"No, Elaine, I can't do that either. The only place near here where they have a telephone is down at Mrs. Hadley's and she has gone to stay a week with her daughter in New York."

"Well, surely you can go down to the drugstore and phone."

"Elaine, if you were dying and the only thing that would save you was a nurse I'd go at the risk of my life, but you're not dying, and what you need is some

sleep. No nurse could get out here anyway tonight.
You know we are a long way out, and—really, Elaine
—I'm just about all in. I feel as if I couldn't drag
another step."

"Oh, really? I don't see what you've done to make
you tired. You've simply been loafing here all day,
haven't you? I didn't think you were selfish! Well, anyway, if you'll go wherever you keep such things and
find mamma's papers right now I'll be satisfied. I
couldn't sleep until I have a chance to look them over."

Lexie looked at her sister sadly.

"I've told you twice that there are no papers. The
only paper I know anything about is the deed of this
house, and that is in a safety deposit box in the bank
out where my college is. It is absolutely the only paper
I have that has anything to do with any financial matters. If you don't believe me you'll have to do what you
want to, but I'm going to bed! I'm just done out!"

Lexie walked out of the room to her own, and
wrapping the only unused blanket about her she
dropped wearily down on her bed, a few steps from the
sleeping Bluebell.

4

But although the relaxation was grateful to Lexie's weary body, she did not fall asleep at once. She realized that her hard day was not yet over. There were things she must decide, many questions that she must settle now, in the silent night, while all her tormentors were asleep. In the morning she would have to have a settlement with her sister, and she must make up her mind beforehand just what attitude she was going to take, and stick to it. That was the only way to manage Elaine. She knew that from her girlhood days.

First, there was the question of finance. Elaine must have some money—perhaps not much—or she would never have come all this way home. But she must have a *little* or she would not have produced some for that nurse and driver. If she had none at all what were they to do? They had the house of course, but could they even afford to keep the house going if there was no money to run it, and nothing to buy food with? Elaine would have to consider that. She wasn't altogether devoid of common sense when she could be gotten down to facts, but at present her mind seemed to be filled with the idea that there was a large sum of money which her father had left, and to which she had a right. Until she got over that obsession there wasn't much she could hope to do with her. But must she go on this way from day to day and wait till Elaine came to her senses? Definitely the question of money was first. She must settle with Elaine the first thing in the morning. But above all, she must *not* give up her college and her job unless it became absolutely necessary.

Before dawn began to creep into the window and lay rosy fingers on the old wall paper above the bed, Lexie had fallen into an uneasy sleep. Out in the offing there was still a relentless sister, and three terrible in-

fants who were determined to bend the earth to their
wishes. But a new day was coming which undoubtedly
would be tempestuous, with decisions to be made that
would be difficult, yet in spite of them all she *must* go
on, through whatever was in store for her reluctant
feet. She must go on and *conquer,* doing what was in
the Almighty's plan for her life. She must not be
blinded by darkness, nor fire, nor opposition of any
sort. It was a war perhaps, between her sister and herself, but she must remember that Elaine was the daughter of her own father, and there was a certain obligation
upon her as the daughter of a beloved father to treat his
other daughter with all kindness and unselfishness,
even if Elaine persisted in being selfish toward her. It
was what was *right,* not what she *wanted.* It was—it
had to be—what God, if He cared about such things at
all—must expect of her! Just why she felt that way,
she didn't know. But she did, and so she must go on.
Even if it meant eventually that she would have to
come back and nurse Elaine, and try to get along with
those terrific children! Of course it wouldn't be so hard
to get along with the children if she had a right to order
their lives and make them behave, but Elaine would
never stand for that.

When Lexie at last awoke and adjusted her mind to
the present day with its problems, she got up hurriedly
and tiptoed out of the room. Bluebell was still asleep,
and looked very sweet without the petulance of the
new day upon her yet, but Lexie couldn't afford to stop
and admire her young niece. She went downstairs,
started some cereal, fixed a tray for Elaine, and set the
table, with as little ceremony as she possibly could.
Whatever this new day turned out to be, it was certain
it would be very full, and she must not be lavish with
dishes that would have to be washed.

But the family was tired, and had not been used to
arising early, so Lexie had a chance to get a real breakfast herself. Toast and scrambled eggs, the lunch she
had prepared for herself the day before and hadn't
eaten. It would taste good now, and give her new heart
of hope for the day's worries. Besides, she would have
opportunity to go over quietly her resolves of the night

before and check up on them. See if they were really wise in the light of day.

Lexie had washed her own cup and plate and written a list of a few things she ought to get at the grocery, when she heard the children waking up. She hurried upstairs and endeavored to greet them and enthuse them with the game-spirit that had worked so well the night before, but they were cross and utterly alien again. So with a mere bright word for them to get quickly dressed and come down to breakfast she hurried back to the kitchen and prepared a generous dish of cereal and another of scrambled eggs, got out the bottle of milk she had saved for morning, squeezed orange juice enough for four glasses, finished the tray for Elaine, and took it upstairs, setting it beside Elaine's bed. She seemed to be still sleeping; so she summoned the half-dressed children in a whisper, and they all went down to breakfast.

While they were eating she talked to them.

"Your mother is sick," she said gently.

"Naw, she ain't sick," announced Gerald. "She's just kidding you. She gets up and walks around whenever you go downstairs."

"I wouldn't say that, Gerry. She's probably trying to help all she can. Now listen. There is a great deal to do today. I wonder if you three couldn't help a bit? Will you try?"

"What doing?" inquired Angelica coldly.

"Well, first, trying to be as quiet about everything as possible so you won't make your mother worse. She doesn't feel at all well you know."

"Will there be a prize?" asked the little girl.

"Well, there might be," said Lexie thoughtfully. "I hadn't thought of that. I felt you would like to do this for your mother's sake."

"*Why?*" asked the child with a hard look in her eyes.

Lexie was startled. Did any children feel such an utter lack of care for their mother that the thought of doing anything for her sake made no appeal? What should she say? But Angelica was waiting with hard impish eyes for an answer.

"Why, just because she's your mother, you know."

"Oh! *That!*" said the Angel-child. "That's no reason at all."

But suddenly the conversation was interrupted by a sharp call from Elaine.

"Here are some apples and pears you can have when you finish your scrambled eggs and toast," said Lexie. "Now, sit quietly while I'm gone, and we'll see what will come next. I've got to go to your mother."

She hurried upstairs.

"Have you sent for a nurse, Lexie? Or have you changed your mind and called my lawyer? I want to get him before he goes out. And you better give an order to have a phone put in right away, then we won't have to bother you to go down town every time we turn around."

For answer Lexie quietly closed the door and sat down.

"Elaine, there are a few things we have got to talk about before I do anything more."

"Oh, *indeed!* Well, make it snappy! I've got my mind on important matters."

"*This* is important. It's about money, Elaine. Have *you* got any? You know we can't do anything without money. Not even telephone. I told you last night how much money I had, and I spent nearly all of it to get those things for supper and breakfast. Now I think we ought to have an understanding. How much money have you got?"

Elaine stared at her disagreeably.

"That's none of your business!" she said angrily. "We'll have money enough when you fork over what your mother salted down. And until then you can *charge* things."

"I'm afraid not," said Lexie. "People are not giving charge accounts much anywhere, not new ones anyway, and if you have had them a long time you have to pay your bills every month *on time* or the government steps in and closes your account for you."

"Oh, *really?* I doubt it. I think we can get by!" said Elaine in a superior tone. "You just charge whatever I ask you to get, and I'll take the consequences."

"Does that mean you haven't any money, Elaine? Because *I* really haven't. My ticket is bought back to college. I got a round trip. And my board is paid at college. That is I have a job working so many hours in the dining room that covers my board and room till commencement is over. And I have a job, a good one, as I told you, after I graduate, but it is dependent upon my graduation. So you see it is important that I get back to college as soon as possible. That is why I am asking about money. Have you enough to take care of yourself and the children and look out for your nurse and everything if I go back right away? I could of course wait till I could get somebody to stay with you and act as nurse."

Elaine looked at her in amazed disgust.

"Do you mean that you would actually *desert* your poor sick sister and her poor little orphaned children, and go running back to your old school, just so you can *graduate*? I never heard of such an unnatural girl as you have developed into!"

"Elaine, how would you think I would live if I don't go? And how could I help you any? I have not been able to save anything, but I knew I had this good job coming if I finished my course."

"That's ridiculous! You could get a job *here*."

"I'm afraid not, Elaine, at least not as good as the one I have. You see I was especially recommended by the college for the one I have, and the government sets the scale of wages, so it is really worth while. And of course I couldn't be of much help to you, even for a little while, without some money. What would we live on?"

"Oh, how absurd!" said Elaine. "There are always jobs to be had. As if there were any better ones out where your college is! And certainly my father's daughter could easily be recommended anywhere. No mere college would have to do it. And what's three months more of college, and a mere trifle of a diploma? You'll never need a diploma anyway. You'll likely be my housekeeper all your life, and I don't care whether you have three months more education or not. Now just put all such notions out of your head and get ready to go on my errands. I've written out a list of them and given you a few telephone numbers I happened to have. You bet-

ter take the two younger children with you. Angelica
can amuse herself with some books out of the bookcase,
and run errands for me if I need her, and I can rest
better with the younger ones out of the way."

Lexie looked at her sister astonished. Then she shook
her head.

"No, I couldn't take the children. It's a long walk I
have to go, and they would get very tired. It would take
me too long with the children. You see I have some errands of my own, too. Let me see your list."

"Well, I must say you are not very accommodating. I
supposed when I came home I would have the care that
the word home generally implies, but it seems not. What
do you suppose I'll do alone with the children? I'm not
able to get up and look after them."

Lexie's eyes and voice were very grave.

"I don't know, Elaine. But they are your children,
and you ought to have enough authority over them to
keep them in order for the short time I shall be gone."

"It won't be such a short time, my dear sister, after
you have done all the things I want you to do. Just cast
your eye over that list."

Lexie looked at the list and her expression grew firm.

"You will notice the order in which I have written my
wishes," said Elaine. "I had a distinct purpose in that,
and I want you to observe it carefully. First, call my
lawyer. I've given you his phone number. Tell him to
come at once! He ought to get here before you do, and
it is for that reason I want you to take the children. I
don't want to be bothered with them while I am talking
to him. Then of course you must order the telephone
put in. And next, I want you to contact the nurse. I've
given you several addresses where you'll be likely to
find one. Of course the best hospitals will know of one.
And Lexie, make it plain that I won't take her at all if
she can't come *right away!* I need her *at once.* Tell her
I'll talk with her about her wages when she gets here.
Tell her to take a taxi. That I'm rather helpless and
need her at once! And next I want you to stop at
Arnolds and get me a box of those lovely caramels he
used to sell. Be sure you get the same kind. You know
what they are. And bring them with you if you can't get

him to send them. If he would send them at once I would have something to offer the lawyer. Or you might get a couple of packs of cigarettes. I'm practically out of them. Any good brand. I don't suppose this dinky town has every kind. And then I wish you would call up Carroll Dayton, and ask her the address of that dressmaker she wrote me about, and if she thinks I could get her to alter some dresses for me at once. I've been too ill to look after my wardrobe, and I need some things at once. And *next*—"

Suddenly Lexie handed back the list to her sister.

"I'm sorry, Elaine, but I'll not have time for all that. I'll try to get someone to stay with you, but I can't do all those other things now. And anyway, unless you have a lot of money, those things will have to wait indefinitely I'm afraid. *I* certainly haven't the money. Now, I'm going, and you'll have to take over with the children. I'll send them to you. I *ought* to get through and get the noon train if possible, but failing in that I *must* get the night train, if I can find you a nurse. You see I'm already twenty-four hours late, and you must remember that I have a job and obligations. But of course I'll find somebody first to be with you. I won't leave you alone. Good by, I'll get back as soon as I can."

Lexie flashed a nervous chilly little smile at her sister, and turning ran out the door, with Elaine calling wildly after her:

"Lexie, Lexie! You can't leave me that way! You can't! You *can't!*"

But Lexie went on down the stairs uncompromisingly. She sent the three children back to their mother with a smile and a promise that she would bring them each something nice if they were good and did what their mother told them all the time she was gone. Then catching up her hat and coat from the chair where she had deposited them five minutes before, she hurried out of the house, resolved not to listen to Elaine's frantic calling. It was the only way! She was sure she was right. They could not go on without money, and the only way she could make sure of that was to keep this job that she had been so happy over only yesterday. Maybe it did seem heartless to her sister, but if Elaine had no money, *somebody* must provide it, and she knew by experience that there was little hope of her getting a job in this vicinity.

And Elaine, convinced at last that it was useless to scream for her sister, arose from her bed of illness, dressed her hair in the most approved style, made up her face with just enough blue shadows under her eyes to look like an interesting invalid, put on a ravishing negligee from her suitcase, a pair of charming slippers, manicured her nails carefully, and went downstairs. She placed herself becomingly on the old couch in the living room that had seen so many years of hard service in the family. Then she called Angelica to her and instructed her to go across the street to Mrs. Wilson's house and ask if she would kindly call up the number written on the slip of paper she carried when she went to do her marketing and ask Mr. Thomas if he would come out and see her at once about important business. Elaine was not one who ever allowed the grass to grow under her feet, and would not be stopped in her endeavors by a mere illness, no matter how dramatically it had been built up.

Angelica was like her mother. She entered into the importance of being trusted with such a message, and went on the errand with avidity. But she presently returned with the news that Mrs. Wilson wasn't at home. The neighbors had said she had taken a defense job, so Miss Angelica had tried other neighbors, who each in turn examined the bit of paper with its unknown numbers, asked several curious questions. Just one finally volunteered to send the message, but came back to the child after she had done so, in high dudgeon.

"Say, little girl, was that lawyer you wanted me to phone to, Bettinger Thomas, do you happen to know?"

"Why yes," said Angelica importantly. "I guess it was. I heard my aunt and my mother talking about him and they called him 'Bett' Thomas. They said they used to go to school with him." Angelica always enjoyed repeating important information.

"Well," said the helpful neighbor, "if I had known that I wouldn't have stirred a step to send that message.

You can go back to your mother, little girl, and tell her that man isn't fit for her to speak to. Tell her her mother wouldn't have allowed her to send for him if she had been alive. Mrs. Kendall was a good woman and she would be horrified to have that man allowed to come to her house. Your mother has been away so long she probably doesn't remember how her mother felt about him. Or maybe she never knew how her mother felt."

"She wasn't her *mother*," said the Angel pertly, "she was only her *step*mother, and stepmothers don't count!" said the child, tossing her dark curls saucily, and flouting away from the neighbor. She went hotfoot back to her mother to report.

"You mean they had the impertinence to say that to *you?*" asked Elaine furiously. "My word! What are we coming to when the neighbors around here would dare to send *me* a message like that! Well, you can just go straight back and tell those old busybodies that they don't know what they are talking about. You can tell them that I've known Bettinger Thomas for years, and I trust him thoroughly, and they better look out saying things like that about him. He is a smart lawyer, and when he hears that he'll certainly get it back on them in some way that they won't like. Being a lawyer of course he knows how."

So, being a smart child, and obedient when it suited her purposes, Angelica went on her way with her retort, and gave it forth with embellishments according to her own sharp little tongue. As the hour of Lexie's absence lengthened into two, there presently drew up at the little white house a costly car, shining in chromium, polished to the last degree, and the hovering neighbors from furtive hiding places, identified the fat pompous man who got out as none other than Bettinger Thomas himself. They shook their heads and murmured sorrowful comments to one another on what "poor dear Mrs. Kendall" would say if she could only know.

"And it's a mercy they can't know such things in Heaven," ejaculated the neighbor who knew the least about it, "because she certainly couldn't be happy knowing it. She was *such* a good woman!"

Lexie, on her way, would have hurried even faster

than she did if she had known what was going on back in the little white house. For though she had known her sister well for years it never entered her head that Elaine would go to the length of getting up from her sick bed and taking things in her own hands to get that reprobate of a lawyer. Trouble, trouble, there seemed to be trouble on every side, and somehow she must go through it and work out a sane and wise solution to all these difficulties. If only God were here to tell her what to do!

Then it came to her suddenly that of course God was here, and He knew all about her troubles. He would know the wise way to work it out. He would know whether she ought to insist on going back to college to finish her course and get her good job, or whether she ought to stay here and look after this unreasonable, unpleasant sister, and her three naughty children.

"Oh, God, won't you please show me what to do?" her discouraged young heart cried out, as she walked down the pleasant street, and wondered that it could seem so pleasant when she was having so much trouble. "God, please help me!"

Her mother had taught her to believe in God. She did of course, but she had never really done much about it. Only said her prayers religiously every night, and gone to church when it was convenient. But she knew in her heart that that wasn't really being even just polite to God. If He were a neighbor, or a mere acquaintance, she would feel that she had to have more of a pleasant contact than just that in order to be really polite. These thoughts condemned her as she walked along. "Please God, forgive me! I didn't realize that I was being rude and indifferent to you. But now, I've nobody else to go to. Won't you forgive, and help me, please? Should I give up everything and let my selfish sister manage my life? Oh, but I can't do that! We wouldn't have any money if I have no job. I'm almost sure Elaine hasn't any money. And anyway I wouldn't want to live on her money. Not even if I worked for her. I couldn't. I just *couldn't,* dear God! And what shall I do about a nurse? They cost a great deal of money I'm sure. And it isn't likely Elaine has enough money for that. Even if she gets a little from her husband's pay in the army, she wouldn't have enough for that, and to run the house. If she had had enough money for all her needs I'm sure she never would have come to me, back to the little house that she always despised. Oh, dear God what shall I do?"

Softly this prayer was going over and over in her heart, with a longing and a kind of wonder that had never come to her before when she was trying to pray. This was just something that breathed from her inner being, from a newborn trust that had come from her great need. A kind of a desperate feeling that she was appealing to the only possible source of help, and if He wouldn't help her she was done.

These thoughts filled her mind as she went swiftly on her way. She was not thinking of the immediate mission before her, for in the hard watches of the night she had settled definitely, step by step, just what that would be.

First, although she felt it was useless on account of expense, she must call up the hospitals, and nurses' agencies, and make careful inquiry about what could be done. That had to be done for Elaine's satisfaction. For she would never give up the idea of having a really important nurse from some established hospital unless she found it was impossible for her to pay such a nurse. So this was the first matter to be got out of the way.

Lexie went to the telephone and called up the various places she had on her list. And of course it turned out to be not only out of the question for financial reasons to get such a nurse, but she found that any nurse was almost impossible to get. So many had gone into war work, that the hospitals themselves were hopelessly understaffed, and they could not suggest any agency, or nurse that would be at all a possibility in the immediate future. They added that conditions were getting more and more strenuous, and nurses were almost impossible to get anywhere.

Lexie tried all the possibilities that Elaine had suggested, and got nowhere so far as a nurse to come out to the little house was concerned, but she carefully wrote down opposite each name on her list every bit of information she had gleaned.

Then, because her watch warned her that this was the

hour when she would likely find the dean of her college in his office she put in a long-distance call for him, and had a five-minutes' talk with him, telling him in brief phrases what had befallen her, and asking his advice. This talk greatly heartened her, for the dean gave her his promise to do all that was possible to help her that she might graduate with her class. He suggested certain preparation she might make in her home, and a possibility of a delayed examination in case her sister was too ill for her to leave at once, or she could find no one suitable to stay with her. He promised also to hold her job for her for a few days until she could let him know just what she could arrange to do, and to use his influence to get her job that was to come after her graduation, transferred to the city near her home, in case she had to stay there. He told her to write him more definitely in a day or two, or better still to come on for a short time, or anyway telephone him again. His words and tone were so kind and considerate that they brought tears of relief to her tired eyes. At least she had one friend who was sorry for her distress, and would do all in his power to help her. Though more and more she became certain that she had to remain for a while at least, and see Elaine and her children safely settled somewhere, somehow.

Then with firmly set lips and determined eyes she started out on her final quest, in search of an old acquaintance who used to live not far from them in the days when her mother was alive. One, Lucinda Forbes, a practical nurse, a staid, elderly woman with a homely face, and somewhat crude ways, but a heart of kindness who would perhaps be willing to undertake even a thankless job, as one attending Elaine would be sure to find it. Lucinda Forbes had loved her mother because of numerous little kindnesses that she had done for the lonely woman, and just because she had loved Mrs. Kendall, Lexie hoped she might be willing to look out for Elaine and her family, at least for a little time until she could finish her course and come back.

Of course Elaine wouldn't like it. She had always despised the woman, who was much too plain-spoken for her ease of mind. And neither would Lucinda like it, because she knew Elaine of old, and had little patience with her selfish ways. But at least she might help out in this emergency for a time.

There was, too, the possibility that she might be sick, or moved away, or gone into war work, or even dead. Lucinda might be rather old for such a job, too, but at least she would try for her, because she knew of no other one she could get at present. So she took a bus to the place where she remembered Lucinda had moved the last time she heard of her.

It was rather a long bus ride, and Lexie was tired and discouraged before she got there, but when she reached the house she found Lucinda was no longer there. She had gone to a single room in a dreary little house in a back street, and when Lexie finally reached her she was just about to leave that and go out to hunt still another abiding place.

"I can't afford this room any longer," she told Lexie with a tired look and a stray tear wandering down her cheek. "You know I'm not able to do so much nursing now. They want younger women, and I can't seem to get in anywhere."

Lexie's hope rose.

"Oh, Lucinda! I'm so sorry for you! But—are you free now? That would be wonderful for us. Would you be willing to come to us for a little while anyway, until you get something better?"

"*You!* Oh, Miss Lexie! Would I be *willing?* But I thought you were away at college! You're not married, are you?"

"No," laughed Lexie, "not married, nor likely to be. And I *am* in college. Or, that is, I *was,* until yesterday afternoon, and still am if I can manage it. You see I've only till spring till I graduate. But yesterday I got a telegram from Elaine. You know she's married, but her husband has gone off to war, and she's sick. She has come home with her three children! I just didn't know what to do. I can't bear to give up my college when I'm so nearly done, and a splendid job waiting for me when and if I graduate. But Elaine is sick! and I don't know what I ought to do. I was wondering if it would be possible for you to come and stay with us—at least with

Elaine and the children—while I go back to college and try to finish up?"

"Oh, *Elaine!*" said Lucinda with a dismal look settling on her grim old countenance. "I'd come for *you* of course, but—*Elaine*—she's another proposition. She and I never did get on you know. She was always too snooty, and treated me like the dust of the earth."

"Yes, I know," said Lexie sadly. "I remembered that of course, and I wasn't sure you would be willing. I know you two never did agree. Of course Elaine *is* rather hard to please. But—she's my sister! I *have* to do something about it. And you were the only one I could think of who might possibly help me out until I can get through this hard place."

"Well, of course," said Lucinda relenting, "when you put it that way—! And your mommie was always so good to me!"

"But there's another thing I should tell you, Cinda," said Lexie, "we couldn't pay you much. Not now, anyway. After I'm through college I hope to be able to earn enough to pay something, but for the present it wouldn't be much but your board and room."

"Oh, I wouldn't stop for the money, Miss Lexie," said Lucinda airily. "Of course a room and a few bites to eat is all I need for a while now, anyway, seein' I've got to move out of this room, poor as it is. And I oughtta be thankful to get a place to lay me head, and a crust now and then. The only thing is that Elaine. I never did favor her. But of course as you say she's your sister, and you can't help that! Well, when do you want me to come?"

"Oh, Cinda, I'm so glad you will consider it! You don't know what it means to me. And I'd like you to come as soon as you can. Now, right away, today. Can you come back with me?"

"Well, no, not just to say *back,* for I've got to wait till me man comes to get me trunk. But he said he'd be here in about a hour or so, and I'll tell you what I'll do. I'll get him to let me ride along of him and bring me trunk and all, and start in living."

"That will be wonderful, Lucinda! It's like a great burden rolled away. I know there are going to be hard things about it, Cinda, but I hope they won't be too hard, and if you find things getting unbearable please try to remember that we are having a war, and things are all mixed up any way, and we've got to win this war. And the way to do it is for everybody to win in their own hearts, and try to keep calm, and not mind when other people are unpleasant."

"I know, Miss Lexie, and I guess I can stand as much as the next one. But when it comes to Miss Elaine, I just know I'll speak me mind too often and she won't like it!"

"Well, try not to, Cinda, and perhaps it won't be as bad as you fear."

"Well, mebbe not. But I'll not bank on that much. I'll just think it's something I've got to weather, for your sake, and your sweet mommie's. Good by and thank ye kindly for remembering me. So long. I'll be seein' you within the day."

Greatly relieved Lexie went on her way back to the house, stopping only to buy a few necessities at the store, and when she came in sight of the little white house, there was that great shining limousine parked before the door, and inside the house, awaiting her return, its obnoxious owner, ready with his little pig-eyes to look her over, and attempt to startle her into admissions that would help him to win this case he was so eager to undertake.

5

WITH QUICKENED HEARTBEATS Lexie hurried on, wondering whose car that could be and what had happened since she left the house. Was something wrong, some accident perhaps to one of the children, and some of the neighbors had sent for a doctor? But that car did not look like one belonging to any local doctor. Surely Elaine hadn't gone to the length of sending for some city doctor!

She hurried in and there sat Bettinger Thomas, and there on the couch reclined Elaine, laughing and talking with the man Lexie felt was nothing short of a moral leper.

Lexie paused in the doorway for an instant, looking from her sister to the caller in amazement, and suddenly became aware that the obnoxious visitor was studying herself with open fulsome admiration in his little pig-eyes.

"Why, it's little Lexie, isn't it?" he said in honeyed tones. "And how you've grown! You're really pretty, aren't you? And I used to think you were awfully plain beside your lovely sister. But you certainly have blossomed out. You're a very handsome girl, Lexie."

Lexie flashed a fiery glance at him, utter contempt in her expression, and turned toward the kitchen with her bundles, vouchsafing no reply. But Elaine stormed out at her.

"You're being rude, Lexie. This is Mr. Thomas. You used to know him in your school days. He has come to talk over our finances with us, and help us to get to a better understanding. Sit down won't you? Mr. Thomas is in rather a hurry, and we mustn't hinder him."

"You'll have to excuse me, Elaine," said Lexie coolly. "I have some things to do, and there is nothing I care to discuss with Mr. Thomas."

61

Lexie turned and went into the kitchen, shutting the door firmly. She walked into the pantry, shutting that door to keep out the sound of her sister's angry voice calling her.

"Lexie! Lexie! You ridiculous child! How rude you are! Lexie, come here this minute. I've *got* to explain to you!"

Lexie stood for a moment with her back to the pantry door, her bundles still in her arms, one hand on her heart, struggling to keep her tears back. The kitchen was very still, and Elaine's complaint was plainly to be heard, but she did not intend to answer it. She could not go into the living room and hear Elaine making complaints of her own dear mother. If Elaine wanted to do that she would have to do it without her as an audience. It was dreadful that Elaine would do a thing like that! Actually charge her mother with being dishonest! And before that great lump of iniquity, *Bett Thomas!*

Then she heard steps coming toward the kitchen. She heard the door open, and heard a man's voice calling her. "Lexie! Oh, Lexie! Where are you, you little rascal?"

Well, she certainly wouldn't answer him. She stood perfectly still, suddenly aware that her bundle-laden arms were aching. But she would not move to reveal her presence. Not until she heard the man coming toward the pantry, heard his prying hand on the knob of the pantry door. The impudent fellow! But Elaine had probably told him where to find her.

Quietly she swayed forward to the shelf and deposited her groceries. Then she turned and faced the man who had dared to come after her.

"Here, you little monkey you, come out of hiding!" he said jocosely. "We haven't any time to waste being coy! I came up here in the midst of a busy morning to discuss business matters, and you'll *have* to come in here and answer some questions. I can't be played with, even if you are a pretty girl!"

"I beg your pardon," said Lexie coldly, tip-tilting her chin haughtily. "I really have nothing to discuss, and you'll please take your hand off my arm. I don't like it! Let me pass, please. I'm busy in the kitchen."

Lexie made a sudden unexpected dash, slipped by him into the kitchen. She went over to the sink where she turned on the water and began noisily to wash some potatoes, and to fill the kettle with water.

"But you don't understand," said the very much annoyed and determined man, "this is an important matter, and I haven't time to waste waiting for you any longer. You'll understand when you are brought up in court how important it is that you should attend to the matter now and perhaps save yourself from an extended trial, where I warn you you will have no friends to save you from trouble."

"Really?" said Lexie. "Just why should I be brought to trial? I'm not aware of having done anything that the law would be interested in."

"Very well, then, you better come into the other room and let me tell you why you will surely be brought to trial unless you can answer my questions in a satisfactory way."

"Questions?" said Lexie airily, although she was inwardly quaking. "What questions are there that you could possibly have a right to ask?"

"Well, you see I am your sister's lawyer, and she is suing you for the money her father left in trust with your mother for his elder daughter."

"Oh," said Lexie, suddenly thoughtful, "is that what she is doing? And just why should she think I know anything about it?"

"Of course you would know, and were probably in collusion with your mother in secreting the money, and diverting it all to your own uses. And now if you will come into the other room and sit down where we can talk, I will explain to you how you can make the whole matter very simple by just being willing to cooperate with us. It will be a great deal easier and better if you will put aside your animosity and cooperate with us. It will be cheaper and better for you in the end if you will come at once and tell all you know about this."

Lexie studied her pompous antagonist for a minute,

and though she was boiling inside she realized that she would get nowhere by angry resistance.

"Very well," she said suddenly, in a quiet tone, as she began to roll down her sleeves and preceded the man into the living room, infuriated by his fulsome flattery.

"That's the good girl!" he commended loudly. "I knew you were too pretty a girl to put up a fight. Now, we shall see how quickly we can get this matter under way. Suppose you sit here," and he indicated a chair close to the one where he had been sitting.

Lexie sat down in a straight chair across the room from the one suggested.

"Now, just what did you want to ask me?" she said in a cold haughty tone, a tone that made her appear so much older and wiser than she really was that Elaine stared at her young sister in amazement.

"That's better!" said the big man with a kind of rumbling satisfaction in his voice. "Now we can get somewhere. First, Lexie, let me ask you to think back to your childhood and tell me carefully what you remember of financial discussions between your father and mother. Way back as far as you can remember. You can remember a time, can't you, perhaps when you were playing about in the room, and you heard your father tell your mother that he had left quite a large sum of money in trust for his elder daughter Elaine, money that had been her own mother's, and that some day he hoped it all went well to leave something for you his younger daughter. You remember that, do you not?"

"No," said Lexie calmly, "I do not remember any such thing."

"Well, suppose you repeat what you do remember on that subject."

"I do not remember my father and mother discussing money in any way," said Lexie quietly.

"Think back. Think hard. Tell us what you do recall."

Lexie did not reply, and the lawyer was annoyed.

"Let us put it in another way," said Thomas. "You may not remember such a conversation, but you knew, did you not, that there was such a sum of money put away in trust for your sister?"

"No," said Lexie promptly. "I did not. Because there was not any such sum put away. My father may have intended to do something like that, but I am sure it was never done."

"And what makes you so sure, Miss Positive?" asked the fat man impudently.

"I am sure because my mother worked hard after my father's death to pay his funeral expenses, and afterward to get money enough to send us both to college. She often came home too weary to eat her supper, but she wouldn't give up her work. She said she had promised my father that we should both have a good education, and she was saving every cent from her own needs to make it possible. I was a witness to all this, and so was my sister."

A cunning look came over the fat face of the man.

"Yes? And what became of that money? Did your sister get her share of it? Did she get her education?"

"No, she got married instead of going to college. But mother gave her her half of the money as a wedding gift. I saw her do it. And then when she got her divorce and was in terrible straits she gave her my share too. I suggested it, and was glad to give it to help her out. But mother got evening work in addition to her day job, and started in to try and save money for my college course. That was what killed her. She only lived another year, and when her funeral expenses were paid I had fifty dollars in the bank to get through college with. I got a job just out of high school, and have worked my way through college so far. I have kept that fifty dollars in the bank, because mother earned it for me, but if Elaine wants that she can have it. It's all I have. And that's all I have to tell you. Now, I'll be excused if you please. I have a train to catch, and a lot to do before I go."

Lexie arose quickly and flashed out of the room before the two astonished listeners could stop her, but before she had closed the door behind her she heard the lawyer say:

"Well, that's a very unlikely story! We'll have to put the screws on that girl and tighten them till she opens up and gives us the truth. You could see she knows where all your money is all righty, or she never would have offered to give up that fifty. You better get at her in earnest and find out just what she knows. Of course I can't do a thing without evidence. And when she finds she has to produce *evidence* for all that pretty story she told, she may come across."

Lexie hurried upstairs to her own room and locked her door. She would not be haled into another questioning.

With swift fingers she put the room to rights, packed her few belongings that she had used during the night, and then came softly out and went upstairs to the one attic room, where Lucinda would have to sleep, for Lucinda would soon be here and there must be a place to receive her or she would vanish into thin air.

Lexie worked rapidly, pulling out bedding, making up the single bed that had stood sheathed in an old bedspread, unused, for four long years. A bright tear or two fell on the sheets as she smoothed them over the old mattress, thinking of her dear mother who was gone away from her forever. What would her mother do if she were here and knew all that she was going through?

But she must not cry like this. Lucinda would be coming, and if she saw her crying it would in all probability bring on a tirade that would wreck all her plans for hoping to keep Lucinda with Elaine, even for a short time.

With firm resolve she wiped her eyes and hurried through the bedmaking, brought a pitcher of water to the little oak washstand, found fresh towels, a piece of soap. She remembered the tears with which she had laid away these things after her dear mother was gone, thinking that perhaps she would never unpack them again, not wanting to recall the precious days of which they reminded her.

She wiped the dust from a little old rocker, plumped up its patchwork cushion, straightened the small mirror, set the window shade straight, and then turned away. The room was as ready as she could make it.

As she went softly down the stairs she had a fleeting wish that she had dared to give Lucinda a room on the second floor. It was surely her due if she was willing to undertake the job of nursing this queer household while she was away. But she knew if she did, it would bring on a torrent of abuse and scorn from Elaine, and probably break up the whole affair even before it was begun. And perhaps Lucinda herself would have chosen the attic room, as a refuge from all that she would surely have to bear even for a little while under Elaine's domination.

So she went quietly down to the kitchen and began to get some lunch on the table. As she did so she heard the children trooping back to the house. They had been across the street playing with some children when she returned, probably sent by their mother to get rid of them while she transacted her business with her lawyer. Well, she would give the children some lunch. That would keep them still for a few minutes, and occupy her troubled trembling hands.

But suddenly she had a feeling that she was not alone, and looking up she saw Bettinger Thomas standing in the open doorway with a fiendish grin on his face.

"Oh, so you thought you'd get by with a tale like that, did you? Well, you've got another guess coming. You can walk right in here young lady and come clean. Walk! Your sister wants you."

6

THE WAY HAD been long and hard, day after day under fire, night after night creeping furtively from bush to bush, from shadow to shadow, sometimes alone, and now and again in contact with others of the same group. It seemed endless, and Benedict Barron felt that he was scarcely human any more. When there was food, coarse and poor for the most part, he wolfed it, and when there was no food he drew in his belt tighter and crept forward. He had to go on! It was so ordered! Just why he who had never been prepared for an existence of this sort, had been selected for this special service he couldn't tell. It was all a part of the bewildering medley of war, he but a cog in a wheel that turned on and on relentlessly. He nothing but an automaton whose business it was to move on and through, no matter how the fires burned, no matter how hot the ground was where he crawled, thankful only that he still had ammunition for a few more shots at the spitfires that peppered him so constantly, thankful that there was still enough blood left in his body to keep going.

And ever and anon there would come a lull in the starlit nights when the fires for the moment had ceased to fall, and a cool breeze would blow. Not for long, but always it would remind him of that cool mountain town back in his homeland, and the little girl in blue swinging on the gate. Then he would remember his intention to write some day and tell her about how the thought of her had helped him through the horror of these days and nights. Some day he would surely write to her, if he lived to find quiet and a pen and paper, or even just a pencil and an old envelope.

Now there was a river in the way, a deep wide river, and he was so tired. If he could only rest before trying to swim. Would he ever get across?

Then as he plunged into the dark cold waters, his senses sharpened and he seemed to be hearing words from long ago. His mother's voice, or was that his grandmother's, reading from the Bible? Ah! It was his grandfather, reading at family worship, a favorite chapter. The words seemed graven in his heart. He had heard them so many times when he was a little boy: strange that after so many years they should come back to him just now when he was going through this experience!

"When thou passest through the waters, I will be with thee; and through the rivers, they shall not overflow thee": Was He here? God? "When thou walkest through the fire," ah, there was fire ahead, on the other side of that river, great walls of fire that he was expected to pass through— Was that God's voice speaking these old familiar words, or just his old grandfather? He couldn't stop to reason now. It took all his energy to get across this wide dark water and keep his ammunition dry. But maybe God had let his grandfather ring out those words from Heaven where he went long years ago, words that he knew God Himself uttered centuries ago. Could they perhaps have been meant for him down in this present modern century stress, and his great need? These deep dark waters were a terrible barrier. He could not get on, yet if God was here perhaps he would get through to his duty, and the fire on the opposite shore. The words went ringing on in his heart, in that strangely familiar voice: "When thou walkest through the fire, thou shalt not be burned; neither shall the flame kindle upon thee."

Were these words really being spoken to him, or was this just a trick of his imagination? His *sick* imagination?

And then the shore, and the fire raging close at hand! Ah! Now the *fire* again!

All through that awful night, the fiercest of them all, those words kept ringing when each man of them felt that the final test had come, the end had arrived. It was a fight to the death, and they expected death, in fact almost welcomed the relief it would bring to have it over. Just the end and the peace that death could bring. But as they fought through that night and the day that followed, and then as another night came down, grim determination, and courage that seemed to be born from above, had kept them going. Dropping down with pain and exhaustion, then rousing and in that vital energy that does not die in desperate need, going on,—even when it had seemed to the enemy that they were conquered. "We must not lose," each said in his heart, "we *must win!* We're dying, yes, all right, but our death must win this war!"

So it was when the fire came over Ben Barron again, and that burning flame fell and went through his very being in one great overwhelming stab, Ben Barron dropped to the blackened hot sand in the deep night, as the fire burned itself out. There he lay through the darkness and pain and sickness that seemed but a lingering death.

But before his senses went out and left him in the blank darkness he saw those mountains of home rise about him, felt the cooling breezes blow over his throbbing temples, and saw again the little girl in a blue dress swinging on the white gate, with a song on her lips and a light in her eyes. He found himself wondering in his pain: Was this Heaven, and was he going in without any more preparation than this? Just a transfer from a battlefield to the Presence of God? Strange that he had never thought of that possibility before. Death? Yes. He had counted *that* cost, had been willing to go, but the thought of what would come after, going into God's presence, hadn't been presented to his mind, either by himself or by any sermon he had heard. And he didn't somehow feel ready for the Presence of God.

In his delirium he looked around—the little white gate—it was there yet, and the little girl in the blue dress. Could she perhaps be an angel? Would she remember him? The little girl on the gate, and the jaunty school boy? Would she perhaps remember him? She had helped him once as he passed on through these fires, could she help him again, now, in case this happened to be Heaven he had reached? He hadn't written that letter to thank her for the help she had given in that wild hot fire, by sending cool mountain breezes. He had surely meant to write that letter. Where was he now? *Was* this Heaven? And how had he dared drift in here, if it was?

Dozing off into delirium it came to him to wonder about the Presence of God, into which he was probably going. How would he be received there? Had he done a creditable job of fighting? Could he pass on his merits as a soldier, or not?

But God didn't care about his courage as a soldier, did He? He was too big and too powerful Himself to care about a little thing a soldier could do, all in the way of his job, wasn't He? It wasn't as if he had done something outstanding, like bringing down his plane in the midst of a lot of Japs and getting away with it. He was only a plain soldier, a fighter, going through fire. Was the fire all done, or would it come again and devour him before he was ushered into the Presence of God? Would God listen if he tried to tell Him how hot those fires had been? How hard it was to keep on with that bullet in his shoulder and the blood seeping away all the time making him weaker and weaker? Or did God know already? Perhaps He did. Those words from the Bible that his grandfather used to read seemed to ring that way. His mother used to think God knew and cared about everything and everybody. "His own" she used to say. "God cares for His own." But that meant people who had done something about it, "accepted him" they used to call it in Sunday School long years ago. And he had never really done anything about it. Not even joined the church when the other kids did. He didn't see standing up before the world and nodding assent to things he wasn't sure of, and then likely going out and acting just the same so the world wouldn't see any difference in him, and would wonder why he did it anyway. But now, perhaps about to approach into the Presence of God, he wished he had. If he could say, "I'm a member of the old First Presbyterian Church in Nassau in good little old York state where my grandmother lived, and where grandfather was an elder and respected," would that make any difference when he was introduced to the Presence? But somehow he didn't seem to feel that even that would make him acceptable. He would be just one of many dead men, and what would God want of a dead church member anyway, since he had never thought about God, nor had Him in mind at all when alive?

If he only knew somebody who knew God well, perhaps that would make a difference. Of course his mother, and his grandmother, but they were already gone. He couldn't likely find them "up there" before he had to make his entrance into the Presence. That little girl in the blue dress? She was here somewhere. He had seen her in his vision. Child or angel? Would she help him? She had brought a memory of dew and cool mountain air down there on the hot battlefield. She had cooled his forehead. Little Lexie. Had that been her cool little child-hand on his fevered brow? Would she introduce him to God? He was almost certain she knew God. If he could just see her again, he would ask her. Where had she gone?

In his delirium he tried to rise, but the pain in his shoulder made him faint, and fall back, and then the world went out and he was a long time in the darkness. But it couldn't have been Heaven could it? Dark like that? He seemed to remember a verse he had learned in Sunday School, "And there shall be no night there." What would a place be like with no night? No falling fires? No bombs?

It was sometime during that night that the Lord came and stood beside him, looking deep into his eyes, speaking gently:

"Ben Barron, I came with you, as I promised, through the water, and through the fire. I am the Lord your God . . . your Saviour. If you want me I will go with you all the rest of the way. For I have loved you. You need not be afraid when I am with you."

The wonder and the awe of it made him forget his pain. Could this be Heaven, here on this scorched battlefield? If not how was it that he was already in the Presence of God? Perhaps Heaven was anywhere where God was? Or was he already dead of his wounds, and this was the Heaven above?

Then even the thought of Heaven vanished and he sank into oblivion. If there were more fires he did not know it. Bombs bursting about him made no impression. If he thought at all he thought he was dead.

He never knew when comrades came to him, touched his forehead, felt for his pulse, shook their heads.

"Take him up carefully, he's got a bad wound. He may not last to get there."

"Do you think it's worth while to take him in? It seems to me only a matter of a few minutes. He may not live to get there. The room is limited you know, and there are so many who stand a better chance of getting well."

"Take him in," said the sergeant. "Give him his chance. He's a good guy. He'd do as much for you."

A murmur of assent, gentle handling, lifted and borne. He never knew any of it. If he had he would have been grateful.

To the swarming semi-privacy of an overcrowded ward he was taken, in a queer foreign hospital, understaffed, undersupplied, and the weary rushing doctors and nurses with too many patients to attend did their best for him in the intervals between what they considered duty toward more important patients. There was so little hope for Barron. He had lain too long on the battlefield. Too long in suffering and loss of blood.

Yet because God had come to him out there on that battlefield and given him a vision of Himself, and spoken a quiet word to his soul, he lived on unexpectedly; and slowly, very slowly began to recover. It seemed incredible to the nurses, even to the skillful doctors who had done their poor best for him with the small equipment given them. All were astonished at the vitality that kept him alive. Until at last one day they began to understand that he was really coming back to life again.

"Well, Barron, you're going to get well!" the head doctor said to him one morning as he made his hurried rounds. "That's swell. You'll be begging us to let you go back to your outfit again pretty soon I suppose."

Benedict Barron turned dreamy eyes to the doctor and studied his face, examined his smile, responded with a comprehending glint in his own eyes.

"Is the fire still there?" he asked after a minute. "Isn't it all over yet?"

The nurse murmured something about where he had been picked up, and the doctor frowned.

"Oh, I understand!" he said. "No, Barron, the fire in that particular spot you manned is out. Definitely out. They couldn't take what you gave 'em. The battle has moved farther on, up over the last mountain stronghold. It won't be long now till we have 'em completely licked!" He gave Ben Barron an affable grin, as well as he could control the poor tired muscles of his face, and Ben tried to smile back.

"Good boy!" said the doctor. "You're definitely on the mend now, and I guess you're glad they don't need you to go through any more fires at present. It was a pretty tough job you had, man! I'm sure you'll do your best the rest of your life to forget all about it."

Ben Barron looked at him startled for a moment, with eyes that had so recently been seeing into another world. Then he slowly shook his head.

"No," he said softly, "I shall never forget. I don't think I want to forget."

"You don't *want* to forget?" said the doctor, astonished.

"Why, that's strange. I'm sure if I had been there I would want to forget it. Why don't you?"

Ben Barron gave a slow smile that lighted up his whole face.

"Because, you see, I met God out there. I had never met Him before. But I met Him, and He talked with me, and now I know Him. I shall never mind dying any more because now I know the Lord."

The doctor studied him, startled, with a strange unaccustomed tenderness about his mouth and moisture in his eyes, and then he said in a grave husky tone:

"Oh, I see!" and he turned away and cleared his throat. "Well, you wouldn't of course if you had that experience! Well, so long. I'm glad you're better. And I'll be seeing you."

Then he went out in the corridor where the nurses were talking together in low tones and went up to one.

"Say, have you noticed, is that guy in the last bed a bit touched in the head?"

"Why, no, doctor," said the nurse who had been attending Barron, "I hadn't noticed it. Why, did he seem wrong to you? He's a very quiet fellow."

"Yes, quiet enough perhaps, but he seems to have been seeing visions, or else he hasn't quite got back to normal yet. Keep a watch on him will you, and let me know if there are any abnormal developments." And then he looked into the room once more furtively and gazed at Ben Barron as he lay there on his cot with his eyes closed and a look of real peace on his face. The doctor went on to other patients, wondering to himself, would having a vision of God bring peace to everyone who was wounded? *Was* there a God? He had always thought he didn't believe there was, but perhaps there was Something. Some Force or Power that worked on weary spirits through nerves that were worn to a frazzle. But that soldier really acted as if he was ready to go out again and fight. As if he really *wanted* to go if there was more fighting to be done. Pity they couldn't have more soldiers seeing visions if it worked like that on them. This Barron must be a regular guy.

From that day on Benedict Barron grew steadily better, and one morning he asked his nurse for writing materials.

"I want to write a letter," he said with an apologetic smile.

"Oh! Do you feel able?"

"Sure! I guess I can manage."

"Going to write to your mother?" she asked as she handed him a tablet and pencil, and arranged his pillows so he could write with the least exertion.

He gave her a sad little smile.

"One can't write letters to Heaven," he said. "That's where my mother is now. She doesn't have to worry about me not getting home."

"Oh!" said the nurse with gentleness in her voice: "I'm sorry! I didn't know."

"Don't be sorry," he said, "I'm glad she's there. She hasn't had to worry about this war at all."

"You've got something there!" said the nurse gravely. But she asked no more questions about the letter. And when it was finished she took it to mail, and studied the address carefully. Miss Alexia Kendall. Nassau

Park, N.Y. U.S.A. An oddly lovely name. Some girl
he knew back in the United States. How interesting!
She held the letter with respect in her face, and started
it out on its long journey.

Ben Barron lay there in his hard narrow cot thinking over the words he had written, and wondering if
they would ever reach the person to whom they were
addressed.

He knew the words by heart because he had been
framing them over and over, reframing them in his
mind, for days and days before he started to write. And
so now he went over them again, questioning each
word to be sure it was just the right one.

Miss Alexia Kendall,
Nassau Park, N.Y. U.S.A.

My dear Miss Kendall:

Do you remember one day when you were a little girl
out swinging on the gate in front of your house and a
high school boy came by and asked your name? You said
it was Lexie, and I've been remembering it all these
years, for I was that school boy.

I never saw you any more because my mother and I
went away in a few days, and I've never been back there,
for my grandmother whom we were visiting, died that
summer. But I've never forgotten the picture of you swinging on the gate in the sunshine with a smile on your happy
little face. You wore a blue dress the color of your eyes,
and there was dew on the grass at the side of the road,
and sunshine on your curls, mountains in the distance.

I'm a soldier now, fighting to keep our world clean and
good for little girls such as you were, and I've been through
fire. One night when I lay wounded on the dark hot sand
where the fire had raged, that picture of the mountains, and
the dew, and you swinging on the gate with your happy
face, came to me, and it was like a breath of comfort from
my home long ago. And then it seemed to me you came and
laid your little cool hand on my hot forehead, and your
hand was like my mother's touch. She's been gone five
years now. Your touch helped me a lot, and I thought I'd
like to tell you, and thank you for it. Do you mind?

Of course I know you're grown up now, and may have

forgotten the laughing boy I was, whom you never saw but
once. You may have moved away, or changed your name,
and this may never reach you. You may have even left the
earth. But if you are alive and get this, you'll forgive me
for writing just to thank you, won't you? Because you
really gave me comfort.

Gratefully yours,
Benedict Barron

Ben Barron fell asleep thinking over that letter, with
a great relief in his mind that he had accomplished it,
for it represented to him a debt that he owed the little
girl. And now, if there were still more fires for him to
pass through, he was ready when they sent him out
once more.

7

Lexie looked at Bettinger Thomas with astonishment, mixed with a deep anger. She was not a girl who was quickly angered, but she knew who this man was, what decent people thought of him, and felt herself insulted by his very tone. Should she go into the other room with him and put herself into his power for even another few minutes? Let Elaine see that she had had to give in? No, she couldn't do that. She could see that just polite dignity wasn't going to make this man understand that he couldn't bully her around this way. She had got to get out of his way, or get hold of somebody who could help and protect her. But who could that possibly be? She wasn't sure of any of the neighbors being at home. Most of them were doing defense work. Besides, Lucinda was due here at any time now, and she must be here to meet her, or all her morning's work would be wasted.

Lucinda would be of no help in this matter. True, she had a sharp tongue and well knew how to use it, but that wouldn't get anywhere with Bett Thomas, nor with Elaine either. It would simply turn Elaine hopelessly against Lucinda, and then where would she be? She didn't know of another person she could get to stay with Elaine.

All this was going through her mind like a flash while she stood and faced her hateful antagonist, and suddenly her mind was made up. She wasn't going into the living room with this man, and she wasn't going to talk finances over with Elaine in his presence. She didn't know just what she was going to do afterwards, but she knew she was going to get out of the house for the moment.

The children were just outside the dining room door now, and arguing with all their might, making a great clatter. Lexie gave a quick glance at the table. Everything was on it they would need except some scrambled eggs she had intended making for them. They could come in and eat without the eggs.

She lifted her chin independently.

"Excuse me," she said almost haughtily, although there was nothing really haughty in Lexie's makeup except on an occasion when she felt desperate. "I couldn't come immediately. There is something I must do first."

Then she quickly opened the door on the clamoring children whose noise drowned any protest the lawyer was trying to make.

"Angelica, stop talking and bring the children in to their lunch. It is all here on the table. Now be a good girl and take care of Bluebell," and as they trooped in Lexie stepped out and shut the door sharply behind her, flying frantically down the walk and out into the street.

She turned sharply into a side street, running as if she were intending to hurry back in a moment, and when she heard the front door open and a man's voice calling her, she was out of sight. He wouldn't know just which way to look. But she did not pause to watch if he would follow her. Of course he had his car there and his chauffeur. They could follow her. What should she do?

She knew that Mrs. Turnbull in the next street just back went early to her job in a riveting plant. No one would be at home there and she could slide through that yard and make her escape to the main highway that led down to the drugstore. If she got there she might be able to hide, or—oh, if there was only someone to whom she could telephone for help! And yet who was there, and what could she say when she found them? The man in the drugstore was no help. He was an old man, a stranger to her, a newcomer since Lexie went to college. But she dashed into the store, and was thankful there were two or three patrons in there talking with the proprietor. She went into the telephone booth and sat down, shutting the door and opening the telephone book, wildly searching her memory for some name she could call where she might at least ask advice. Some of her father's or her mother's old friends, who for their sake would be kind enough to advise her what to do. But suddenly her eye fell on a name. Foster. That was a familiar name. Judge Foster was her father's old friend. Was he still alive, and would she dare call on him for advice?

Her hands were trembling as she turned the pages, and tears blurred into her eyes as she tried to think what to do. She simply could not go back and face that obnoxious man, and listen to his slanderous words about her dear mother!

Then there was the name Judge James Foster, and the old address where she had often gone as a little girl with her father to see his friend, and perhaps on business. Dared she call him? There were two addresses. His residence, and his office. She would try the office first. Perhaps this wasn't the right thing to do, but what else was there for her?

Her fingers were trembling as she dialed the number, and her voice was shy and frightened as she asked the severe lady secretary at the other end of the wire for Judge Foster.

"Who it is, please?" came the response.

"Oh," said Lexie, "I—tell him it is the daughter of his old friend George Kendall. Tell him it is important, and I won't take but a minute of his time."

"Hold the wire please," the severe voice said.

A moment more and she heard the man's kindly voice, an old, kind, dependable voice, and her frightened heart leaped thankfully.

"Oh, Judge Foster, is that you? Really *you*? This is Lexie. You wouldn't remember the little girl who used to come with her father, George Kendall, to your house sometimes, but surely you would remember my father?"

"Why certainly, I remember my dear old friend George Kendall, and *of course* I remember you, little Lexie! I remember you well. You used to have such a happy little smiling face and sunny curls. Yes, I remember you, and have often wondered where you were? What can I do for you Lexie? I'd like to see you again. Where are you?"

"I'm out at our little house. That is I'm at a public

telephone now, not far from the cottage. But I'm in awful perplexity, and I thought perhaps you would let me ask you a question or two, and tell me what you think my father would want me to do."

"Why of course, little girl. What is the matter?"

"Well, you see, I've been working my way through college and am ready to graduate in June, but my half sister—you remember my father had another daughter—Elaine?"

"Yes, I remember Elaine. She was older, was she not? And she did not have a very happy face, though she was quite pretty."

"Yes," gasped Lexie, and felt that her counselor understood the situation fully. "Well I came back here to put the house in shape to rent, and while I was here got a telegram from Elaine. Her husband was in the army, and word had come he was missing in action. She said she was sick, and she was coming home with her three children. And before I could do anything about it she arrived with a trained nurse, who left as soon as they got here. Elaine seems to have no money, and says she is too sick to do anything, and I am due back at my college where I have a job, and important examinations to take, finals you know. But the worst of it is that Elaine claims that our father told her when she was a little girl that there was a large sum of money left by her own mother for her, and that when she was of age she would get it. And now she is obsessed with the idea that the money must have been left in my mother's trust and that mother has spent it on me and herself."

"Impossible! Outrageous! Absurd! Of course there was nothing of the sort!" ejaculated the judge.

Lexie caught her breath.

"And now," she said, her voice trembling full of tears, "she says she is going to sue me for it. This morning she sent her oldest child to a neighbor and got her to telephone for an awful lawyer she has been corresponding with. He is a bad man, a man we knew in school when he was a boy. Bettinger Thomas. Perhaps you have heard of him."

"I should say I have!" said the judge, indignation in his voice. "He is a villain if there ever was one."

"Oh, I am so glad you understand!" gasped Lexie gratefully. "I was afraid you wouldn't. Well, he is at the house now. He has been asking me all sorts of insulting questions about what mother did with that money, and putting words into my mouth to which he wants me to assent. I told him I knew nothing about any such thing, never heard my father speak of any such money. I said I knew he was in financial trouble when he died, and that mother worked very hard to pay the funeral expenses, and then to put aside money for us both to go to college. When Elaine married instead of going to college she gave her share to her as a wedding gift and started in to do extra evening work to get money for my college. But she died from overwork. I told him that and then I went out of the room, but the lawyer chased me into the kitchen and insisted I come back to answer more questions. I made an excuse and slipped out of the house to this telephone. I'm very much ashamed to bother you but I knew that you understood my father's ways and wishes, and that you would know if there was ever any money left to Elaine that we did not know about. I do so need someone to advise me what to do, how to answer that awful lawyer. He is very crude and tries to bully me into saying what he tells me to. Please, do you think I should answer him? And what should I say?"

"Say nothing, my dear! Just refuse to answer his questions. You say you have already told him you never heard of any such money, and so, if you cannot get away from him then simply tell him: 'I have nothing further to say.'"

"Oh, thank you! I am so relieved," said Lexie with almost tears in her voice. "I had hoped to get away, but I can't go till the woman comes whom I hope I've secured to stay with Elaine. Do you think I ought to go at all when she is sick? You see I have a job out there when I have finished my course."

"I certainly think you should finish your college course if possible," said the Judge, "but I'd have to know more about this to rightly advise you. When and where can I see you? Should I come out there? Or can you come to my office?"

"Perhaps I could get away to come there," said Lexie. "I can't be sure whether we could talk at home without Elaine hearing everything. Of course she ought to hear everything, but how she would act when she heard it is another thing. Can I call you this afternoon and let you know if I am free to come?"

"You certainly can. I'll be here at four o'clock. And until then, if I were you I would keep away from that lawyer if you can. If that's impossible just sit quietly, calmly, and do not answer his questions, beyond saying once or twice, 'I'm sorry, that's all I have to say,' or, if necessary again, 'I do not know.' Don't lose your temper, or try to make smart answers. He has a way of nagging people into that. Just be calm. Even a vacant smile is better than getting excited or frightened, or making unwise answers. Wait until we can talk together. Keep your answers for a trial, if it has to come to a trial. But personally I don't think it will. Certainly I know all about your father's affairs. He told me everything when he was first taken sick, and asked me to look out for you. I'm so glad you came to me. I had rather lost sight of you."

"Oh, thank you, Judge. This is a great relief to me to know there is someone who will help if I get into trouble."

"You won't get into trouble, my dear. Not from that man. I'll look out for him. But your sister. Remember she will be likely to do some goading of you also."

"Oh, yes, she has already!" sighed Lexie.

"Well, don't be goaded. Just take it smiling as far as you can and keep sweet. There is no point in getting angry, though I grant you there will probably be plenty to make you angry."

"Yes," said Lexie, "there will! But I'll just keep quiet and act dumb."

"That's the idea, child! And now, will you be all right till four o'clock? Well, call me up if anything unforeseen happens, and meantime don't worry."

Lexie went quietly back to the house and entered through the kitchen to the dining room where the children were squabbling over which should have the biggest cooky, and suddenly there came upon her a new strength to deal with the situation. She went over to Gerald and putting a firm hand about his wrist, folded her other hand over the cooky he had just taken from the wailing Bluebell.

"Oh, no, we don't do that!" she said in a low voice. "Gentlemen don't snatch cookies from babies. And you are the only gentleman of the party, so you must act like one."

Bluebell had ceased to howl and was listening, and suddenly broke into a joyful smile.

"Oh, is this a party?" she inquired happily.

"Why yes, I suppose you might call it a little party," said Lexie. "Suppose you try to act as if you were at a party, and that will make it a party you know."

"*She* don't act nice at parties," said Gerald pointing his crummy finger at Bluebell.

"Oh, but gentlemen don't try to bring out other people's faults," said Lexie. "Suppose you pass the plate to Bluebell and say 'Bluebell, will you have another cooky?' "

Gerald was intrigued by this suggestion, and took the plate with zest, imitating Lexie's little speech with an effective tone till Angelica giggled.

"Oh, but you mustn't laugh when a gentleman is being polite," said Lexie. "Gerry did that very nicely. Now, Gerry pass the plate to Angel."

Gerald entered into the game eagerly, and Angelica went one better and reached gracefully for her cooky, with a slight bow and said: "Thank you very kindly, brother!"

They were just in the midst of this little game when the door opened and there stood the lawyer, pompously glaring at Lexie.

"So!" he said irately. "You keep your sister waiting while you play a game with the children. Is that your important duty that hindered you from responding to your sister's urgent call for you?"

Lexie looked up coldly.

"I'll be there in a moment," she said, in a tone of decided dismissal.

"I'll say you will!" said the man, striding over to

where she stood and laying hold of her arm to draw her along.

But just as he did so Bluebell reached out her short fat arm to snatch Gerald's cooky, and unheeding, knocked against and swept her brimming glass of milk across the edge of the table and straight onto the immaculate suit of the lawyer, deluging the front of his coat, and pouring milk gaily down his perfectly creased trousers.

The fat lawyer's hand dropped suddenly from Lexie's rigid arm, and with an angry ejaculation he stood back and looked down at himself in dismay and fury.

Then he lifted his eyes to the staring baby who was giggling delightedly at the catastrophe she had wrought, and a look like a thundercloud passed over his fat flabby face.

"You little *brat!*" he said furiously. "You little *devil you!*" and he lifted his heavy hand and administered a sound slap on the round pink cheek of the baby. The sound reached into the next room to the excitable mother who was languishing on the couch, waiting for her annoying sister to appear. But when she heard the resounding slap she sprang furiously to her feet and dashed quite agilely over to the door, which she opened with a snap.

"What are you doing, Lexie? Slapping my baby? You outrageous girl! To think you would vent your fury on a baby! A poor little innocent. What can she have done to deserve a cruel slap like that?"

Her indignant tones were drowned by Bluebell's first heart-rending shriek of horror at the chastisement she had suffered at the hand of a stranger. It was the "stranger" part that was to her the most terrible, added to the fact that she hadn't at all intended to douse the gentleman's elegant suit. There were plenty of times when she *had* intended to do terrible things, when she *should* have been chastised, but this was not one of them. In fact it hadn't entirely dawned upon her that she was in the least to blame for this catastrophe. She had only been trying to snatch Gerald's cooky, and the deluge had been a mere incidental consequence. So why the slap? Besides, it hurt! And as this fact became more and more evident to her stinging facial nerves Bluebell howled the louder. In fact one might call the noise she made a roar, drowning everything else completely out.

Lexie opened her mouth to deny any part in that slap, but saw there was no use. It would not even get across while the child was crying. It was maddening. Elaine stood acting the plaintive mother part, flashing her eyes at her sister, casting apologetic glances at the lawyer who was wholly engrossed in mopping up his new suit with a pair of expensive imported handkerchiefs, and ignoring everything else. Nobody was doing a thing to comfort the distressed baby.

Then suddenly Lexie caught a glimpse of Bluebell's puckered lip, and came over with a soft old napkin snatched quickly from the sideboard linen drawer, dipped it in a glass of water from the table, and gently wiped the bruised cheek that distinctly bore the red imprint of heavy fingers, with a wide bleeding scratch where a sharply manicured finger nail had ripped the delicate skin.

Elaine watched with jealous eyes.

"Oh, yes," she sneered mockingly, "you're making a great show of trying to be kind and gentle, now that you've slapped her! Even brought the blood! That's you all over, Lexie! Slap an innocent little baby till the blood comes, and then pretend to be so sorry for her! *Slap* a *baby!* How *could* you? For what, I'd like to know? And then pet her up in the presence of others! I'll teach you to slap my child! How *dared* you?"

Suddenly Angelica spoke up shrilly.

"Aunt Lexie *didn't* slap Bluebell! It was that man slapped her." She pointed an accusing finger at Bettinger Thomas. "Aunt Lexie was standing over on the other side of the table, and that man was trying to make her go in the other room. Bluebell reached over to snatch Gerry's cooky, and knocked her glass of milk over on his pants, and it made him mad. He slapped her hard, and *scratched* her. I *saw* him! He's a bad old man! That neighbor-lady told me he was. She said you

oughtn't to have him come here, he was a bad man!
She said your muvver wouldn't like it!"

"Be still, Angelica! You're a naughty girl to say
things like that! I've told you not to repeat things the
neighbors say. The neighbors are bad people to talk
that way! And of course it was your Aunt Lexie that
slapped Bluebell. You mustn't contradict me!"

"No, it wasn't Aunt Lexie that slapped her. I saw it.
It was that bad old man. He was mad because his
pants got all milk."

Bettinger Thomas lifted a very red face and angry
eyes. There was no apology in his glance, only annoyance.

"This is a new and very expensive suit!" he declared
in furious explanation. "I am attending an important
luncheon at the Country Club this morning, and now
my suit is ruined! It is all that girl's fault too. If she had
come into the other room when I told her you wanted
her this never would have happened. I am sorry. I
shall have to put the price of this suit on your account.
It was quite expensive!"

"Well, if it was Lexie's fault she will of course want
to pay for it."

"Yes, and it won't be the only thing she has to pay
for if she keeps on in the way she has started. It may
be that we shall have to resort to having her arrested
and put under charge if she continues to refuse to tell
what she knows."

Lexie caught her breath softly, and closed her trembling lips. Then she remembered what her friend the
judge had said. She must not talk. And certainly she
must not cry.

She closed her lips tight in a thin line. She put her
mind on the effort not to look angry. Anger at present,
and in this company could not help. Neither must she
look frightened. She wasn't frightened, now that Judge
Foster was her friend, and going to help her through
this trouble.

The trembling that was in her fingers came from her
frightened heart. It was crying out to God to help her,
to show her what to do, to save the situation for her,

since she did not know what to do herself. Crying out to God as she would have cried to Judge Foster if he had been there. She was glad that God was always present. She could call to Him when she had not time to reach her father's friend the judge.

And then, most unexpectedly Lawyer Thomas stopped mopping his elegant clothes and gave a quick glance at his watch.

"I shall have to ask you to excuse me," he said looking at Elaine. "I must go home at once and change to another suit. I shall have to hurry, as it is most important that I should be on time. You will excuse me, won't you? I'll try to return tomorrow morning. Or at the latest the next day. Meantime get all the evidence together that you can find and put the pressure on your sister. She is the key to it all you know. But I'll have to say good by now."

"Oh, but I can't possibly wait till tomorrow!" wailed Elaine in distress.

"Sorry my dear lady, but tomorrow will be the very first moment I can spare, if indeed I can come then. I'll bear you in mind however, and come as soon as possible. And now brace up and get your evidence. I can't do anything without that you know. Good morning!" and hastily the obnoxious lawyer went out the door and down to his car.

8

ELAINE STOOD APPALLED and angry as he vanished, and then she turned her fury on Lexie:

"Well, now I suppose you think you've done it! You hateful cruel thing you! Torment a poor sick sister this way! Get up little trifling silly devices to have your own way and get rid of my nice kind lawyer. Spoil his wonderful new suit for him, and send him off before we were done with our business! I hadn't told him half the things I wanted him to know. And you *intended* this to happen of course. *I know you!* You always did work against me whenever you could. I remember that since you were a mere baby! You and your mother before you! Oh, why did my poor mistaken father every marry that scheming determined woman?"

Lexie stood there for a moment and listened aghast. Elaine rattled on. Long ago she had formed the habit of letting Elaine finish entirely whatever she had to say on a subject, for she had found by bitter experience it was the only way ever to get done a matter. If you interrupted her she would only go back and say it all over again. So, remembering, she stood quite still and waited until Elaine had talked herself out. And then suddenly Elaine, troubled by Bluebell's low wail that kept on bleating from her cooky-crumbed lips, turned toward her baby.

"You poor child! Poor little baby! Her own auntie slapped her when she hadn't done anything at all! Naughty auntie! Aunt Lexie doesn't love you. She doesn't care how much she hurts you."

Lexie winced at that, telling the baby lies about her, but she knew if she tried to speak her indignation would come to the front and take control of her, and that must not be. So she kept still, till finally Elaine turned toward her again with a direct question.

"Tell me, Lexie, just *why* did you slap the child so unmercifully? I can't understand it. I thought you were always kind to children. That was the reason I felt perfectly safe in coming to you while I was so sick I couldn't look after the children myself. Why did you do it?"

"But I didn't slap her," said Lexie quietly. "I wasn't even near her. I was trying to get away from that man. He had hold of my arm and was dragging me across the room. What made you think I slapped her, Elaine?"

"Of course you slapped her, Lexie. There is no use in lying about it, even if you are angry. Have a little sense."

"No, she didn't either slap her!" maintained Angelica, and Gerald hastily joined his word.

"No, Aunt Lexie *didn't* slap Bluebell, Elaine," he said. "That old man slapped her. I saw him! He was mad 'cause his pants got all milk."

"Yes, I see you have bribed those children to side with you. I call that pretty rank, for you not only to slap the baby, but bribe my children to lie for you!"

"Stop!" said Lexie. "Elaine, you must be crazy to say such things. Now, I'm not going to talk any more about this. I have told you the truth. I *didn't* slap her, and if you won't believe it I can't help it. Suppose we just forget it all, and try to get this family straightened out. Would you like some lunch, Elaine? Why don't you go and lie down again and I'll bring you a tray?"

"No, *thanks!* I don't want you to bring me a tray. I'm sure I couldn't eat anything you brought. Where is that nurse you were going to get?"

"She will be here in a little while, as soon as she can get packed. Do you feel able to sit down here at the table and take just a bite? How about a glass of milk?"

"No!" said Elaine sharply, "I detest milk. You know it always disagrees with me. I want some coffee. Where *is* that nurse? *Where* did you locate her? At one of the hospitals, or an agency?"

"No," said Lexie quietly, "there wasn't one to be had at any hospital or agency. The hospitals are suffering for lack of nurses themselves. But I finally found a woman who was about to take another job. She is an elderly woman, and doesn't mind being where there are children. I think perhaps she'll be willing to stay if you are all very pleasant to her."

"*Pleasant* to her! The *idea! Really,* I don't care to have a nurse like that! I want a regular trained-nurse, a graduate nurse! A young strong woman! I can't endure an elderly woman with set ways that has to be coddled."

"Well, I'm sorry, Elaine, I tried every place on your list and there wasn't one. They all gave me the same story. The young strong nurses have all gone to war, and the hospitals are suffering for lack of them. I think for the present everybody will have to put up with what they can get, or get on without help."

"Oh, fiddlesticks!" said Elaine angrily. "I'm quite sure I can find a regular nurse if I try myself. And as for this woman, if I don't like her I shan't stand her for a minute, do you hear?"

Lexie turned hopelessly away from her sister and went toward the kitchen:

"Suit yourself," she said with a sigh. "I've done the best I could. Now I'll go and make you another cup of coffee. There is just a little left in the canister. We'll have to use it carefully, for we can't get any more till someone goes to the ration board."

"Oh, how utterly silly!" said Elaine, walking languidly into the living room and flinging herself on the couch. "I certainly wish I had stayed in the west. I never had any trouble like this there. My housekeeper looked after all such annoying questions. I wish I had stayed there!"

And Lexie, in the kitchen, could not fail to hear, and echoed in her heart with a sigh:

"I certainly wish you had!" But she faithfully shut her lips tight and did not let the words out.

By the time Lexie had the coffee ready and took it in to her sister, Elaine was ensconced on her couch again with a handkerchief in her hand and great tears rolling down her cheeks. She paused in her grief long enough to announce again to her sister that if she didn't like the new nurse she didn't intend to keep her, and Lexie needn't think she would.

"Well, that's all right, Elaine," said Lexie, "but you see I have to go away at least for a few days, and wouldn't it be well for you to have somebody who could at least get you something to eat while I am gone?"

"You have to go *away!* How can you? You wouldn't leave me in this helpless condition would you?"

"That's it, Elaine," said Lexie trying to be patient. "I shall probably *have* to go. If there was any way to avoid it for the present, or to put it off a few days, I certainly would. I'm not sure I can. But while I'm gone there ought to be somebody here with you, that is if you intend staying."

"Staying?" yelled Elaine. "What else can I do? I'm here, and I've spent practically all the money I have to get here. Of course I'm staying. I never thought you would dare go away and leave me alone."

"I'm not leaving you alone, Elaine. I've got a woman who is entirely able to make you comfortable if you will let her, and I'm just suggesting that you'll have to put up with her, even if she doesn't happen to take your fancy, at least for a little while."

"Well, I like that! Talking to your poor sick sister that way. What would your precious mother think of that kind of talk, I'd like to know."

"I'm sorry, Elaine, but this seems to be necessary. Even if I don't finish college I've got to go back and get my things, settle up my bank account, report about the job I have, and the job I'm supposed to get after I'm through."

"Oh, that's all nonsense!" said Elaine petulantly. "That's just an excuse. That could all be done by mail or telephone."

"Elaine I have no money to telephone until I go back and get it. There are people for whom I have been doing things who owe me, and I would likely never get it at all unless I went. It may be that I won't have to stay long, but while I am gone there must be somebody here with you. So please don't antagonize her."

"Oh, *indeed!* Well I'll just let you know that I don't intend to toady to anybody if I don't like them. And as for your jobs you can send them postals that you can't come back. I can lend you money enough for that myself."

Lexie gave her sister a steady look, but said no more, and began to tremble for the meeting of Lucinda with Elaine. Would Elaine remember her? If she only wouldn't perhaps they could get by for a little while, but probably there was no such luck as that.

Lexie made short work of her own lunch, and the putting the kitchen to rights after it, trying meanwhile to think her way through the rest of the day. Though she ought not to make any definite plans until she had talked with Judge Foster.

It was just as she was putting away the last dishes that a little boy came to the back door and peered in.

"That you, Miss Lexie?" he said in a low tone. "Say, Mr. Maitland sent me over from the drugstore to tell you there's someone on the telephone wants to speak to you. Name's Foster."

"Oh!" said Lexie softly. "All right, I'll come right away."

She wiped her hands on the roller towel and dashed softly out the door, running her hands through her soft brown curly hair as she ran, for she knew it was awry. She wasn't vain, but she knew the neighbors would probably be looking out their windows, and she hated to look disheveled.

It was Judge Foster.

"Lexie, I find I have to drive out your way at three o'clock to see a business friend who is very ill. It is important that I talk with him before tomorrow's court session. Could I pick you up somewhere near your home and take you along? Then we could talk. It isn't a long drive, but it's about the only time I can possibly spare today. Will that be all right with you?"

"Wonderful!" said Lexie. "I could meet you at the drugstore. Then Elaine needn't know where I have gone. I'll tell her later but I don't want to be questioned till I have talked with you."

"That's the best thing to do. Yes, I remember where that store is, corner of Main and Cooper streets, isn't it? Be there sharp at half past four, and I think I can promise to get you back in an hour."

"All right. I'll be there!" said Lexie with a ring of relief in her voice, and then she hurried back to the house again, wondering what she should do when she had to leave if Lucinda hadn't come yet. But of course that would have to settle itself somehow. Perhaps it would be just as well for Lucinda to come while she was gone, although Elaine *might* send her off. There was no telling. But perhaps she would come before.

Back at the house she found Elaine had cried herself to sleep, which relieved the situation for the time being, so that she could finish putting the kitchen in order. Then she sat down at the kitchen table and wrote a list of things she must attend to before she went away to college, if indeed she found she could get away at all.

It was just as she finished her list that she heard a truck drive up to the door, and hurrying out found that Lucinda had arrived. She could dimly hear the children's voices across the street arguing with the neighbor's children, and was thankful that for the moment they were absent.

The truck driver who was an old friend of Lucinda's, accommodatingly carried Lucinda's trunk to the attic, and Lexie took Lucinda up and was glad that she was pleased with her simple little room.

"It isn't much of a place to put you, Lucinda," she apologized, "but I thought you would rather be up here by yourself. You would have more privacy. There's nothing else up here but the big storeroom, and no chance for you to be interrupted when you want to rest."

"Oh, it suits me fine!" said Lucinda. "I'm real pleased to have this much of a room over me so soon. It's just Providence, I can't help thinking. Somehow He always did look out for me when I got in a puzzlement. Leastways it must be Providence, for there isn't anybody else bothering about what becomes of me. So it must be Providence. And now, Miss Lexie, I'll be changing my dress, and then ya can show me the ways about, and I'll take over. You just tell what you want of me and go on about your business. You'll want supper got, and anything else you have in mind just write me a line on a paper. I can read real good and then I needn't trust to me forgettery."

So Lexie told her briefly about the location of rooms, and that there wasn't very much in the house to eat till she could go to the ration board.

"Oh, we'll make out," said Lucinda. "I know more ways to get meals out o'nothin' than you can shake a stick at, and good enough for that Elaine-one, too. Get me a lemon, an' a mushroom, an' a pimento an' I'll make out. Me hand's right in it when the pocketbook and the pantry is low."

"Oh, Cinda! That sounds good!" said Lexie with relief. "I've been so worried. You see I came down from college for just a day, and we haven't any ration cards yet. I haven't had time to find out where to go for them even, and I've got so many things to do. This afternoon I've got to see an old friend of father's and find out about some business matters, and I'm not sure whether I can get in touch with that ration board yet or not."

"Don't you worry, little girl," said Cinda. "Trust me! I'll scare up some kind of a meal, and if she don't like it she can lump it. But I'll risk but what I can make something she'll like. What have you got on hand? Any canned goods?"

"There's some fruit of mother's canning, a few cans of soup and vegetables I guess, too. I haven't looked them over very carefully. There's been so much else to do. But there are eggs and potatoes, and a loaf of bread."

"Well, I'll make out with those for a time or two, and if worst comes to worst, there's me own ration card. I been savin' up a point or two, and a bit coupon fer coffee and sugar. You can take *them* down and cash 'em in. Being out on a case, and then having to move, I didn't have any chance to cook. Get half a pound of butter, and a bit of meat, even a quarter of a pound ground, will go a good ways. I guess I could find me way to the stores if I got stuck whiles you are gone. But anyhow, where are the childer you was telling about? Can't they go errands?"

"Why, they're mere babies, all but Angelica, and they don't know the way anywhere yet. You better not count on that. They are across the road playing with a neighbor's children, but I hear them fighting. I suppose I ought to go and get them, and introduce them to you, but I'm afraid they'll bother you a lot while you're trying to work."

"That don't make any matter. I'm here to work, and to stand what's to stand. You run along and I'll make out. Don't bother about the childer. They'll turn up. If they don't I'll go hunt 'em. And you needn't bother to wake up that Elaine. Leave her lay an' sleep. I'll interjuice meself, and mebbe it'll be that much better fer results. Got any lemons here? I'll make her a nice cold drink. Too bad you haven't got any ice. But we'll manage. You run along. Here! I'll get those coupons for you before I go down."

Very quietly they went downstairs, and Elaine was either still asleep or simulating it very well.

Lucinda stood for an instant in the doorway looking keenly toward the invalid, and then with nodding head and set lips went her way, following Lexie to the kitchen. Lexie showed her all the meagre stores, whispered a moment with her, and then caught up her hat and coat left on a chair in a convenient shadowed corner and went out.

She did not go out the front gate nor take their street, but crossed the back fence into the fields, and got herself down to the drugstore without the danger of Elaine's discovering she was going out. She certainly didn't want Elaine to know about this interview with Judge Foster. It would bring on a tirade she was certain.

Lexie thought she was far ahead of the time named, but she had scarcely reached the corner next to the drugstore when she saw the judge's car coming from the opposite direction and drawing up to the curb.

She hadn't been at all sure she would know him, for it had been a number of years since she had seen him. But when he swung out of the car and glanced around him and toward the store, she knew him at once. She ran toward him just as she used to do when she was a little girl downtown with her father, running to greet her father's friend.

Oh, the judge's hair was a little whiter, and the fine lines around his eyes were graved a little deeper, but there was the same keen twinkle in the wise blue eyes, the same kindly look about the strong smiling lips.

He whirled to look at her, and the smile beamed out. "Little Lexie!" he exclaimed reaching out a hearty hand to grasp hers. "You haven't changed a mite, only grown a little taller! Hop in, little girl, and let's get on our way. This is a beautiful day and I'm anticipating a pleasant ride. I'm sorry it had to be your troubles that brought us together, but I'm mighty glad to get in touch with you again. And now, suppose we get the business out of the way first and then we can really enjoy our ride. Suppose you begin at the beginning and tell me the whole story. Begin when your mother died and tell me what you have been doing since."

So Lexie told her simple story, and the wise old man watched her, studying her lovely expression as she talked.

When she came to her college life he asked a few questions that put her whole present situation before him. Working her way through by doing little menial tasks here and there, and now and then tutoring some other student. She told it all most briefly, answering the judge's questions in few words, and hastened on to the main issue, the story of Elaine's arrival with her three children, just as she herself was about to leave to go back to college. And then the amazing claim of her sister, and her demand for money.

Very carefully now she answered every question the judge put to her, and then settled back in the car.

"That's all," she said with a troubled sigh. "Now, what shall I do? I meant to go back to college today at the latest, but I had to stay till Lucinda came. She wouldn't have known where things were nor what to do. I knew I could trust Lucinda, but she had to understand."

"I see! That was wise. And now, you say she has come?"

"Yes, she came just a few minutes ago."

"And how did Elaine take it?"

"She's still asleep, or seems to be. She doesn't know I've gone away. I slipped out the back door, and across the fields."

"Good girl! And now, let's see about this money business. You're right my dear. Your father didn't leave any money at all, not that I know of. Your mother finished paying for the little house you own. That's right isn't it? I thought so. I have all the papers that showed what your mother spent since your father died. She took great care to send me everything, as it came on the calendar, and I have kept them all together in a safety deposit box, so they are safe and can be used in court if they should ever be required. But really, my dear, I don't believe it will ever come to that. I think if it seems to be getting that far I will have a little talk with that rascal of a lawyer your sister has secured, and show him just where he can get off. I know he is a rascal, and I know too many things about what he has done to trust him for one minute. Of course he is very tricky, but he probably has been made to feel that there is some large sum of money involved, or he never would have wasted his precious time monkeying with it. Has your sister by any means told him how much she thinks is involved in this case?"

"I'm afraid she has," said Lexie with trouble in her eyes. "But I don't know how much she is claiming. She seems to think I have it hidden away somewhere and am using it for myself. They are going to sue me for it, and he has done his best to make me own up to whatever he says. He even told Elaine that if I kept on refusing to talk, the quickest way to make me tell the truth would be to have me arrested, and regularly charge me with being a party to the theft. He said that would bring me to terms quicker than anything he knew."

"Yes," said the judge gravely, "that sounds like his tactics. But my dear, there is a great deal of boasting about that. I scarcely think he would try a thing like that with you. However, we'll take steps to make that thing impossible. And now, my dear, if I were you I would go to college right away. Tonight, if there is a train, or certainly tomorrow morning, and see what arrangements you can make there, in case your sister is really as ill as she makes out, and you find you have to be at home for a time. But anyhow I would go at once and get what matters you have to attend to out there in shape, so you will be ready for any emergency. Perhaps that too will avert a clash about this maid you think she won't like. If she is sick she'll have to accept whatever services she has till she can get in touch with you again. And meantime you can put your business in order so you can return if necessary."

"Oh," said Lexie with relief. "You think I have a right to go? You think my father and mother wouldn't blame me for running off and leaving Elaine sick? And all her naughty little children to be looked out for by a woman who couldn't possibly love them enough to make it really pleasant for them?"

"Yes, I think you are right to go and get your affairs arranged. I think Elaine needs to understand you have to. I certainly think your mother and father would want you to do this. Maybe you can't stay there, of course, but if not there may be some way for you to go on studying and run back a few days for examinations. That can probably be arranged. And about your job, well, I don't know. I might be able to get that work transferred to this vicinity. And again, I might be able to offer you something even better in my office. It depends on the movements of the woman who is now my secretary. I might let you take over later. However, we will look into this and see how things come out. Certainly I won't let you down, my dear."

"Oh, that would be wonderful!" said Lexie wistfully. "But I never have had experience as a secretary. I'm afraid I wouldn't be worth much to you."

The judge looked at her with a kindly smile.

"Don't worry! I fancy you could learn, and I often have more than one secretary. Now, here we are at the house where I have to stop. I'll let you sit in the car and wait if you don't mind. There are a few magazines in the back seat. Help yourself. And I won't be any longer than I can help."

But Lexie did not spend any time reading magazines.

She had too much to think about, too much to be thankful for that she had found her father's old friend, and he was so inclined to be helpful. She sat still and thought her way ahead.

She decided not to tell Elaine anything about Judge Foster. She was sure she would immediately tell Bett Thomas, and there was no telling how he might involve Judge Foster. She must move as cautiously as possible.

But anyway she would have to see what had happened during her absence before she decided definitely what she would do. It was rather late for her to get the night train of course, but if she could slip off in the morning before Elaine was awake it certainly would be easier. That would have to depend largely on whether there had been a terrible eruption between Lucinda and Elaine. If there had, and Cinda refused to stay, she would have to wait and make some other arrangement, but she hoped she had made the woman understand how necessary she was to her plans, at least for a few days.

Lexie returned from that drive greatly heartened. She had met with kindly sympathy, and keen common sense, a promise of help if it should be needed, and sane advice. Her conscience would no longer trouble her if she went to college, at least for a few days.

But as she neared the house she began to have an uneasy fear of what might have happened while she was away. Oh what should she do if Elaine had sent Cinda away? There wasn't anybody, not *any*body that Lexie knew of who would be willing to come as Cinda had, without pay, and who would stand Elaine's imperiousness even temporarily, like Cinda.

So as she bade Judge Foster good by, and promised to let him know at once how things came out, a shadow was beginning to creep into her eyes, and a worry into her heart.

9

LUCINDA WAS IN the kitchen beating up biscuits with some prepared flour she found among Lexie's purchases. That didn't take shortening of which there was as yet none in the house, and it would provide something more interesting than the continual diet of dry toast without butter. She was trying to think what she could make that would be tasty and take the place of meat, which of course had not been purchased yet. Then suddenly she discovered a package of spaghetti and cheese preparation that ought to make an attractive dish. If Elaine didn't happen to like it, why, that was just too bad. It was the best she could do. But she hastened to make a pitcher of good strong lemonade. It didn't take much sugar, and would be heartening for an invalid perhaps—if she really was an invalid, Cinda had her doubts. She knew Elaine of old.

She wished as she finished stirring the concoction, that she had some ice, considered going to the neighbors to beg a tiny piece and decided against it. Instead she wet an old napkin and folded it about the pitcher setting it in the open window where there was a good breeze. Give it a little time in that breeze, and the evaporation from the wet cloth would make the lemonade almost as cold as if it were iced.

Then she set about preparing the table as if she were expecting a real dinner with all the fixings. There was lettuce. There were apples and nuts. And a little jar of mayonnaise dressing. Some cottage cheese, too. She could make a fine salad with those. Even a raisin or two might be added to give it character. Cinda tramped quietly about that little kitchen quite pleased with herself, thankful that the children had not yet appeared. Although she was not unmindful of them, and prepared three little jelly tarts for them when they should arrive.

The tarts were in the oven baking when Cinda heard a sharp call:

"Lexie! What on earth are you doing out there in the kitchen so long? Aren't you *ever* coming in to see me? Do you realize that I haven't had a mouthful to eat since breakfast? *Lexie!* Where *are* you! *Why* don't you answer me?"

"Coming!" sang out Cinda in as good an imitation of Lexie's voice as she could manage. She stepped to the window, flung off the napkin from around the pitcher, placed it on the tray already prepared, with a couple of vanilla wafers on the thin old china plate beside the pretty crystal glass. Then she tramped into the living room bearing her offering.

Elaine looked up startled.

"Oh! Who are you?" she said coldly. "And where is my sister? Didn't she hear me call her?"

Cinda drew up a little table to the couch and laid her tray upon it quite within reach of the invalid. Then she poured a nice glass of lemonade into the glass from the frosty pitcher, before she answered.

"Why, I'm the new nurse," she said pleasantly— more pleasantly than she felt. "Your sister had to go on some errands. She'll be back in a little while. You can tell me anything you want done."

"Oh! Indeed!" said Elaine. "You're the nurse, are you? Where's your uniform? I like my nurses to wear their uniforms. I'm very particular about that. Which hospital do you come from?"

Cinda looked the younger woman down, contempt beginning to dawn in her eyes, till suddenly she remembered her promise to Lexie, and she said in her heart, "Well, if you wantta act biggity, then I can act biggity too!" and she lifted her belligerent chin proudly and spoke in honeyed tones.

"I'm not from no hospital. I'm just a private nurse. A very *special!* I been on duty too long to be dependent on hospitals and agencies and the like. And I don't hold with wearing uniforms fer everyday work, especially in small houses. I think they're out of place, and too pre-

tentious. A uniform's all right if you don't do nothin'
but nurse, but if ya havta cook some, and look after
the family, it makes too much work to be washing uniforms all the time. Me, I didn't bring me uniforms with
me. I didn't think they'd fit the job. Not unless there's
two or three servants to help with the work. Is that drink
cold enough? Sorry I didn't have ice, but ya see we
haven't got that-is-to-say-organized yet, and I understand the ice man don't come around every day these
war times. It's awful, ain't it, what we havta put up
with, but then it's war, and we gotta be patriotic. Is
there sugar enough in the glass? I didn't dast use too
much because I wasn't sure just when yer ration card
would come through, an' I wouldn't want ya to be without sugar in yer tea. Could I be gettin' anything else fer
ya?"

Elaine turned and looked at the woman.

"Haven't I seen you before?" she said. "What's your
name?"

It was just at that moment that Lexie arrived at the
back door and Cinda turned and hurried away.

"Excuse me," she said. "I think I hear somebody at
the kitchen door," and she vanished from the room
leaving Elaine's question hanging in midair.

Then Lexie breezed in quietly and pleasantly, bearing in her countenance enough of the cheer from her
hour with the judge to give her an appearance of authority.

"Oh, Elaine," she said in an interested tone, "you've
had a nice long sleep, haven't you? Do you feel better?
I hope you do, and that you're going to be able to eat a
little supper. You've scarcely eaten a thing since you
came."

"There hasn't been anything fit to eat!" said Elaine
grumpily. "It does seem to me that you had time enough
after my telegram arrived to get some decent food in
the house, when I took all that trouble to let you know
I was coming."

Lexie drew a deep breath, and tried to smile.

"Sorry, Elaine, but I didn't dare do anything about
it until I was sure you were going to stay more than an
hour or two. I didn't think you would be satisfied with

a closed up house, and everything packed away, and I thought it best to wait till I could talk to you about it. You see I didn't understand that you would feel you had to stay here when you found that I was not living here."

"No," said Elaine, "I didn't figure on anything like that, but I knew you would *have* to stop college when I got here and you found what you were up against."

"I see," said Lexie, refusing to argue the matter. "Well, now suppose we put the matter aside and try to see what we can make out of things as they are. It really isn't worth while to argue about it. Are you ready for something to eat yet, or do you want me to go and get the children? It seems they must be tired and hungry by this time, and I think the new nurse has dinner almost ready, if I may judge by the nice pleasant odors that are filling the house. I think I'd better go out and see if she found everything, or maybe needs my help in anything. I'll look for the children, too, and bring them back with me. I'll be back in a minute!" and Lexie vanished, not heeding her sister's fretful insistent call.

She came back presently with the three children trooping after her and escorted them to the dining room where their mother presently heard them clamoring happily that they wanted "some o' that, an' that, an' a *lot* of honey." Real honey in a honey comb, Lexie had bought the last time she went to the store, and it went well with the hot biscuits Cinda had made, and the milk that filled their glasses. So Elaine called in vain for her sister, and finally started to rise and find out why Lexie didn't answer her call, but came face to face with Cinda and such a tempting looking tray that she suffered herself to be arranged with a table by her side and a napkin tucked in at her neck and a plate put within her reach. There was a cup of real coffee filling the room with its delicate aroma. For Cinda had some precious coffee from her own rationing, which she had brought with her, and had used a tiny bit of it to "work her lady" as she told herself grimly. She wanted with all her might to help Lexie, brave little Lexie, and she determined if good food and giving up her own cup of coffee now and then would help, she would do it. Lexie wasn't going to be the only one to sacrifice.

So Elaine ate her supper quite interestedly, and Lexie and the children ate theirs in comparative peace, save for the gossip that Angelica and Gerald retailed from time to time, concerning the misdeeds of "that bad old lawyer" who had come to see their mother that morning and of whom they had that afternoon overheard not a little that was not intended for their ears.

But Lexie managed those children into bed very soon, for they were really tired from hard play, climbing trees and digging in gardens where they shouldn't have been, and piling wood by other people's back doors where it wasn't intended to be. They were tired and dirty. So Lexie, tired as she was, managed a bath apiece, and got them into bed, one at a time, and they were very soon all three sound asleep, and the mother none the wiser. Perhaps that was one secret of their subjection, for they and their mother did not seem to get on at all well together.

Very tired at last Lexie responded to an angry call from Elaine, and went in to sink in a chair and let Elaine complain.

"Lexie, did you know that maid out in the kitchen isn't a trained nurse at all? She says she is something special, but I know better. She hasn't even a uniform. At least she says she left them all packed up at home, but I'm inclined to think she never had any. She hasn't the least sign of real training, and I told you I wouldn't have any other."

"I know, Elaine," said Lexie wearily, "but there really wasn't anybody else to be had."

"Fiddlesticks! I'll wager *I* can find somebody when I get well enough to take over the matter. However she brought me a very creditable supper when you consider what she had to make it with. But Lexie, did you know she was the old woman who used to live down the lane behind the mulberry bushes? She says her name is Lucinda, and I began to remember about her. I should have thought you would have known she never would do. She was half crazy or something, wasn't she?"

"No, she wasn't crazy. She's a very wise old woman, and very kindly if you don't antagonize her. But Elaine, she was the only one I knew to go after. You know I've been away from this region for almost four years, and it isn't easy now to pick up anybody to do anything. Besides, she was just about moving and it meant something to her to have a room at once. That was the only reason she was willing to come. That and because she knew us. And besides, I had to tell her we hadn't anything to pay her with at present, and most people wouldn't come to a place like that anyway. And by the way, Elaine, we've simply got to talk about money. Have you enough to pay the grocery bill while I'm gone away to see how I can get my affairs straightened out? Because I have hardly anything left and I'm not sure there is enough food in the house to last more than a couple of days. But if you say your ration books are in your trunk why we ought to be able to get things as soon as they come, but they will have to be paid for at once. They have no charge accounts at any of our stores out here any more, and even the larger stores in the city insist on having charge accounts paid up every month or you have to give up the account."

"How perfectly horrid!" said Elaine. "I'll speak to my lawyer and see what can be done about that. I simply won't buy where I can't have things charged."

"But you don't understand. *All* the stores are that way now. *Everybody* is obliged to pay, no matter how wealthy they are."

"Well, we'll see. Bettinger will be out in the morning. He telegraphed a little while ago and said he would, and if he can't make some arrangement with a store near here, I'll just borrow some money from him, that's all."

"Borrow of *him!* Oh, Elaine!" cried Lexie in despair. "Please, *please* don't do that! You just don't understand. It is all wrong."

"Nonsense! It's you that do not understand, my prissy little sister. I've always known how to get what I wanted from any man, and I shall get it this time too! I'd thank you not to say any more such things about my lawyer, and not to poison the minds of my innocent little children about him either. I mean that! And what's more if you don't stop this nonsense, I'll tell him what you are saying about him, and I'll tell him *right before you,* too! It's time you stopped passing on such slanderous gossip. Do you understand?"

Lexie caught her breath and closed her eyes for an instant.

"I understand that I'm very tired and I've simply *got* to go to bed or I won't be fit to get up in the morning," she answered desperately. "Can I help you any before I go, Elaine, or can you manage alone?"

"No, you needn't help me. I don't care for such unwilling assistance as I get from you anyway. You can send that so-called nurse in to help me to bed. If she's a nurse she ought to be able to do that at least."

Lexie looked at her sister aghast for a minute. Would Cinda be willing to perform menial services for Elaine, or not? Then she turned and went softly out to consult with Lucinda.

But before she could say anything to Lucinda that dignitary spoke first in an indignant whisper:

"Sure I'll do it. This once, anyhow. Yes, I heard every blessed word she said, and it's no more'n I expected. If I was you I'd go your journey the first thing in the morning, and not let her know you're going till you're gone. That way you'll be out of the house when that dratted lawyer comes, and you won't have to bother with him. And you leave the rest to me. Them childer'll be all right. I can get on with 'em, an' ef I can't I know how to spank good and proper, and keep their mammy from finding out about it too. So you don't need to fret. I'll carry on till you come back, anyway, and if it gets so bad I have to quit after that, why I'll just quit. That is if you say so. You're my real boss, you know. Not *her.*"

Lexie smiled a tired little smile.

"All right! Thank you, Cinda. I'll go as you suggest. Early. You'll know how to order and save points won't you? And if I find I can't return at once, at least I can send you a check for five dollars right away when I get my checkbook, and perhaps that'll go till I can send you more. Though *perhaps* my sister will have *some* money to pay for things. I don't know. You might ask her, if you need anything very badly. I do hope she won't borrow of that terrible man, but I'm afraid I can't do anything about it, not till I can get some money that some people owe me, anyway."

"Now, Miss Lexie, you go right along, and I'll manage somehow. There's canned goods in this house enough to keep from starving for a long time, and if your sister wants something better let her get it! Doesn't she get something off the government for her husband being in the army? Or doesn't she? She'd oughtta, I should think."

"I don't know, Cinda. She doesn't tell me things like that. Even if I ask her she doesn't tell me. She's got an idea in her head that our father left some money for her, and that my mother and I used it up, and she's trying to get it out of me somehow. I don't know how she ever got that notion, but she has it, and unless she can find out the truth about it and know there never was any, I'm sure I don't see how I'm ever going to get along with her."

"Well, Miss Lexie, you just run along to your college and get your matters straightened out, and then if you want you can telegraph me what you want I should do, and I'll do it. You trust me. I can hannell things all right. Now go right to bed, an' I'll wake you up in plenty o' time in the mornin'."

So Lexie finally went to bed, creeping in softly beside the sleeping Bluebell, and praying that God would somehow bring her affairs out right, thinking with great gratitude of Judge Foster as she fell asleep.

But Judge Foster was lying at that very moment in a hospital bed, unconscious, as a result of an automobile accident.

Lexie, happily ignorant of this, went on her cautious way the next morning, rejoicing that she had so strong and wise a friend as Judge Foster, who had made her see so plainly that she need not be frightened, but might go safely on in the right way.

10

LATER IN THE day, after Lexie had had a long talk with the dean of her college, and he had given her two propositions to choose from, she went to her old room and sat down in perplexity. Should she try to stay here in college now for three months more, and get through with her examinations before she went home, trusting that she could get another job at home afterwards? Or should she accept the dean's offer to make arrangements with the university in the city near home to let her finish her course and take examinations with them? Or what would be best? At last she went to the telephone and called up Judge Foster's office to ask his advice. He had told her to do so if she felt at all worried about anything. But when she finally succeeded in getting the Judge's office, what was her dismay to be told by that cold-voiced secretary of his that Judge Foster was unable to talk with her as he was lying unconscious in the hospital and they were not even sure he would recover.

She hung up the receiver and sat limply down in a chair in the quiet office room where she was phoning. Not only was she filled with sorrow because this dear old friend of the years was in danger of his life, but she was also overcome with a great dismay. This newly-found old friend was gone again, taken away from her need, and she had to go on *without* his help, at least until he got well. Perhaps he might *never* get well, and she would have to go on through her sea of perplexities alone! Suddenly Lexie put her head down on her folded arms on the desk and wept.

"Oh God! You'll have to take over for me! I haven't any other friend to guide me, and I don't know what to do. Should I stay here and finish and let Elaine see what a mess she's made of things, or should I go home and try to help and see this thing through? Is this some-

thing you are expecting—wanting me to do for You?
For righteousness? Won't you please show me right
away?"

It was just then that the telephone girl from the dean's
office opened the door and said:

"Oh, you're still here, aren't you, Miss Kendall? I
was afraid you had gone. There is someone calling you
from your home town. They want to speak with you
right away. They say it's very important. Will you take
it on this phone?"

Lexie sat up and looked at the girl in amazement. It
seemed so much like an answer to her prayer, that call
from home. For of course no one would have called her
unless something had happened. Or would they? She
tried to summon up reasons, but her tired brain could
think of nothing but that this message would decide one
way or the other what she must do."

Yes, it was Lucinda's unmistakable voice.

"Miss Lexie, that you? Now ain't that somethin', to
think I could get you right away! Miss Lexie, I'm that
sorry, but things has been happenin' thick an' fast ever
since you left this mornin', an' I'm sorry, but I guess
you gotta come back right away. First, Elaine she took
on somethin' terrible when she found you'd left without
tellin' her, an' she cried herself sick. An' then her lawyer, he sent a message he couldn't come out today,
'count of a court case he hadta try, an' that angered
her. An' then Miss Angelica had a fist fight with that
boy that's visitin' acrost the road, an' got herself a
black eye, an' Miss Elaine went out an' give that boy a
regular jawin', an' finally hit him with a broom when he
was sassy. Then his aunt come out an' give back words,
an' threatened to send fer the p'lice. An' then the police come an' made a lotta talk and threats. An' while
that was goin' on, Gerry, he went out an' monkeyed
with the neighbor's lawnmower, an' cut his foot bad,
an' I had ta send fer the doctor. An' whiles he was
comin', Bluebell, she went out, an' got stung by a big
bumblebee in the clover, an' she was cryin' fit ta raise
the dead, an' her mamma all in hystericks when the
doctor come. An' meself that near crazy I wasn't know-
in' which ta do first. An' then ta crown all, that Elaine

went up ta the attic and pulled out every blessed thing from the boxes an' trunks and bureaus an' left 'em all strewed around the floor. She told me she was looking among your mother's things for some very important papers she needed for evidence, an' she claimed to have found what she wanted in your mother's diary book. So I guess you better come back an' set things goin' straight. I'm awful sorry ta havta call you, but it's me that don't know what ta do first."

So! Her orders had come. This was her duty, obviously, to go back home and take over. One couldn't expect Cinda to do everything. She must go at once.

So, God had undertaken, and this was His order! But He would go with her! He would be there to show her step by step what to do. Was that it?

She closed her eyes for one breath of a second, and then drawing a deep breath and glancing up at the clock, she said:

"All right, Cinda! I'm taking the first train in the morning. I'll be there a little after two o'clock. You carry on till I get there, please, Cinda."

"I sure will, Miss Lexie. An' don't you worry none. I'll do just as I would be done by, an' no mistake. Me heart is all right, even if me brain don't always work the way Miss Elaine thinks it should. Gooby. I'll look out for everything." And she hung up.

Lexie turned from the telephone and went swiftly back to the dean's office.

"I've got to go back," she said breathlessly. "I've just had a phone call. I must leave on the morning train. Will I have to come back here again to get my credentials for that examination, in case I find opportunity to take the examinations in my own city?"

The dean shook his head and smiled with his characteristic kindness.

"No," he said kindly, "I'll fill out the paper for you right away, and I'll write my friend in the University in your city tonight. I'm sure it can be arranged. I'm sorry you can't finish with us however, for I had counted on using you later in our college. I felt you would fit right in here. Nevertheless if the way opens later for that you will let us know, please."

Much relieved Lexie came away with her papers, and hurried to her room to pack, trying not to think about what she might be returning to, doing her best to keep her anger from rising when she thought of Elaine mauling over her mother's precious papers, and reading her own intimate words not written for other's eyes.

It was a sad confused time, hustling the simple belongings into her trunk, stopping to say good by to the friends she had made in the college, trying to explain breathlessly about a sick sister with her children. And then back of it all in her heart there was an ache of worry about the kind old friend of her father's who was lying unconscious and in danger in a hospital. Oh if she could only ask his advice about this. But that was out. Nobody to go to now but God. Would God care, and go with her and guide her, she wondered fearsomely? She hurried with her packing, praying that all would be well. This was something she *had* to go through. It was going to be hard, and maybe long and disappointing, but it was right she should do it, and she *must* do it even if everything else she had wanted had to be given up. It was sort of like the boys who went to war. They *had* to go, even though it wasn't a pleasant prospect. They had to stay and fight it out, even though it might end in death for themselves. And in a way, this was like that. This was death to herself, and her own life and plans. Giving up for righteousness' sake. She *must* go, but perhaps God would go with her. Surely it was He who had answered her prayer by letting her know that she was needed at home at once. Only, what was she going to be able to do when she got there? Oh, if Judge Foster would only get well so she could talk to him for a little while. But perhaps, if she talked to God in the same way she would have talked to Judge Foster, He would somehow make her know what she ought to do.

So all the way of the journey she sat with closed eyes, her head back on the seat, trying to talk the situation over with God, and to realize that His Presence must be there with her, ready to help, if she would only put herself into His hands and be willing to hand over her own wishes.

When Lexie reached the street in which the little

white house was located, she sighted the shining limousine again parked before the white gate, pompous liveried chauffeur and all, and with quick resolve she turned and skirted that end of the street and slipped into the field behind the house. She did not intend to encounter that lawyer again, not if she could help herself.

But now she had the advantage of coming in quietly by the back door when they thought she was far away, and had no idea she was returning. Yet she wished she knew what was going on, and just what line Elaine was taking. There was no telling how she might have twisted words of her mother's diary to serve her own purposes.

Very quietly she entered the kitchen and put her suitcase down in the laundry entirely out of sight from even a casual observer passing through either the dining room or kitchen. Then cautiously she went over to the side wall close to the dining room door.

The door into the living room was wide open. She could even see the large flat foot of the lawyer as he lounged in the big chair by the table, but she kept well back so she could not be seen herself. It was obvious that she could not go upstairs without being seen by him. She would have to stay here until he was gone. Softly she swayed back again, entirely out of sight, and suddenly she became aware of another figure across in the dining room, unobtrusively planted just inside the partly open china closet door. This china closet was next to the living room door, but its doorway opened in such a way that one could stand inside and reach dishes without being seen from the living room. And that was where Cinda was standing. She was absolutely motionless, and in such an attitude that upon the appearance of anyone from the living room she could in an instant appear to be exceedingly busy picking out the right dishes, and selecting the linen from the linen drawer for the meal she was preparing. But in the meantime, she was motionless, listening with all her might! It was all too apparent that Cinda had no scruples against listening in on any conversation that went on in that household, of which she was for the time the custodian.

And while Lexie would not have justified a listener under ordinary circumstances, nor have felt justified in arranging to listen herself, somehow she couldn't help being glad that Cinda was there, ready to be a witness, should there be need of a witness to anything that went on. Anyhow, there was nothing she could do about it, unless she should walk right in and reveal to her sister and Mr. Thomas that she had arrived home, and was in a position to hear what they were saying. And after all, hadn't she a right to hear if there was a conspiracy going on against her, that involved using evidence Elaine imagined she had found among her mother's papers? Certainly she must understand this thing fully.

So Lexie kept very still, and listened through the long silences while papers rattled and the lawyer cleared his throat and coughed a little now and then. At last she heard a final page turned in whatever papers he was reading, and the whole bunch were laid down on the table. Lexie wished she dared step over nearer the door to see if that was really her mother's diary he had been perusing, but she knew if she should be discovered now it would only precipitate trouble, so she remained as still as stone and listened.

"Yes, well, Elaine," said the lawyer with his offensively intimate tone, "that is valuable, of course, especially that reference to yourself, and the distress you seem to have caused her by asking for money. But there is no definite evidence. Nothing decisive enough. I will say however that there are three or four distinct sentences there that if elaborated upon somewhat, might prove to be just what we want. How good are you at imitating handwriting?"

"Well," said Elaine, "I used to be good at that sort of thing at school. They said I would make a great counterfeiter," and she laughed excitedly. "What is it you want me to write? I used to try and imitate mamma's handwriting. I remember several times when I wrote excuses for absence from school and signed her name, and the teacher never knew the difference."

"Well, I should think you would be quite clever at this, then. Just the changing of a word here and there and the evidence is perfect. See here! There is plenty of room right here to make this read, 'Her father wanted her to have this money,' instead of 'I want her to have this money.' And where it says 'it was her father's wish,' make it read 'it was her mother's wish.' And then if you can insert on this line below, '*It was her mother's money left to her,* my husband said before he died.' Then down on this next vacant line, 'My conscience will be clear if I give her *some* of it, and give the rest to my own child.' "

The hot blood rolled over Lexie's cheeks and receded leaving her white and stricken, as she listened to this perfidy, and she waited for her sister to reply, hoping against hope that Elaine would demur. But Elaine's only answer to all this was a light laugh.

"Is that all, Mr. Thomas? Why that's easy. And it doesn't seem at all wrong. It just makes the meaning of what is written clearer, doesn't it? But would just those little changes give you the evidence you want?"

"Well, they certainly would make a great difference. But you must be careful to make the writing so like the rest that there will be no questioning it. Would it be possible, do you think, to use the same kind of ink? Would there be an old bottle of ink about that might have been used to write the rest of this little book?"

"Why, yes, I wouldn't be at all surprised if I could find some. In fact I think I saw a bottle of ink standing on mamma's desk when I was looking through it for this book."

"That would be very good," asserted the lawyer importantly. "But now, Elaine, you know there is one very important matter still unsettled. You do not know definitely how much money is involved in this matter, nor where that money is located. I shall have to know that of course before I can be sure that it is worth my while to go deeply into this at all. You know of course there are expenses involved. This matter alone of hiring witnesses to prove these things. That takes plenty of money. And you haven't given me any but the vaguest idea of how much money there will be when we get track of it."

"Oh, but I told you I was willing to give you ten percent of all that I get, regardless of how much it is," said Elaine sweetly, "and I have always supposed that my mother's estate which she left in trust for me was from thirty thousand dollars, to perhaps seventy-five or a hundred thousand! That of course is what I have hired you to find out for me."

"Well, but suppose the money cannot be found, or suppose it has been spent? Then where do I come in?"

"But if it has been spent you can sue my sister for it, can't you?"

"Well, yes, I suppose we can, provided we can prove beyond any doubt that the money was there when your father died, and that it was in his wife's trust, and left entirely to you."

"Oh, but I'm sure it was," said Elaine in her sweetest most confident tone. "Of course I wouldn't have sent for you if I hadn't been entirely sure."

"But my dear, why didn't you look up these claims several years ago? I should have supposed you would have done so as soon as you were married, and while you had a husband to help in looking up your evidence."

"Oh, but you see I didn't think of such things then. I had a husband to support me, and it didn't occur to me that I would be left alone with three little children to support on simply nothing! But I'm sure you'll be able to work this out, won't you? You wrote me that you were sure you could."

"Why, yes, of course, but again, Elaine, as I told you, it will cost you something to get witnesses to substantiate your claims. Well, now I think that is all for today, and I'm very glad you found this diary and if you will work these changes out as I suggested, and as quickly as possible, we will get right to work on the case. Of course, in case you find that your sister has spent all this money that ought to have been yours, has she any money or property that we can levy on?"

"Oh, yes, she has a part ownership in this house, or that is, I believe she claims it is all hers, since she says her mother paid for it. Of course we know she didn't. But if worst came to worst we could claim on this house, couldn't we?"

"This house?" said the lawyer. "Why yes, I suppose

so. But my dear, surely you know that this house would be a mere drop in the bucket when we are talking in terms of fifty or a hundred thousand dollars. You couldn't possibly expect to get more than five or six thousand dollars out of this plain little house in this locality, you know. Seven thousand at the most."

"Oh, *really?* Is that all? But I always supposed this was a very valuable property indeed. My father used to say it was."

"Well, that was a number of years ago, and property depreciates. But of course there would be other ways to get money out of your sister. If she had a job we could arrange that a certain percentage of her wages would be paid directly to you. There are ways to make such arrangements. However, that we can talk over later. And now I really must go. I am late for an appointment already. And you, my dear, will get right to work on that diary and make the changes, please. By-by, and take care of yourself, darling!" Heavy footsteps went out the door and down the path to the street. At once the expensive engine began to turn and was soon on its way and the obnoxious lawyer was speeded away out of sight.

Lexie had waited during the talk, silent, but boiling with rage, appalled at the lengths Elaine was willing to go to accomplish her ends, and wondering what she ought to do.

Of course if Judge Foster was well she would have carried the story at once to him, but since he was in the hospital, even if he was better, she must not worry him with her affairs now.

But God! God was there! She could send a quick SOS for help from Him, and there was nothing to do but trust Him fully, and go each step as He seemed to direct.

But now suddenly this interview had come to an end, and something must be done. She must decide just what she was going to do. She must be wary, and careful. She must not let Elaine know just yet that she was at home, nor that she had heard the interview between the lawyer and her sister. And yet she must contrive some way to get hold of that precious diary before

Elaine could mutilate it in any way. However, that was something that would take time and thought to work out, and the first thing she must do was to see Cinda somewhere—out in the yard perhaps where Elaine could not hear them talking. And it wouldn't be impossible for her to slip out the back door now without making a bit of noise, but she must attract Cinda's attention before she left for she must find out if anything more had happened. Also if Cinda had heard this shameful talk between the lawyer and her sister.

But before Lexie could make a move she heard Cinda stamping out into the kitchen, making her footsteps sound as if they came from the cellar door and had not been near the dining room. Cinda was clever. She had come across that room so silently that not even a fly could have heard her. And when she saw Lexie she lifted one eyebrow and winked one eye as if she had known all the time that Lexie was there. Had she? Dear old Cinda!

So with a quick motion Lexie covered the space between herself and the back door, and crooked her finger at Cinda to follow, and Cinda without a sound beyond a slight nod of her head rattled some pans on the stove and then slid out of the door into the back yard.

They went out behind the old chicken house far enough from the house so that their voices could not be heard.

"Aw, but I'm that glad to see you home!" said Cinda. "Such goin's on as there has been! Did you hear all that stuff they was gettin' off just now? How *much* did you hear? I didn't hear you come in, but I was hopin' you'd get in on some of it. And I was that glad when I got out here an' saw you."

"I got in while the lawyer was reading the diary. Was there much before that?"

"Not so much. Only he come in and told her she was havin' ta pay somethin' down or he couldn't do anythin'. An' then she cried an' said she didn't have much. She said she'd give him twenty-five dollars, but she had ta keep somethin' ta live on till she got her fortune. Then he give in an' said okay, he'd do it if she'd pay ten down, an' the rest as she got it from the govern-

ment. She cried a lot but she give him the ten. I hid behind the portiere an' seen her. An' then she told him
about the diary. It seems he put her up to lookin' in the
attic whilst you was gone, an' he ast her a lot of questions about didn't she find any deeds of property, ur any
receipts of your ma havin' paid any large sums to anybody, an' she cried a lot more an' sobbed out no, she
hadn't, an' then he took the book an' began to read.
That musta been about the time you come in. I thought
I heard a little click of the kitchen latch, but I didn't
dast move enough to look. I figured it was better I
should hear the rest. But I'm mightly glad you come."

"Oh, so am I, Cinda! But if I only knew what I am
to do now! I thought I had a friend to help me when I
went away, a judge, a friend of my own daddy's, and
he promised to help me, but when I tried to reach him
after you telephoned, they said he was unconscious in
the hospital, from an automobile accident, and they
weren't even sure he was going to live."

"Now ain't that a shame, Miss Lexie! But don't you
worry none. I'll stick by you, and somethin'll turn up."

"Thank you Cinda. I knew I could count on you.
And now, there is one thing I've got to do, and that is to
get that diary of mother's away from Elaine. I can't
have that tampered with!"

"Of course not, Miss Lexie. And you can count on
me for that. I can snoop around and find out what she
does with it, and snitch it away somehow and hide it
for you."

"Well, be careful, Cinda. You don't want to get
mixed up in this. That lawyer of hers can make trouble
for *any*body, and if he *wants* to he is capable of putting us all in jail."

"Don't you worry about me, Miss Lexie. I didn't cut
me eyeteeth just yesterday. I can take care of meself.
Now, go your ways, whatever that is, and I'll keep a
watch out. Where you going? To the store? Because
you don't need to today. She give me some ration cards
an' money an' I went an' bought her a steak. That was
what she said she wanted. An' I got plenty other things,
butter and coffee and sugar, and some canned stuff and
more vegetables. I figured it would be better to have

some things on hand than to be continually having to run down to the store and leave them three babies to wander around alone without anybody to look after 'em. You might however get me a bit of cinnamon and ginger. There's a can of pumpkin in the closet and I thought a pumpkin pie might come in handy, seein's there's some molasses that needs eatin', so the ants won't be prancin' all over the shelf."

"All right, Cinda. I'll get anything else you need. I've a little more money now, if Elaine didn't give you enough. But I shan't be gone long. I just want to telephone and find out about Judge Foster."

"Yes, you do that," said Cinda understandingly. "If there's anybody needs a good friend I'd say it was you, and I guess the good Lord understands that, too. You might ask Him to see to that!"

"Oh, I have, Cinda! All the way home. Oh, Cinda, I'm glad you know Him too."

"Well, I ain't sayin' how well I know Him, but I've always felt when it come to the last pinch that the Lord wouldn't let me down. Now you run along, and I won't let her know you've come back yet."

So Lexie hurried down to the drugstore to telephone to the judge's office, hoping it wasn't closing time yet. She wouldn't feel free to telephone his house.

She was greatly relieved to hear the cold-voiced secretary.

"Oh, is this Judge Foster's secretary?" she asked eagerly.

"It *is!*" said the cold voice.

"Well, I'm just the daughter of an old friend of his, and I'm calling to know how he is. Has he recovered consciousness yet? I've been so worried."

"Oh!" said the cold secretary, giving her voice a space in which to warm up a little. "Why yes, Judge Foster has recovered consciousness somewhat. That is, the doctor thinks he is a trifle better, and he has a chance to recover. Of course that is not certain yet, but it is more hopeful than yesterday."

"Oh, that is so good!" said Lexie, with tears in her voice. "I was so worried."

"Of course he won't be able to talk with anyone, not now, nor probably in a long time."

"Of course," said Lexie sadly. "But if you should have a chance when he is better will you tell him Lexie Kendall sent him her love, and tell him—I've been praying for him."

The secretary evidently was embarrassed by the message.

"Why, yes, surely," she said formally. "I'm sure he'll be much pleased when he hears that. Suppose you give me your name and address. It's my business to keep a record of all calls."

So Lexie gave her name and address, and turned sadly away from the telephone. Of course she hadn't really expected that she would get even as good news as that he was a little better, but it saddened her to feel so utterly cut off from her only earthly friend, now in this new perplexity.

11

MEANTIME CINDA FELT that this was her time to act. Great interests were at stake and she seemed to be the only one who could do anything about it. She resolved that she and she only would be responsible for securing that little diary book which seemed to be taking such an important part in affairs.

So Cinda prepared a delicious drink, a combination of grape juice and ginger ale and one or two other small spicy ingredients known only to herself. By this time she had arranged to have plenty of ice on hand, and the drink was cold and sparkling.

Elaine was just about to settle down at the desk to experiment with the writing she was supposed to do in the little blue diary that lay closed before her on the desk, when Cinda entered bearing the drink.

Cinda was all honey and smiles, with oily words.

"Miss Elaine, my lady," she said obsequiously, "I brought you a nice pleasant drink. I'm sure you'll like it. It was always a favorite of my best patients, an' this mornin' when I went to the store I made out to get the ingredients so that you could try it. And now I thought, she's tired, with all that discussion with her lawyer, an' she oughtta lie right down an' take a rest, so I'll take her drink in to her and get her to drink it an' then lie down on the bed in her quiet room an' have a little sleep, an' then she'll feel real better. Now you go into your room and I'll draw the shades for ya and keep the childer real still when they come home an' not let 'em bother. An' when you wake up you'll feel like a new woman."

This was Elaine's language. She simply thrived on such talk.

Graciously she accepted the glass, for she was thirsty

and the frosty crystal tempted her after her hectic discussion with Bettinger Thomas.

"Why, yes, this is really delicious, Cinda. I'll have to get you to make some of this for me when I have callers," she said.

Oh, if Cinda could just keep up this line of talk Elaine would be as putty in her hands, but Cinda was so raring mad inside that it was a question how long she could endure in honeyed tones. Still, Cinda realized the necessity for strategy, and she was ready to endure as long as the time required her services. Amazingly she was able to coax Elaine into her bedroom, making her lean on her arm as she led her there. She lowered her gently to the bed, threw a light blanket across her shoulders, adjusted the shades, opened a window where there was a pleasant breeze, and tiptoed out, closing the door after her gently.

As she passed the desk she noted the little book that had figured so largely in the afternoon's affairs. She moved with extraordinary stealth across the room. Her large capable hand enveloped the small leather-bound book, and swept it up under her apron, conveying it in safety into the outer kitchen. She secreted it, wrapped in a clean dish towel, down in the capacious pocket of Lexie's coat, that was bulked above her suitcase in the little laundry down on the far side of the laundry tub where Elaine would never in the world bother to go.

With some satisfaction she turned to the kitchen and prepared an unusually fine supper for the silly dupe who by this time must be sound asleep, as there came no sound at all from the bedroom where she had stowed her. Fortunately the children were making a victory garden with the children across the street, a neighboring daughter of the house having decided that something ought to be done with those children if the whole neighborhood was not to suffer. So she had set them all at something really worth while, and the children were greatly intrigued. It was probably the first time in their young lives that anyone had ever set them at something that was worth doing, and they liked it.

But Cinda was thinking hard and fast. Something

must be done with that book to make it impossible for Elaine to find it again. She didn't understand just what all this trouble was about, but she was keen enough to know that something very crooked was about to be put over upon Lexie, and the book was a part of it all. So, having purloined the book, she didn't intend to have her efforts fail.

She planned her work at the sink under the window looking toward that back way across the fields where Lexie had disappeared, and when she caught a glimpse of the slender figure in the dark blue dress that she knew was Lexie, she took opportunity to slip out the back door and meet her down by the fence, the book still wrapped in its dishtowel, and further hidden in a paper bag.

"Here it is," she said in a low eager whisper, "and you'd best take it and put it in the bank out of harm's way, before you get home and she knows you're here. Can't you put it in one of those little boxes they keep jewelry and valuables in at the bank? I should think that would be the only way. Then they would never know you had it. I didn't tell her you had come home. She's asleep, and she won't know what's become of it. Maybe she'll think the lawyer took it."

Lexie peered into the paper bag, turned back the dishtowel and then with a mist of sudden tears in her eyes said: "Oh, Cinda! You're wonderful!"

"That's okay with me, Miss Lexie, but don't waste precious time now. You've just about enough to get to the bank before it closes. I looked at the clock before I come out, an' you can't tell what minute herself will wake up an' come yellin' out the back door, an' see you standin' here with the book. Then the fat's in the fire! *So go!* An' don't you dare bring that book back with you! You leave it in the bank, even if they're closed, an' you havta pound on the door to make 'em let you in. Hurry, *quick!* An' if you can think of something to do to stay away a while longer, that would be all right too, an' let her get over the excitement of not finding the book when she wakes up, before *you* are home, so she can't connect it with you. Now, go! Leave the rest to me!"

Lexie turned with quick thankful comprehension, and sped across the field back toward the village, laying plans as she went. Why, Cinda was really a wonder! She had planned the whole thing out cleverly, for Lexie really couldn't have hidden that book in the house where Elaine could not have found it. Just what Elaine would say, who she would blame, when she discovered it was gone, Lexie hadn't stopped to think. At least *she* had the book, and she needn't tell her sister where it was. Elaine needn't suspect that she even knew about it. Trust Cinda for that.

Lexie arrived breathless at the bank almost ten minutes before closing time, having done some very rapid running. She paused inside the door to get her breath. Then she walked up to the cashier whom she had known for years, and said she wanted to put her small account in the bank, and she wanted a safe-deposit box to keep some valuable papers in.

It didn't take long to arrange the whole thing, get a new check book, make out a check from her college bank to put in her new account, take over the safe-deposit box and lock the book safely inside. Then Lexie went out into the street again and tried to decide just what she would do next.

She had her handbag with her, for she had taken that when she first went to telephone about Judge Foster. And in her bag were the letters written by the dean of her college. Why shouldn't she go down to the university in the city, and see what arrangements they were willing to make for her examinations? It was just as well to get it settled now as any time, and it really would be well of course to keep away till Elaine had gotten over her first excitement about the loss of the book.

So she took a bus down to the university, and spent an interesting two hours meeting different college dignitaries and explaining her situation. She was greatly relieved to find that her credentials would be accepted and arrangements would be made for her necessary work if she would come down next week.

Lexie went home quite relieved about her examinations. It looked as if everything was going to be all right for her getting through without going back to college, although she was going to miss sorely the friends and associations she had made there. But still it was a relief to know that the people in the university were going to be cooperative and kindly. And she was so elated about it that she almost forgot that she was going home to face Elaine and a trying situation.

As she turned the corner into her own street she began to wonder what Cinda had had to meet. Would she have had sense enough to evade Elaine's questioning, or had she let a small tempest arise that would make the night intolerable? Well, as she was just arriving Elaine would not likely blame her with the loss of the book. At least not tonight. Not unless Cinda had been tricked into admitting too much. But she felt pretty sure Cinda could be counted on to keep secret what she knew.

Lexie entered breezily, and found the three children noisily eating a very pleasant-looking meal of corn meal muffins, soft boiled eggs and honey, with brimming glasses of rich milk, and big dishes of applesauce peppered with cinnamon. It looked very nice and the children were going into it with zest. The little group at the table seemed very calm, and not as if there had been any kind of an emotional upheaval in the house lately. Lexie wondered if Elaine could still be asleep, or what had happened.

But a twinkle in Cinda's eye assured her that everything was all right so far, and a slight wave of Cinda's hand, with a little grin, sent her into the other room.

Elaine had wakened late in the afternoon after a refreshing sleep, probably made possible by the talk she had had that morning with her lawyer, and his assurance that a little writing in a good imitation of the rest of the diary would work wonders. But when she awoke, and found herself rested, and came around in due course to the train of thought that had put her to sleep, she arose. She spent a few minutes in beautifying herself just in case her lawyer changed his mind and decided to return that afternoon, and then sauntered into the living room. She went over to the desk, intending to practise writing the lines the lawyer had suggested, and then finish them off so they would be ready for him when he came tomorrow. But when she sat down there was no book on the desk where she thought she had left it, and after pulling out the desk drawers, and poking around in the cubby holes to find it, thinking she herself had put it away out of sight, she grew a bit frantic. She arose and went to the door, her hand on the knob, thinking to ask Cinda if she had seen it, but her natural caution warned her. Perhaps she had carried it into the bedroom with her and slipped it under her pillow. But why should she do that? There was nobody in the house who would be interested, or know what significance that special book could have. But she went into the bedroom and searched the bed and surroundings most thoroughly without result, and then went back to the desk and searched the whole room, more thoroughly than Elaine had ever looked for anything in her life before. At last, utterly exhausted, she dropped herself down on the couch and wondered just what she should do about it? Was it at all possible that Mr. Thomas could have taken it with him? Put it in his pocket absentmindedly? She tried to visualize him doing it, and yet wasn't sure at all. If they only had a telephone! If she could only call him up and ask if he had taken the book without knowing it! Would she dare go across the street herself and try to telephone? Of course if that should get to Lexie's ears she would not be able to carry out this idea of being an invalid and needing not only care, and nursing, but money. Finally, after due thought she called Cinda.

Cinda appeared promptly and cheerfully with the most innocent expression on her face.

"Cinda, were any of the children in the living room while I was asleep?"

"Oh no ma'am. I didn't see none of them in there."

"Has my sister been home?"

"No ma'am, she's not been in the house."

"Well, I don't understand it, Cinda. There's an important little book of mine gone. I had it there on the desk. I'm positive I left it there, and I can't find it anywhere. It's just the kind of thing Gerry or even Bluebell might take a fancy to, and carry off. I wish you'd call them and we'll ask them."

So Cinda marshaled the children over from across the street, and their mother conducted a most thorough examination, but they all declared they hadn't seen any little book at all.

"Didn't *you* see it here, Cinda? You didn't put it away or anything, did you? It's very important that I find it at once!"

"No ma'am, I never monkey with *your* papers. I never took notice of anything at all of *yours,* my lady! Too bad you lost something important. But mebbe it'll turn up in good time. Aren't you gettin' hongry, Miss 'Laine? I got a nice supper planned. Go an' read awhile an' I'll be bringing in your tray after a bit."

If Lexie could have heard her she would have stood in awe of Cinda's histrionic ability, for she certainly was playing her part well, and really getting away with it. Her innocent air, and her willingness to please, threw Elaine entirely off her guard. Elaine loved to be served in this spirit. Perhaps Lexie was too honest-hearted to try to gain her end by subtlety, although she had had years of suffering under Elaine's selfishness and greed, and she had watched her own dear mother suffer also. When she thought it over honestly she knew that one should not always yield to such greedy demands.

Well, Lexie wasn't there to see it all, but was greatly relieved when she reached home to find a comparative calm in the house, and Elaine quietly reading a magazine that Cinda had cannily brought and left around to further her own purposes.

It was after supper that Elaine tried a new line with her sister:

"Lexie, I suppose you are tired and I hate to ask you to do anything more tonight, but *would* you run across the road to one of the neighbors and phone Mr. Thomas? I have something very important to tell him, and I think he would come out tonight and see me if I knew. Would you just say that I have a matter of importance to tell him that he ought to know tonight?"

Lexie looked at her aghast for an instant, and then a

sudden remembrance came to her that she was not alone. God was with her. His Presence was there, even if Elaine couldn't see it. But *she* knew He was there, and she would be strong in *His* strength.

Then Lexie smiled pleasantly, but her lips took on a new firmness, her voice an assurance that was not too natural to her.

"No, Elaine, I'm sorry to seem unaccommodating, but I cannot have anything to do with that man!"

"Now, Lexie, don't be silly. You will just be carrying a message for me, your sister. He needn't even know who you are."

"No," said Lexie, "I do not care to approach him in any way, even as an unknown."

"But that is silly! It's childish!"

"No, it's not silly. I do not like the way he speaks to me, and I do not intend to give him another chance to insult me. It's useless to argue, Elaine, I simply *won't* do it. If you want to have dealings with him you'll have to do it without me. And now, would you like me to help you to get ready for bed, or shall I wait till the children are in?"

"Oh, don't trouble yourself!" said Elaine coldly. "I'll get to bed somehow. Though I'm not going yet. But if you can't do the one thing I want I shall have to hire somebody to do it for me, or else go myself."

"Sorry," said Lexie briefly, "but what you ask is out of the question for me," and Lexie went quietly out of the room and upstairs to get the beds ready for the children.

Cinda was Elaine's next choice of a messenger. She called Cinda in and endeavored to inveigle her into carrying the message to the telephone across the street, but Cinda had been listening to the conversation between the sisters, and was prepared with her answer.

"Now, you know, Miss 'Laine, I'd like to accommodate you, but I'm that shy of a telephome, I just couldn't do it. No ma'am. I can't get over it. I'm what they call mikerphome-shy, only with me its telephome-shy. Besides, those folks across the street have all gone to the movies. I heard 'em go, an' their house is locked up. I saw 'em lock it. An' no ma'am, I wouldn't care to go down to the drugstore this evenin'. I'm that tired I thought I'd go right to bed, an' get rested up for tomorrow. I don't wantta play out on you. You can ast me most anythin' to do fer you but phome. I jest can't learn to phome."

So Elaine had to resign herself to writing a letter to her lawyer asking him if he carried the little book away with him, and while Lexie was putting Bluebell to bed and Cinda was clattering the dishes in the kitchen, Elaine stole out herself and went down to the corner where there was a mail box. She mailed her letter, but she took pains when she got back to see that both Lexie and Cinda knew that she had gone to the mail box, and that she was worn out in consequence and was sure she was going to be sick that night from the exertion, and the chill damp air. She also complained of having twisted her ankle crossing the street.

Lexie went to bed early that night. She didn't want to enter into any more discussions, and she lay in her quiet room with little Bluebell by her side and wondered how long this sort of thing was going on. She felt almost like a criminal, not telling her sister that the little book was in safe keeping where she would not find it again, but she knew this was the wise way. It was her book, not Elaine's and she had a right to put it beyond use against her.

But in the dark room, as one by one the noises of the street toned down, the neighbors came home and went to bed, and the lights around went out, somehow she had a stronger feeling than ever that the Presence of the Lord was in the room, and that He was going to watch over her and guide her. If it had not been for this it seemed to her she could not have gone on, into days that would of necessity be filled with bickering and strife. Yet she must, and if He was there was it true that His Presence could protect her? She would see.

12

ABOUT THE MIDDLE of the next morning there came a telegram from Lawyer Thomas.

I do not have the book. You will probably find it if you search carefully. If not I suggest a reproduction from memory of as many pages as possible. Let me know as soon as you have completed it.

                                                        B. Thomas

Cinda found the telegram in the wastebasket when she took it out to empty it, and she relayed the contents to Lexie, which caused her to sigh heavily, and finally run down to the drugstore and call up Judge Foster's office again.

When the secretary answered, she said:

"This is Lexie Kendall again. Am I troubling you very much if I ask how Judge Foster is this morning?"

She was thrilled to hear the answer:

"Oh, you are Lexie! I was about to write you a letter, since you have no telephone listed. Judge Foster is quite a little better this morning and he has been asking for you. At least he has several times murmured your name, with a worried look in his eyes. The doctor wondered if you would care to come down to the hospital and see him for a minute or two. He seems to be worried about you in some way."

"Oh, that's very kind of you to tell me. Of course I'll come. Just when and where should I come?"

The secretary gave the necessary directions, and Lexie hurried back to get ready to go. As she passed through the dining room she caught a glimpse of Elaine at the desk nibbling the end of her pen and looking perplexedly at the paper before her. Ah! Elaine was taking her lawyer's advice!

131

All the way to the bus line she was puzzling to know if there wasn't some way she could stop Elaine doing this preposterous thing. Oh, if only Judge Foster was able to talk and she could ask him what to do! But of course they wouldn't let her do anything but just step into the room and say she was so glad he was better.

She trod the marble halls of the hospital with her heart beating wildly, because in spite of her desire to see Judge Foster she was frightened at the idea of visiting a very sick man. She was afraid she might do or say something that would make him worse, and she read herself a great many warnings as she walked sedately toward the room to which she had been directed.

She tapped at the door and waited. The nurse opened the door and she asked in a soft voice if that was Judge Foster's room, and the nurse's face brightened.

"Oh, are you Lexie Kendall?" asked the nurse. "He's been asking for you. I'm glad you've come!"

It was nice to be welcomed. She went in shyly, and there was the judge looking every bit as friendly and judge-like as when he was sitting in his office. But his face was white, and there were worn lines that gave him a gaunt appearance. Her heart smote her that she had come hoping to get help from him, but of course that was impossible. She must be very careful what she said.

She approached shyly and put her hand in the big white one he held out to her.

"Well, I'm glad you've come, little Lexie," he said, his voice almost natural in its cordiality.

"Oh, I was so glad to be allowed to come. I was terribly worried when I heard you were in the hospital."

"Well, they're fixing me all up fine here," he said with a smile. "I think I'll be ready to go home pretty soon," he smiled.

"Oh, I hope so, Judge Foster!" said Lexie earnestly.

"But how about you, child? As soon as I came to myself I began to think about you, and to worry lest I wouldn't be able to help you as I had planned. How has your affair come out? Did you go to college?"

"Yes, I went back," said Lexie cheerfully, "and they were very nice. They said if I found I had to return here that they would arrange for me to take my examination here at the university, and they gave me papers, credits, and letters to people of the university. I went there to-day and it's all to be arranged next week."

"But why did you come back, child? I thought you were planning to stay away from that lawyer."

"Yes, I was, but—well, Cinda telephoned me I *ought* to come back."

Lexie hesitated, and looked worried.

"But I oughtn't to trouble you with my small worries," she said, trying to look exaggeratedly cheerful. "It's nothing, I'm sure, and I guess it will be all right. But I thought I ought to return."

"Child, you needn't be afraid to tell me. They won't let you stay long, I know that for I heard what the doctor said, but it's best that I should know all, for I've been worrying about you, and if there have been any new developments I want to know them."

"But I know you ought not worry about me. I want you to get well. I'll tell you all about it when you are better."

"No!" said the judge in his most judgely tone, "you will tell me *now*. I am your father's friend, and I *must* know *at once!*"

"Oh, well, I guess it wasn't anything to worry much about, but I did want to ask you if I did right. Cinda telephoned that Elaine had gone up in the attic and pulled out all my mother's things, her private papers and everything, and when I got home I walked in the back door and overheard her talking with that lawyer. She had found mother's private diary, and she showed it to him. There were little items about the money she had earned and how she wanted to give some of it to Elaine, and some to me, and they twisted it so it seemed as if she was referring to something father had said to her about Elaine, about saving up and having money to send us both to college."

The judge nodded.

"Yes, that was your father's desire," he said with a sigh.

"Well, the lawyer read the diary nearly through and then he showed Elaine where she could write in words that would make the meaning entirely different. Elaine has always been clever at imitating writing and she agreed to do what he suggested, and then he went away. Cinda was in the dining room and overheard the whole thing, and I heard most of it, but they didn't know that I was home yet, nor that Cinda was where she could hear them. They wouldn't have thought she mattered anyway. But she was very bright. She told Elaine she needed to lie down and rest, and she brought her lemonade, and took her into the bedroom and tucked her up. Then as she came out she picked up the diary, brought it out to me, and told me to go quick to the bank and put it into a safe-deposit box before my sister knew that I had come home. And so I did. Do you think it was wrong? I hurried across the fields and got to the bank just before it closed, and the book is safe in the bank now. Elaine doesn't know where it is. Do you think that was a wrong thing to do, to let Cinda take that book, and for me to hide it and not tell Elaine?"

"Certainly not. You did just right. And now, this puts things in a little different light. What was Elaine's reaction to the loss of the book?"

"Oh, she thought the children had taken it first, till she found out they hadn't been home. They were across the street playing. She asked Cinda, but Cinda said she never took notice to anything belonging to *her*, so there was no more said, but when I came she tried to get me to call up her lawyer, and I declined to do it. I told her I didn't like the way he talked to me, and I didn't want anything further to do with him, and then I came away. Was that right?"

"Yes, that was right. Keep that up. Don't let him get any chance to talk with you if you can help it. And now, if anything more happens and you need help I wish you would go to my friend Mr. Gordon. He is a fine man and a keen lawyer, and I have told him about you. I felt it was necessary someone else should be wise about you, and I spoke a few words to him on the phone again this morning, so he will understand. Now, I wish you would go right down to his office. Here is the address. I asked the nurse to write it, and this card with my name on it will admit you to his office right away, without waiting a long time. I am talking rapidly because I think the nurse is coming back and she will drive you out. But I'm so glad to have had this talk with you. It's relieved my mind a lot, and now I can rest better. I seemed to have a psychic warning that you were still in trouble."

The nurse entered quietly and came smilingly to stand beside the bed.

"Now," she said looking apologetically at Lexie.

"Yes, I'm going," said Lexie smiling and rising. "Good by, Judge Foster, and you've helped me a lot. I'm relieved to think you feel I did right."

"Yes, you did perfectly right," said the judge happily, "and now, will you go at once to Mr. Gordon's office?"

"Yes," said Lexie, "of course."

"Well, please tell him everything, the whole story. He knew your father slightly, and I want him to get every detail you have. And if anything further occurs report it to him *at once!* That is, until I am back in my office. Gordon's telephone number is on the card. You will find him most sympathetic and helpful. Now, good by, little girl. Come and see me again soon. And please call up occasionally. I might have a message for you about something, you know."

"Oh, thank you," said Lexie, a bright pleased color in her cheeks. He was so pleasant, so fatherly it almost brought the tears.

"I hope I haven't tired him," she said to the nurse as she got to the door.

"No, I think not," said the nurse with a quick glance at her patient. "I believe he almost looks more rested. He worried a lot about you that first night. You seemed to be on his mind."

So Lexie went on her way to Mr. Gordon's office and found her talismanic card opened the way to him almost at once. He proved to be all that the judge had said he would be, a man of keen eyes, quick understanding, and a friendly smile. When she left Lexie felt a great burden had been lifted from her shoulders. God had sent her an adviser to whom she could go! Oh, she would still go to God with it all first, and then if an earthly adviser was needed here was Mr. Gordon who would if necessary talk it over with Judge Foster, and she wouldn't have to bother Judge Foster with things that he didn't need to know.

So Lexie went back to the house, feeling that whatever had happened she was fortified to stand it.

Cinda was washing the kitchen floor, with a face like a thunder cloud.

"Them childer," she murmured as Lexie came in the back door, "they went out an' jumped up an' down in a puddle of black oil some old truck left in the road, an' then they come in here to me nice white floor just scrubbed yesterday, an' they walked all around makin' what they called patterns on my floor, an' crowin' over it to beat the band. Even that oldest kid, that 'Angel-child' you call her, she was walkin' around makin' circles of her footprints, an' runnin' out to the road to get more oil on her shoes when it got dim. So I up an' spanked her, good, an' she screamed for her mother, an' that neighbor-lady across the street come over to see was she hurt 'ur somepin' an' then they all howled so I spanked the other two. I guess I spanked pretty hard fer their mom she come out from her nap, an' she was pretty mad, an' said I was to stop hurtin' her childer, an' then she fired me! *Me!* She had the nerve to *fire* me. An' then I up an' told her I wasn't workin' fer her, I was workin' fer her sister, an' I wasn't fired till *you* fired me, an' fer her to git outta me kitchen, ur I'd swash some water over her feet. So she got, but she said when you come home she'd tell you ta fire me, an' I might as well go git packed, fer it wouldn't be many minutes 'fore you'd come home an' give me the gate. So, Miss Lexie, you better go right in there an' git yer orders, an' then I'll know what ta do."

"Oh!" said Lexie in dismay, and then *"Oh!"* with a little laugh at the end of her breath. "Well, Cinda, don't you worry, I'm *not* giving you the gate. Not unless you feel you can't stand it here any longer. I wouldn't blame you of course, but I'm sure I don't know what I would do without you."

"All right, me lamb, don't you worry none. I'm

workin' fer *you,* an' ef you still want me, here's where
I stay."

"Oh, that's good, Cinda!" said Lexie. "Now, tell me
the rest. What else happened and where are they all?"

"Well, Miss Elaine, she's on her bed cryin' her eyes
out, an' groanin'. Can't ye hear her? The childer are
acrost the street as usual. That Angel-child is probably
tellin' all that happened. Drat her! I could whale her
good ef I got another chancet. But whut else happened? Well, that fat lawyer come back, and he had
words with my lady. It seems she'd writ a whole lot
more an' signed yer mom's name to it, an' he said she'd
got ta get you to okay it or somepin', so it would carry
more influence, an' she tole him she *couldn't* get you to
do *any*thin', an' he said there was *ways* ta *make* ye. He
ast her did you have a lawyer, an' she said 'Oh no, you
didn't have any lawyer,' an' he said well in that case
maybe she better go easy an' coax. But he tuk her ole
papers she'd been writin' all mornin' an' said he'd see
what he could make out with them. An' he ast her
wasn't there some rich relative she could borry of ta pay
the advance fee, an' she cried a lot more, an' said *every*-
body was against her, an' she didn't know what she was
goin' ta do, so he just tuk her in his ole fat arms an'
hugged her, an' kissed her three four times, an' petted
her like she was a baby, an' said he'd do his best to get
her the money somehow, an' then he went away. An'
then those childer come over an' worked that oil-act
on my nice clean floor, an' that's how 'tis. Now, I'm
sorry fer you, but I guess you better go in an' settle
with her, an' after you're done if you really think you
better fire me why I'll go quiet-like an' not make you
any trouble."

"Oh, bless your heart, Cinda. No, I'm not going to
fire you. I'm much more likely to fire myself. This certainly is an awful household, and I don't wonder you'd
like to leave, but please don't, Cinda, for I just can't
go on without you."

"Okay!" said Cinda with a crooked triumphant grin.
"I'm here fer the duration, so put that on yer pianna an'
play it. Run along now, an' don't lose yer nerve."

So Lexie put aside her outer wraps in the dining

room, and went into the living room and over to the bookcase where she selected three or four books, and sat down to run over some of the work she would likely be tested on at the new university.

But Lexie didn't have long to study. She heard Elaine's studied sobbing being audibly wound up, heard stirrings in the region of the bed, and then slippered footsteps, and the door opened.

Lexie sat very still absorbed in her study till Elaine spoke:

"Well, so you've finally got home *at last!* Where on earth have you been?"

"Oh," said Lexie looking up pleasantly, "why, I had a few errands to do. Did you want something?"

"I certainly do," said Elaine. "I want you to go out in the kitchen and fire that outrageous impudent woman you hired. She is simply insufferable! I can't stay in the house with her another night! She is not fit to have around. I'm afraid to trust my babies near her. Do you know what she dared to do? She *spanked my children! All three* of them! Imagine a girl as old as Angelica being subjected to that! And the whole neighborhood was roused by their screaming! So, Lexie, I won't stand another day of that insolent woman. I told her to go. I told her we didn't want her here another hour, but she said you hired her, and she was working for you, and nobody but you could fire her, so now for pity's sake go out there in the kitchen and fire her, and then you go down town to the best agency there is and get a real servant. Offer good wages. You simply can't get anybody worth her salt unless you promise to pay for it."

Lexie looked up with mild troubled eyes:

"I'm sorry you've had such a time, Elaine," she said, "but perhaps you don't know what the children did to make Cinda spank them."

"Oh, she's been blabbing to you, has she? I thought so. And of course you take *her* side. I might have known you would. You always go against me if there is any possible way to do so."

"Listen, Elaine. Did you know that Cinda had just scrubbed the kitchen floor the last thing last night, and the children found a puddle of dirty black oil in the road and they all stepped in it and then came into the kitchen and walked around making patterns on the nice white floor. You don't think that was right, do you?"

"Oh, the idea! A little trifling thing like that, and she gave them the most cruel chastisement I ever saw. She left the imprint of her ugly coarse hand on their tender little pink flesh. It was terrible. I had to anoint them with oil and the poor little things were in agony! Simply *agony!* And I demand that that woman leave this house at once! I wouldn't feel safe another day with her and my babies in the same house together! Now, go, and fire that creature and then come back and I'll tell you what I suggest we do next."

Lexie looked at her sister steadily for a minute, took a deep breath as she had prayed she might remember to do when a time of stress arrived, and then answered quietly:

"I'm sorry, Elaine, I can't do what you ask. You see, Cinda is the only one we could possibly get without wages for the present, and neither you nor I have money to pay a trained servant. Besides, I told you I went carefully into that matter before I went away, and I could not find a single servant who was willing to come out to this suburb where there is so little bus and train service. I talked with several applicants at several agencies, because you had insisted, and because I did not know certainly but you might have some secret source of money that would change things, but I simply *couldn't* find a single servant who would come out here. And I thought you felt you *had* to have somebody when I am away."

"Away! You're not still thinking of going away again are you? I thought you had gone up to college to close that business all up."

"Oh no, I didn't close it up. I tried to arrange to take the rest of my work nearer by, and I may be able to do so, but even then I would have to be away a good deal, and you are not able to do the housework yet, are you?"

"Yet? *Me* do the housework? Well, I should *say not!* So! You thought you were going to be the scholar and I

was to be the household drudge! Well, you've got another guess coming, and if you think that I'm going to
fall for any such idea as this you're badly mistaken!
You can go out there in the kitchen and fire that vam-
pire, and then come back and I'll tell you what to do
next."

Lexie took another deep breath and looked at her
sister steadily.

"Elaine," she said, "I'm not expecting to be a scholar, nor have you slave for me. I'm just trying to get my
diploma because in these days one is not sure of any job
that's worth anything unless they have finished college.
So, as there are only three months of hard work now to
finish my college course I am going to stick to it and do
the best I can. And to that end I intend to keep Cinda
here. I haven't any money to pay a maid or a nurse,
and we shall have to get along with Cinda, even if you
don't like her. That is, unless you can lay down enough
money to cover the weekly wages of a better maid.
Even then you'd have to find the maid, for I've exhausted my resources in that line."

"The idea!" snorted Elaine. "What have you done
with all that money of mine? That's what I want to
know. *Some*where you have it stowed away, and now
you are trying to get money out of me to run this house
and you're not going to get it! Do you hear? You're
not going to get a cent more out of me for anything."

Lexie drew a weary breath.

"I'm sorry, Elaine, that you have such a mistaken
notion. I can't think where you got it. But you evidently
think it is true. And it isn't! Really it isn't. I have only
a very little money that I have earned in hard work,
saved to get myself a graduating dress because I didn't
think it was fair to the other girls in the class for me to
go on the platform with them in a dark dress when they
were all in white. I didn't have a single thin dress left
that wasn't simply in rags."

"Oh, *really!* What earthly difference would that have
made? You probably would never see any of those girls
again, and they would never hear of you. I declare,
Lexie, you seem to have gotten very worldly. I'm sure
your mother would never have approved of that. But

however, whatever you have become, I really don't credit that story of yours about having no money except enough to get a simple white dress. So you might as well understand it, and it is time that you came across with some of the money that belongs to me. You said you had fifty dollars that mamma left you, and that you would give it to me, but I haven't seen it yet. Suppose you go and get it for me now. I need a new dress myself, and I want to go to a beauty parlor and have a facial and a shampoo and a permanent. I am ashamed to meet my lawyer looking like this."

"I'm sorry, Elaine, but I've spent every cent of that fifty dollars on you and your children, since you came, to get food for you all to eat, and I haven't any more to spare. And now you'll have to excuse me. I don't want to continue this discussion. It only brings hate in our hearts and it isn't good for the children to hear bickering all the time. They are coming in now."

"Oh yes, you are very clever to get up excuses to change the subject, but you'll soon find out that it would have been much better for you if you had come through and told the truth, because if you go on like this you'll not only lose every cent of the money yourself, but you'll find yourself sadly in debt for interest on all that money. You see, my righteous little sister, I have definite proof now, and we know pretty well just where you have parked that money, and are going to have no trouble in getting possession of it."

"Yes?" said Lexie, lifting her eyebrows. "Just what evidence could you possibly find of something that doesn't exist and never has?"

"Sez you! Well, my dear little sister, I have evidence in your own mother's handwriting, stating the whole thing, when and how she took possession of the money, and what she did with it. But of course you know all about that."

"No," said Lexie steadily, "I do not know anything about any such thing, and I don't believe you do either. I'm sorry to speak this way to you, but I know what I am talking about, and I'm quite sure if you keep on in this way I shall have to take steps that will make you know also, just what you are doing. You know I am not entirely without friends even though I haven't much money, and if you persist in acting this way to me I shall be obliged to appeal to them to put an end to it. Certainly I'm not going to stay here and run this house for your benefit, and feed you and take care of your children when there is need, if you are going to persist in being unfriendly. I would rather go away by myself than to live in continual bickering. I'm willing to forget what you have said without formal apologies, and to try to forget what you have said about my mother, who was as kind and good to you as she was to me her own child, if you will try to be decent to me. But to stay here and take insults like this is unbearable."

"Oh well, if you are going to take that attitude of course you will have to bear the consequences, but I was just trying to warn you that it is a great deal simpler to come clean and tell what you know, and you will be treated with far more leniency, than if you persist in lying about it, and won't tell what you know."

"Very well," said Lexie quietly, and got up to go out of the room, but Elaine detained her.

"Wait a minute, Lexie, there is something I want to ask you. Do you remember a friend of father's, a Mr. Harry Perrine, a financier who made investments for father?"

Lexie looked at her sister thoughtfully.

"Yes, I remember a man of that name who *wanted* to make investments for father, and father wouldn't have anything to do with him. He said he was rotten and not fit to handle money for anybody, and mother couldn't bear the sight of him. He was always coming here at mealtime and hanging around to be invited to dinner, and coaxing father to invest in this and that."

"You're quite mistaken, Lexie. He was a successful financier, and my father put some of my money with him at your mother's suggestion. I have had this investigated, and he owns that father put money with him intended for me, and after his death your mother drew it all out and invested it elsewhere. He has all the papers to prove it, and he knows just what your mother did with the money after she drew it out to use for herself."

Lexie was very angry by this time, but she knew she must not let this be seen. Her talk with Mr. Gordon had fortified her for such a scene as this, so she closed her lips and turned toward the door again.

"Oh! You haven't anything to say to that!" taunted the angry woman. "I thought that would finish you. There is nothing further you can say!"

"No," said Lexie gently. "I just felt that I would rather not talk any more about this matter lest I might say something unpleasant to you, and I don't see that that would do anything but make you more angry. I think if this has to be talked about any more I will let you talk to my lawyer."

"Your *lawyer!*" laughed Elaine. "Since when did my kid sister have a lawyer. Send him on. I'm sure I can give him a few facts that will astonish him and he will certainly wish he hadn't taken you on as a client."

The sentence ended with a hateful taunting laugh, but Lexie had gone quietly out of the room, shut the door, and did not hear the meanest part of it. She hurried upstairs to her own dark room and stood for a long time looking out into the starry night, wondering if God really cared for her, and was going with her through all this.

And then she bowed her head on the window frame and prayed softly, "Dear God, help me to trust even when things are like this. Help me to remember You are here, walking with me every step of this hard way."

13

THE LETTER THAT Benedict Barron had written to Alexia Kendall, reached her the morning after her fiery talk with her sister, and almost precipitated another.

In fact Lexie almost didn't get that letter at all. Elaine had been watching for the postman, as *she* expected a letter from one Harry Perrine, and she was close by the front door, ready to fly out before anybody in the house knew that he was there. But Lexie had been watching for the postman also. She had written a letter to Lawyer Gordon as she had promised she would if anything arose at home that she felt he ought to know, and she wanted to get it off in the next mail. She was worried lest she ought not to have let slip those words about her lawyer. Maybe it could do no harm, but she must keep watch on her tongue and not let an angering word break her silence.

Lexie had hurried out from the kitchen door by the side entrance with her letter as soon as she sighted the postman, and met him at the gate. So she got her letter first.

But all these days since that letter had started on its way, Ben Barron had lain on the hard little cot, of the ramshackle place they called a hospital, slowly recovering from a serious wound and its resultant illness. The depressing condition had been brought about by his long exposure and the lack of food and rest, following his unremitting fighting of fire and fiends, without any assurance that he would sometime reach safety.

Most of the convalescing time he had dreamed and slept by turns and in snatches. He had eaten a little of whatever they gave him, apathetically, slept some more, and waked again to dream of the past. But sometimes there came to his mind the thought of the letter he had sent out so blindly into his old world, to a girl who did not know him, and whom he scarcely knew at all, and he would wonder if it would ever reach her. And if it did whether she would be minded to answer it.

Of course it had been a crazy unconventional thing to do to write that letter. If he had waited until he was really well and strong he never would have written it at all. Though in these war times plenty of girls were writing bright cheery letters to boys they had never seen nor heard of before. They were just given an address by somebody, and asked to write to a lonesome soldier. So he hoped this little Lexie-girl would be moved to answer his letter, if it ever reached her.

He sometimes dreamed of what she might think or say or do, if the letter reached her. But as the days passed by the letter faded into the past, and new thoughts about going back to the fight again began to take form in his renewed brain as his body slowly healed. The letter took on less significance. It had been a vagary of his sick mind, out there in that fiery field, a brief respite from the heat and terror. God's cool mountain with the dew on the grass at the roadside, and one of God's children smiling and swinging on a little white gate. Just a symbol of home it had been. But he still was glad he had written the letter, if only to get it off his mind.

Lexie, holding that letter in her hand, seeing her own name in an unfamiliar handwriting on it, noting the strange foreign stamp with the war insignia upon it, wondered. She read her name again to make sure, and slid it into her apron pocket, one hand safely guarding it as she turned to go back to the house.

Then Elaine's sharp voice interrupted her.

"Give that letter to me!" she said, stepping out to the small front portico and holding out her hand. "How *dare* you put it into your pocket, and take it in to examine!"

Lexie looked up in surprise.

"But it isn't your letter," she said sweetly. "It is *mine!*"

"*Your* letter! That's a likely story. I was expecting an important business letter, and I don't want to be delayed in reading it. I *demand* to see that letter instantly!"

Elaine was very angry, and was talking in loud piercing tones. Lexie was aware instantly of furtively opened doors and windows from neighbors' houses. They would be too polite to stand around and listen, but they could not fail to hear that an angry altercation was going on between the sisters, and pursed lips and shrugs would be exchanged between those women who heard. Oh, this was terrible!

"Why certainly, Elaine, look and see my name on the envelope," she said, and held the letter up where she knew her sister could easily read her name.

Elaine leaned over the porch and looked, reached out her hand for the letter, but did not quite touch it.

"Give me that letter!" demanded Elaine again. "There is some trick about this! You are as sly as can be. You've exchanged the envelopes or something, and you're trying to open my letter and find out what I'm writing to my lawyer about. Give me that letter, I say!"

"Why no, I won't give you my letter," said Lexie. "Why should I? It's my letter, not yours. Oh, Elaine, why will you go on acting like this? You're fairly driving me to leave. Is that what you want me to do? It would be much easier and cheaper for me to go, than to stay here and submit to all this from you. It is shameful for you to act this way, and there is no point to it. What is your idea anyway?"

"Who is that letter from?" demanded Elaine. "I insist that you tell me at once. I don't want any more underhanded business. After all your threats of yesterday are you doing some fool thing, writing to some man and trying to get help?"

Lexie laughed.

"Why no, Elaine, I haven't been writing to any man, and I don't know yet who wrote me the letter. You haven't given me a chance to go into the house and open it. It's probably from someone I met at college."

"It's from a *man!*" insisted Elaine. "That's a man's handwriting! You went to a *woman's* college."

"Yes, but we had men callers and several men teachers, and often met men in the town and at games and so on."

"Now don't try to tell me that you had some incipient

lovers out in that dull college town of yours. You aren't the kind of girl that attracts men, and never will be."

"Oh," laughed Lexie amusedly. "Does this look like a love-letter? No, I didn't have any lovers out there that I know of, but I did have a few friends, and this is probably from one of them, or it might be from the dean."

"No!" said Elaine sharply. "That's an overseas envelope. I know their look, you know."

"Oh, yes. It is overseas. But there were a number of the girls' brothers who are overseas of course. It really isn't important, though, I'm quite sure," and Lexie slipped the letter into her apron pocket again, with her protecting hand over it.

"Give me that letter! I want to see for myself that you're not fooling me."

"No!" said Lexie firmly, and sudden as a bird in flight she flew down the path to the kitchen door and fled up to her room where she locked her door and sat down to read her letter.

She did not, however, stay upstairs long. She knew that to make much of that letter would only be to continue the controversy with Elaine. She must make light of the whole thing. With fingers that trembled just a little at the thought of a letter from anybody for herself, she opened the envelope and unfolded the letter. Later she would read it more carefully of course, but just now it was as if she must take the whole thing in at a glance and be ready to be composed about it, if Elaine should venture to climb the stairs and try to investigate.

Lexie had a trained eye, used to taking in a good deal at a glance, and the whole lovely idea of the letter burst upon her mind like a sweet picture. That boy, with his books in a strap, and his handsome laughing eyes. Yes, she remembered him! Of course! She even remembered his asking her if her name was short for Lexicon. She laughed and swept her eyes downward to the quiet, wistful, respectful closing, and then folded the letter and locked it quickly inside her old suitcase under the bed. She ran downstairs and began to help Cinda in the dining room, making out a list of small necessities that must be ordered from the store.

Suddenly Elaine entered like a frowning Nemesis.

"Who was that letter from? I insist on being told."

"Why should you be told?" asked Lexie innocently. "It was from an old friend I used to know in my school days. He's in the armed forces now, and he was just sending me a greeting the way all the boys in the army do. It isn't important."

Elaine gave her an angry suspicious look but Lexie went out the back door and down the field to the store, and presently Elaine went back to her own scheming. On her way Lexie had opportunity to think over this remarkable surprise, remember more definitely the boy who had accosted her on her white gate so long ago, and try to think just how he had looked. A nice smile, a twinkle in his eye, pleasant words—to just a little girl! And to think he had remembered it all these years!

When Lexie came back from the store with the yeast cake Cinda had sent her for, there was a look of unexpected brightness in her pretty wistful face that quite gave old Cinda pleasure. She knew there had been some sort of a quarrel between the two sisters, and she was glad to see that Lexie no longer looked as if she had been crushed. There was a lightness and a brightness that was more what Cinda would like to see in Lexie's face.

And all the morning as Lexie went on her sunlit way across the meadows and did her other errands at the store, and back again, she was thinking back to the day she had swung on the gate and seen the nice big boy! And to think he had written to her! Remembered her all these years, and thought of her when he was under fire! He said that the memory of her face had helped him bear the heat and fire and terror. Thanked her for just being herself, a little girl with a smile in her eyes for a stranger boy.

As soon as lunch was over and the children started off to their play again, Elaine retired in a huff to her bed and a nap, Lexie stole upstairs to her room and locked the door, and there in the quiet she read that letter over again. Read it several times, and reveled in the fact that she had a letter from a young man across the sea who remembered her.

When she knew the letter by heart she took her fountain pen out of her handbag, hunted up some stationery from her little old desk in the attic, and wrote an answer to that letter. Somehow it seemed to her that she must answer at once. That a letter like that demanded an immediate reply. A lonely soldier boy who turned back to his childhood for a bit of comfort! She would let him know that she remembered too.

Dear Sergeant:

Yes, I remember you. You were a tall boy with curly black hair and a nice smile and twinkles in your eyes. I was wonderfully surprised that you noticed me, just a little girl.

I remember what you said, too. You asked me if my name, Lexie, was short for Lexicon. I laughed over that a lot, all by myself, afterwards.

But I am very much surprised that you thought of a little girl when you were under fire, and quite pleased that the thought of my mountain helped you through hard places. Dew on a hot forehead would be pleasant, and I'm glad I was that to a brave soldier, for somehow I know you were brave. You looked that way the day I saw you.

Your letter came to me here at the little white house, down by the white gate where I went to meet the postman. I just happened to be here or I wouln't have got the letter. I'm glad I came.

I've had some hard times too, and your letter came on one of the hardest days and made a bright spot in what would otherwise have been a very dark day. I thank you very much for taking the trouble to write me.

Some day perhaps the war will end, and you will come home, and then perhaps you can come to the home town. I would like so much to see you again.

Your little-girl-friend,
Lexie
(Alexia Kendall)

Lexie slipped out the back door and whisked across the fields to the post office with her letter, and when she returned she went straight up to the attic to put things to rights. She hadn't had time before, and Elaine hadn't even gone back to attempt clearing up the mess she had made. Lexie was appalled. Blankets and pillows and papers and books spread out in a heterogeneous mass, papers and old letters all scattered over the top. She stood still for a moment, angry tears springing into her eyes.

Then she remembered.

Her Lord was with her. He would know how hard this was for her to bear, seeing her mother's precious things that had been so carefully guarded and put away in such lovely order, now all crumpled up and thrown around, some of them crushed in balls and thrown under the edge of the eaves.

Lexie dropped down in the midst of all the disorder and struggled with her tears. "Dear God," she prayed softly, "please help me now. Help me to forgive her, and not to let her know I am angry."

Then she lifted her head and went to work.

First of all the precious letters, gathered into a neat pile. The box they had been packed away in was sprawled at the other end of the room with its sides torn down, and its cover bent in two. Elaine was evidently angry because she couldn't find what she was searching for, perhaps. Well, why think about it? Just get things in order as quickly as possible, and then put them all under lock and key and hide the key, or keep it always about her. That would be the only safe way. She would probably have to go down to the hardware store and buy some more locks. Or perhaps a hammer and some nails would be better. That ought to make things safer, for she was well aware that Elaine could never pull a nail out of a board, and it wouldn't be easy for her to open a box that was nailed up. She must be prevented from pulling things to pieces again.

So, carefully, thoughtfully, she put her precious belongings into safekeeping, and finally nailed up the boxes securely.

She was almost done with her work when the stair door opened and Elaine's shrill voice complained:

"What on earth are you doing upstairs, Lexie? Here I lie down to rest and just get to sleep, and you set up the most unearthly noise right over my head! It seems to me that you are just doing this to be disagreeable, and you know how easily I get one of those awful head-aches. I feel one coming on now, and I just know I'll have it all night."

Lexie stopped in dismay.

"Oh, I'm sorry, Elaine. I thought you were still sitting out on the porch."

"But what are you doing?"

"Why I was just nailing up some boxes so things won't get all over the place."

"You mean you are nailing up boxes you don't want *me* to look into. That makes me quite certain you have something more that you are afraid I will find."

"No," said Lexie sadly. "I just wanted to put things away. It looked terrible up here. I'm only straightening up. But I'm quite sure there is nothing up here you would want to find. Oh, Elaine, I wish you wouldn't be so unfriendly. You give me the feeling that you are just here to fight me."

"Really? Well, if you want me to treat you differently, you know what to do. Come clean. Tell me all you know about that money. Then I'll be as friendly as I always used to be."

Lexie sighed.

"I've told you all I know already and you won't believe me. What is the use of talking any more?"

"Well, there isn't any use. Not if you keep to that attitude of course," and the stair door closed with a slam. Then she could hear Elaine's footsteps clicking back to the living room.

Lexie took a deep breath, and turning went on with her work. But she drove no more nails at that time. There was no need to make her sister angrier than she already was.

When the attic was in neat order again, and all traces of the onslaught were removed, Lexie went quietly downstairs and marshaled the children home from the neighbor's sandpile, which had become the unfailing rendezvous of attraction to them. Their mother seemed to pay no more attention to them than if she had never heard of them, unless she thought somebody else was finding fault with them, or attempting to punish them, and then she roused to a scathing sarcasm. But Elaine, after her tempestuous outburst, had gone back to her bed and was soundly asleep at last, an old mystery-story novel lying open by her side. So Lexie was free for the time, and after the children were fed she coaxed them off to bed by telling them a couple of stories, while Cinda reluctantly prepared a special tray for Elaine, to tempt her to relax and stop tormenting Lexie.

But after the tray had been administered, Elaine still refused to be on good terms with Lexie, to Cinda's great disgust, and went back to her bed and her novel. So Lexie sent Cinda off for a walk, and a little time to visit an old friend in the neighborhood, and Lexie sat on the quiet porch and had opportunity to think over the remarkable letter she had received. A soldier in the midst of the fire! She likened his situation to her own. For in a way they were alike. Although of course no physical harm was coming to herself, she was in no danger to her health, she had no pain nor actual fear to endure, yet on the other hand what could be hotter than her sister's scorching words, what could be more lonely than this existence day after day in company with one who apparently hated her, and lived only to do her harm, to subjugate her?

But she must not get to pitying herself. Her soldier boy was not doing that. He was drawing comfort from a distant picture of mountain strength, dewy grass, and a child's small cool hand. And *she* must find the comfort that surely was somewhere about for her. And if she didn't find it she must press on anyway. Oh yes, there was comfort, there *must* be comfort in the thought that God was with her, and God cared, had promised to be with her through water or through fire. Yes, this lad from out her childhood past had helped her, even as he claimed that she had helped him. The thought of him was pleasant, like something out of a story, when all had been unhappy prose before it came. It certainly was a strangely beautiful thing for that grand boy to have grown up, and yet to have remembered her, an insignificant little girl, remembered her well enough to take the trouble to write her a letter.

There was one thing that made her sad for him. He

must feel strangely alone in this world, that he should bother to write to a mere thought-shadow of a child he had seen but once. There must be something almost occult about this. Lexie couldn't understand it, but she liked it. Perhaps God had made him do it! What a wonderful thought!

And then she heard Elaine groaning, heard her flinging her book away upon the floor and bursting out into heartbreaking sobs.

Lexie hesitated for just a moment. Should she go to her? And then she heard her calling Cinda petulantly, like a child's wail, and she hesitated no longer. Stepping to the bedroom door she said gently:

"Is something the matter, Elaine? Are you feeling worse? Can I do anything for you?"

Elaine stopped her sobbing and looked up.

"Oh, it's *you*, is it?" she said in a voice like an icicle. "I didn't call *you*, I called Cinda. I wouldn't want to trouble *you*, who are so utterly unaccommodating. Where is Cinda?"

"Cinda went out for a little while," said Lexie pleasantly. "Tell me what you want, Elaine. I'll be glad to do anything I can for you. I don't want to be unaccommodating."

"Oh, you *don't*, don't you?" taunted the unhappy woman. "Well then, come clean, and tell me what I want to know about that money!"

"I'm sorry, Elaine. I've told you all I know. You don't believe me. There is nothing else to say!"

"Oh, *be still!*" snapped Elaine, kicking her slipper off at her. "I'm sick of such lying prattle. I wish you would go upstairs and let me alone. Here I am, a widow if there ever was one, or worse than a widow perhaps. The only man I ever loved either dead or a prisoner of war, and I all alone having to battle my way with an unfriendly world, and penniless, having to fend for my poor dear little children. And my only sister, instead of showing sympathy and kindness, and being ready to sacrifice some part of the fortune which she has been enjoying, remains silent and smug, and refuses to divulge what has been done with the booty!"

Elaine was working herself up to a fine fury now, and turned upon Lexie fiercely. "Get *out!*" she cried. "I say, *get out!* I don't want to see you again, *ever, anymore!*"

Lexie quietly stepped out of the room and said no more.

What was she to do with a situation like this? There seemed to be no possible way of making Elaine believe what she had told her. How could she go on from day to day under conditions like this? Certainly she couldn't hope to do much worthwhile studying.

But then, this wasn't any worse than that soldier boy over on the other side of the world had it. There was no actual fire here. And God let that young man go through that, probably for some reason she wasn't wise enough to understand. And He wanted her to go through this, and walk worthy of Him, worthy of having God for her Companion, Christ for her Saviour. Could there possibly be glory in this walk? Would any witness she could manifest be a testimony, to her unbelieving sister, for instance? What and if somehow by her life she might show forth to Elaine what Christ wanted to be to *her?* It didn't seem possible that anything she could do would do any good, but if it did, wouldn't it be worth doing? Of course she could never do it alone. It would have to be Christ living in her, and not herself.

Then she knelt down by her bed and talked to the Lord about it, and it really seemed as she knelt in the dark room that the Lord Himself stood there and showed her how this might be, if she would yield herself utterly to Him.

14

WHEN BEN BARRON received Lexie's letter he was sitting up in a very crude deck chair, on the meagre little upper veranda of the tiny hospital, a building hastily assembled from what material could be found in the vicinity.

He had had a long hard seige, a bad time getting well, and perhaps little heart to help the doctors, who were doing their best with the supplies at hand, and within the necessary limitations of the war. But now it seemed fairly certain that he was to recover, and to that end he was ordered out in the chair, to do nothing, which wasn't very helpful to a person of Benedict Barron's eager restless temperament.

For Ben Barron was lonely. Definitely lonely. This wasn't like being among his comrades in camp, or on the march, or even under fire, with a lot of friends who had grown to be closer than brothers because they had fought together, had bled together, and some of them had died. His clan had grown during this season of war to be a part of him. But now they were none of them here. The few who had come to the hospital when he came, had either got well and gone, or died from their wounds. He had no one here. He was looking forward to going away himself very soon, he hoped, yet he had no special place to go, unless they would let him go back into action, and the doctor had said that must not be for some time, if ever. He would have to await developments in his recovery. So, he had to sit here and try to build a new philosophy of life.

When his thoughts turned back to home they seemed to come up against a blank wall. His father had died three years before he went to war, and his mother died in the hospital while he was fighting fire. He would never see her again on this earth. The thought of his native country was gloomed with sadness because she was gone. There seemed to be no one left over there whom he wanted to see just now. No one who would really care whether he lived or died. Oh, there were a couple of aunts and an uncle, several cousins. The girls had written a letter apiece to him after he entered the army. Just stupid sort of formal letters, because they had a duty toward all soldiers, and he was moreover their cousin. One of them had recently written him that she was married to a flier and described her elaborate wedding in detail, said she wished he had been there to add his uniform to the procession. Another one had joined the WAC's, and still a third was an army nurse and going overseas. They were enthusiastic and eager over the war, as if it were a new game. They spoke of their uniforms and training as they used to tell him about their new permanents and lipsticks. They were giddy girls full of rollick with no thought for serious things, though perhaps if they got into the real war it might put some sense into them. But they and their crowd were not interesting to him now. He might get over this feeling during the years perhaps, but just at present he was not interested in them at all.

There had been another girl, a girl he had almost decided to take for his girl. Then, one day just before he left for camp, she came smiling to him to show him her new ring. She was engaged to another soldier boy. He had waited too long. He had lost out! Or had he? He hadn't been sure she was the girl he wanted, till somebody else got her, and that put a gloom on things for a while until he got interested in war. He had nearly forgotten about her now, the way she lifted her sunny lashes, the dark look of her big soft eyes, but it had closed one volume of the book of regret for him when he went away from his own land. Perhaps that was why it had been so easy to take the thought of a little child in a blue dress from long ago to think about out there on that dark hot field of fire when memory needed a relief, instead of some girl of his own age who had been a companion. That girl who had shown him her new ring had been a friend of years, yet she had turned so easily to the new soldier who had only been in town a week or two visiting some of her friends, when she got that ring. He felt she had been rather faithless to him. But perhaps she had never counted him as closer than just a playmate. Well, he had a feeling that women were rather undependable. And so after he had waited for several weeks since writing his letter and sending it out into a world that had likely forgotten him, he had come to class Lexie with all other girls. She wouldn't likely even bother to acknowledge his letter. She was grown up, maybe married, no longer a little girl, and never really knew him anyway. So he must forget that letter. He had acknowledged his debt for her little memory, and that was that. It had been a crazy idea to write to her anyway.

And that was what he was thinking when the nurse brought him the letter. Her letter. Little Lexie!

He gave a quick glance around after the nurse had handed him the letter, to see if anyone near was looking at him. But the man in the next chair was sound asleep, and the two chairs on the other side of him were vacant. Somehow he felt half silly getting a letter from a little girl, and on his own initiative.

He had known at once that it was her letter, partly because there were so few others who would be likely to write to him now, as the relatives had all done their kinly duty, one letter apiece; and partly that he had sensed the familiarity of the postmark even before he was able to read it clearly.

So, slowly, carefully, he tore open the envelope and pulled out the sheet of paper, folded so neatly, traced over with such characterful handwriting. He was conscious of being glad that the letter was not too short. He must savor every line of it, for whether it was pleasant or not it was the only letter he had had in a long time, and he wanted to enjoy it, even if it was a cold haughty rebuke from a grown-up young woman who did not like it that he had written to her, recalling such a childish thing as that she had been swinging on a gate!

"Dear Sergeant," she had written, familiarly, pleasantly, like any girl in a social center, being friendly with a soldier who was lonely!

He read on eagerly now. Yes, she remembered him.

She recalled what he had said and had laughed over it by herself! Bless her little heart! Then the next paragraph. Yes, she understood the strain he had been under. She knew what dew on a hot forehead would mean. She did not resent it that he had thought of her and acknowledged that she had been a help to him.

As he read on he was thrilled to think she had answered, glad that he had written her. He had worked a "hunch" and he was glad he had. He shut his eyes for an instant and now he could see her in a blue dress, walking down to the little white gate to meet the postman.

She had just happened to be there or she would not have gotten the letter. Then she must have been away. Where? Had she moved away? Or been away to school, or working somewhere like everybody else?

He opened his eyes and read on. Would the rest of the letter tell where she had been, and why she would not have received his letter if she had not been there?

Ah! She had had hard days! Poor child! She was going through some kind of fire too, though she didn't say what kind of fire it was. Her letter really told him nothing about her daily life and circumstances. Yet it did give the general background of a common experience, hard times, dark days, a life under fire that had to be gone through with. She acknowledged that his letter had made a dark day bright for her, and that was as good as making a fiery day cool and restful for him.

He drew a long breath of pleasure and reflected to what a pass he had come that a letter from a young unknown could bring such pleasure to him. He read on to the end. She hoped the war would end and he would come home some day, that she would like to see him. Well, that settled it. He would go home when he got that promised leave that the doctor had hinted might be in the offing for him if he continued to improve as he had been doing lately. Yes, he would certainly go home and seek out the little white house with the white gate, and the little girl with the blue eyes, and they would get acquainted, get really acquainted. That would be something to look forward to.

He lay back in his chair with his eyes closed and the letter held tight in his hand, and when the nurse came padding along on her rubber heels with his glass of milk he did not hear her. His thoughts were absorbed in what he was going to write back to the little girl.

Yes, he was going to write back at once! He wouldn't need to wait for courtesy's sake because a letter took plenty of time to travel across the world and get there, without putting unnecessary time between. He would start tomorrow morning and write a good long letter this time, because her letter would likely be longer if he made his long, and he needed good long letters to get through these days until he could go home.

So the next day he wrote a really long letter, taking it at intervals as the nurse would allow, and writing as if he had known her always. It was quite plain from everything he said that her letter had been a great delight to him, and so he wrote:

Dear Lexie:

You don't mind if I call you that, do you? Because you know you told me that was your name, and I'm not so well acquainted with the Kendall part; and it doesn't seem right to call you "Miss," though of course you must be by this time.

I can't tell you how glad I was to get your letter, for you see I had worried a good deal lest you would think me presuming, now you are grown-up, to dare to write to you, right out of the blue, when you weren't the little girl I remember any more. But you see I felt as if I had a proper introduction because you came to me in my troubled vision of you that dark night among the fire and pain. So when the nurse brought me your letter I was greatly glad. And when I read the letter I was doubly so.

I am sitting up now a little while every day. I was in a deck chair on a sort of scaffold they call a porch, when your letter came, and it seemed to me the sky looked bluer, and the few trees around were greener, after I read the letter. I suppose that may sound childish to you, but after you've been in a hard narrow bed for weeks and weeks, and wondered if you would ever get up, and after you've wondered if anybody would know or care if you didn't, a voice from the faraway home-place seems very sweet, and very nearly puts one out of his head. So, thank you for the letter.

It would be nice if you had sent me a little snapshot of yourself. I'd like so much to see how you look now you've grown up, so I will know you if I ever get home and have a chance to see you. And I'm sending you one a fellow took of me in London, before we came out here. I've been keeping it just as a sort of souvenir of London, but I'd like to send it to you. It will be more as if we were talking to one another. I'm not sure they will let it get by the censors, but if they don't it won't be much loss, so I'm sending it.

This letter is getting pretty long, but there's one more thing I'd like to tell you before I close, because I'd like somebody to know about it, and there is no one else I'd care to tell it to, or who would likely understand, but I have a feeling you will.

It's about an experience I had while I was lying out in that hot dark field with fiery pain in my shoulder, and more planes bringing more fiery bombs coming on and on. One had just exploded near me, and I was thinking that the next one would be the end for me.

And then suddenly there was a great stillness and I wondered if perhaps I was dead after all. But then I heard a voice speaking. It said "*I* am here with you!" and I looked up and saw that it was the Lord!

I had never seen Him before, of course, but I knew Him by the nail-prints in His hands, and by the great glory-light in His face, I wonder if you have ever seen Him, or heard His voice? Please don't think I'm crazy. I'm just an ordinary fellow, but my mother used to talk about Him, used to read me stories from the Bible. A verse I had learned for my mother came back to me then. "When thou passest through the waters; I will be with thee; and through the rivers, they shall not overflow thee: when thou walkest through the fire, thou shalt not be burned."

I had been through a river, a deep wide river, but it did not overflow me, though I had thought at one time it would; and then I had been through fire, fire after fire, but I was still alive! I had not been burned. I was startled. That verse had come back into my life, spoken just for me, spoken by the Lord Himself! It wasn't anything I had just imagined. I had *heard His voice* speaking the words! You don't know what it did to me. It is something I can never forget. And because you are the only friend in touch with me now, I want you to know about it. Do you mind?

Just today I got to thinking those words over that I heard

Him say to me, and I asked the nurse if she knew whether there was a Bible anywhere that I could read for few minutes. She said yes, there was a chaplain in the next ward had one, and she would borrow it for me. So she did, and I looked up that verse, and then I read on. A little farther on there was another verse, almost like a signature to a letter. It said "I, even I, am the Lord; and beside Me there is no Saviour."

So, I have that to think about. He is the only Saviour. He saved me from fire and water. There'll be other things farther on that I'll need saving from too. He saved me when they thought I was dying from my wounds, so there'll be other times ahead when I'll need saving. I'm going to trust Him from now on.

I wonder, do you know Him? Did you ever see Him? Do you trust Him too?

Forgive me if I sound crazy, but I wanted to tell you. I'm going to investigate this, because I know it's real.

Please write to me again.

Your friend,
Ben

The letter went off, and then Ben began to worry himself lest it would sound crazy to her when it reached her. People didn't talk about seeing the Lord in the workaday world where she lived, nor where he had lived either, yet people didn't have such experiences as he had had every day. They didn't go through such fire, they didn't stay alive afterward, and they didn't meet the Lord. It wouldn't make any difference how long he lived afterward, nothing, nobody, could ever make him believe the Lord had not come to him. If they didn't believe it they just didn't know, that was all. Well, he had given the story to Lexie and this would be a sort of test of what she was. If she made fun of him he probably wouldn't write again, at least not more than once or twice. He would know she just hadn't met the Lord and couldn't understand until she did.

So he tried to put the matter out of mind, but he had a sunny feeling in his heart continually, that he was no more alone in a strange land, with no place anywhere that wasn't strange. He had the Lord with him continually. He had found another verse in that borrowed

Bible before he sent it back to the sick chaplain. A verse that said "Lo, I am with you always, even unto the end of the world." So, what did it matter whether he had anyone else or not?

Perhaps Ben Barron wouldn't have come so fully to believe in what he had been through if life had always been full of fun and joy to him, but the loss of so many things he had cared for when he was younger and the terrible strain through which he had passed, had opened his mind to receive. And then too, that vision had been very vivid.

So the days went on and the patient was docile and quiet and content. He was not restless, though he knew that as soon as the doctor felt he was able to travel, and the journey could be arranged, he was to be sent home to America on furlough. It was wonderful to look forward to, but he was not impatient, because secretly he wanted to wait till there could be a chance of another letter from Lexie. But when he realized this he told himself he was a fool. She was only a child. Well, grown-up of course, but nothing to him but an idea, a vision. And why should he care whether she wrote again or not? And if she wrote whether she thought him silly or not?

And then one night, in the still darkness, it came to him what was behind this whole feeling, but it came to him clearly then, and he acknowledged to himself what it was. It was because he was troubled that perhaps he should not have told that sacred tender experience to anyone, even a girl who was in his mind but a child with innocent lovely thoughts. Perhaps it was a desecration of his Christ that he should have told that experience at all. And why did he choose that memory-child to hear it?

But the days went on and the doctors watched and rejoiced over this patient who had seemed at first so hopeless. He was really getting well, and he was being very docile and doing everything he ought to do willingly, and that was an unusual state for a patient to be in. Most of them were so impatient to go away, to get home, but he seemed content to lie here and wait.

Then one day the nurse brought him another letter,

and she studied it as she carried it across the hall to his
room where he was lying down resting. It must be from
a girl. It was a girl's handwriting. And when she handed
it to him she had the pleasure of seeing a brightness in
his face, lighting up his handsome features. He was thin
and somewhat wasted of course, but he was still handsome, and she wondered what the girl was like? Or
would she be his sister? Perhaps. But he only thanked
her and smiled and she had to go her way without
having her curiosity satisfied.

Ben Barron sat up on his cot with interest and
opened his letter. It was from Lexie. She *had* written
again! And out of the envelope as he opened it carefully, there fell a small unmounted photograph of a
lovely girl. Yes, it was the same little girl with the
sweet eyes and the charming innocent smile. She hadn't
thought him quite a fool or she would never have sent
him the picture, and there was a look in those eyes of
trust and understanding, just as he had hoped there
would be. Just as he had seemed to read in her child-
eyes so long ago. He had taken a girl on trust from
memory and now he was looking into the pictured
face of that girl, and she came fully up to what such a
child should have been. He was thrilled with the picture.

Then suddenly he bethought himself that he had not
read her letter yet, and he unfolded the pages. Yes, it
was a good long letter, and he felt a great joy. Just why
he didn't understand, only he had been so lonely, and
now there was someone who was interested enough to
write him, interested enough to take hold of the slender invitation he had thrown out and respond to it. He
was crazy of course, but he was very glad. He had been
waiting and the letter had come before he was gone. So
he read.

Dear Sergeant Ben,

It was wonderful to get your letter from such a far land,
and I was so glad to have the little snapshot you sent. It is
very like what you were when I saw you. I'm sure I remember you well. Looking at the picture made me sure. Your
nice smile is just the same. And I think it was such a good

idea for you to send me the picture and ask for mine, because it sort of identifies us for each other.

So I am sending you a little picture that was taken for our class book in college, and I happened to have one left over. It's not a very wonderful picture but it will give you some idea of what the little girl swinging on the gate looks like now. You see I've been very busy lately and I haven't swung on the gate for a long time of course, so I don't know whether my smile has changed or not, but you can play the picture is smiling as you, because I am so pleased that you wrote to me.

And now you have told me a wonderful thing about your experience that night of so much fire. I am glad to know it, because it makes me sure you are a Christian, and your experience matches something that has happened to me. I'd like to try and tell you if you don't mind.

You see, my father died, and then my mother, just a little over a year ago, while I was still in college, and now I am on my own. There hasn't been much money, but I found some work, and was getting through. I've just a few weeks more to go now before the end, with a nice job promised when I finish. But my half-sister telegraphed me her husband was reported missing in action, and she was very sick and was coming home with her three little children.

I couldn't stop her. She didn't give me time, and the house is half hers. Of course I knew I must stay and help her out. Things haven't been easy. I haven't been through fire, but sometimes sharp words can burn your soul very like a flame of fire. I've had to give up going back to my college, but have been able to arrange to finish and take final examinations at the university down in our nearby city. Still it is not going to be easy to stay here. My sister does not approve my finishing college. She feels I ought to go to work. But I can get a better job if I have a diploma.

Things have been rather awful sometimes, and one night when I couldn't get to sleep, thinking it over and wondering how long this kind of thing could go on, suddenly I seemed to feel the Presence of the Lord in the room, and to realize that I wasn't alone in this. God was here, and He knew why it had to be, and If I trusted Him it would all come out the way He has planned.

You see, though I've never seen the Lord, the way you describe, I've known about Him always, and when I was a

little girl I took Him for my Saviour. But I'm afraid I
haven't done much about it since. Of course I've prayed
and sometimes read my Bible, and gone to church when I
could, but I haven't taken the trouble to get better acquainted with Him. And while I lay there with the feeling
of that Presence in my room, it came to me that God was
letting all this happen to me to call my attention to Him,
and to His love for me. While I had had comforts and good
times I had practically forgotten Him, and it seemed there
was nothing would call my attention back to Him but
trouble and sorrow, and it even took a lot of that. So I
began to see it all, that He really loved me, and wanted
my loving service.

My sister wasn't ever interested in religious things. She
didn't join the church when I did, and never wanted to go
to Sunday School, and she used to taunt me saying I
thought I was so awfully good because I went to church,
whenever I did anything she didn't like. And I began to
see that perhaps the thing that I had to do was to show her
how I had a Saviour who could help me through hard
places. I knew I hadn't been doing that at all. And somewhere I had heard that the only thing God has put us here
for is to witness for Him.

So I knew, there in the darkness, with the feeling of
God's Presence in the room, that henceforth I was going to
try to do that.

But I knew I could never do it of myself. It would have
to be Christ, living in me, instead of myself, and living my
life for me.

So that's how it is with me now. I've just started, but
I'm trying to let Him have His way in me. That's why I'm
glad you told me about meeting the Lord, for if you hadn't
I never would have dared tell you all this. What you have
told me has made me feel that we are really friends, because
we both belong to Christ.

I've never talked about such things to anybody else but
my mother now and then, and she was very shy of it. So
maybe I do not know how to say such things, but it
certainly makes me glad to know someone who can talk
the way you do.

I am so glad you are getting better, and I do hope you
will not have to go back and fight under fire any more, but
I know if you feel that it is needed you will go. But God
will be there, and nothing can hurt you. You may not

always be able to see Him, but He will be there, and I am glad.

Your friend,
Lexie

There was a grave sweet look in Ben's eyes as he finished the letter, and then he thoughtfully turned back to the first page and read it over again. In his heart there was chiming a pleasant thought. "Dear little girl," it said, "I never knew a girl could be like that." And later when he thought it over again, he said to himself: "If Norine had been like that she never would have done what she did to me. That is she never would have led me on to believe she cared, the way she did, when she didn't really care at all, only wanted me for an added trophy."

Ben Barron had read the letter through three times before the nurse came back, but he had such a renewed, happy look that she could not help but notice it.

"Well, I guess you must have had good news in your letter," she said as she handed him his glass of orange juice.

"Why, yes, thank you, I did. By the way, when is that doctor coming again?"

"Well, he said he was coming in tomorrow again. Why, don't you feel as well?"

"Oh, sure! I feel as if I could go into the fight again."

"You do?" she said with surprise. "But I think you're due for a furlough before you go into any more fights. At least that's what I heard the doctor say the last time he was here."

A happy grin dawned on Ben's lips.

"Suits me all right," said Ben. "I'm getting right fed up on lying here in a hospital."

"Well, you've been a pretty good patient, and we'll all feel sorry to have you go. Not sorry for you, you know, but sorry for ourselves. We're going to miss you."

"Thank you," said Ben with satisfaction.

"Do you know what I think about you?" said the nurse, lingering a moment with misty eyes upon her-patient. "I think if there ever was a real Christian, it's you, even if you *are* a soldier."

Ben Barron looked startled.

"Oh!" he said embarrassedly. "I'm not much of a Christian. I never claimed—"

"No, you didn't claim to be, but you just acted like one. You don't always have to go around talking about what you believe to make an impression. It's when you stand pain with courage, and don't get mad when you can't have everything to eat you want. It's when you speak kind to the nurses even if they bring your bath water too hot, and forget to bring you cold water when you're thirsty. You live like you knew God. Not just been brought up polite, but as if you had a real gentleness in your soul like they say Christ had!"

"Yes?" said Ben Barron, wonderingly. "Well, that's extraordinary of you to say that, because I just had a letter from a friend I used to know in America, and she talked something like that, but not about me, you understand. She was talking about some of the hard things she had to bear, and it seemed to be her idea too that it wasn't all in profession whether one was a Christian or not. She seemed to think a Christian had to go through fire, like a soldier, to prove the Lord was his Saviour."

"Well, there's soldiers and soldiers. Plenty of them are brave to stand fire, but not everyone can keep a civil tongue in his head when he's suffering. It takes something more than human nature to do that at times. I know for I've seen plenty of 'em."

"Yes," said Ben Barron thoughtfully. "I guess it does. It takes a divine nature. And if you've seen anything like that in me I guess it was because I met the Lord out there on the field of fire."

"You—*what?*"

"I met the Lord. He came and stood beside me. He spoke to me. And I guess it's up to me, since then, to act a little different from what I used to act when I was just on my own and acting out what I felt."

The nurse stared.

"That might make a difference! You certainly are different. I am sorry to see you go! We need more like you. You're a loyal soldier if there ever was one," and brushing away the mists from her eyes she hurried out to get another man's orange juice, another man who definitely was *not* a Christian.

But Ben Barron sat still with his glass of orange juice in his hand and stared into the distance. She thought he was a Christian! Lexie thought so too. *Was* he? He certainly had not known he was. He certainly had done very little about it in the past. And yet he had given a testimony to that nurse! Was it all because he had met the Lord out there in the fire under the stars? Well, it was time he did something definite about this! When he got somewhere where they had such things he would buy himself a Bible. That ought to help!

15

LEXIE WAS ENTERED now in the university, and very busy every day with her study, and doing what duties she could find time for between about the house. Elaine found a great deal of fault with her, and hindered her in every way she could. When she would discover Lexie studying she would demand some service from her, lemonade made, or cakes brought, and would she please go across the street and see what the children were doing, and bring them home and give them baths and dress them up?

Lexie made protests now and then, urging a heavy schedule at college, and examinations imminent, but this only brought scorn from Elaine.

"Such silly nonsense! A great big girl like you going to school at your age! You ought to be back at home getting the meals and cleaning the house and helping me with the children."

"*Helping* her!" Lexie complained to herself. "As if she ever lifted a finger for those children, except to scold them, or protect them against other's protests!"

But what was the use of protesting? Elaine always won in the end, unless, as on a few occasions when there was great stress in her own work she simply ignored Elaine's request and went on with her study. But she always paid bitterly for this in reprisals, and sharp words that scorched her very soul. Oh, it was not easy to live this kind of a life, and so far as she could see she was getting nowhere in making any impression on her sister. She only grew sharper day by day, and more exacting. She complained continually, and Lexie's nerves were on edge all the time. Oh, would this ever be over?

The one bright spot now in the happenings of the

day was the occasional letters that came from abroad, from Benedict Barron.

Sometimes Lexie wondered what her mother would say to her keeping up a correspondence with an utter stranger. Yet somehow she couldn't help but feel that it was all right, and her mother would approve of the letters that passed between them. He was so very respectful, and he was a Christian. He seemed so sincere, and so sort of lonely, just as she was. And yet she sensed through it all that there was danger in such sort of blind friendships. He was lonely now, and so was she, but sometime, when he would perhaps come home, and meet his old friends, and get into his old life again, would he forget her, and was she laying the foundation for sadness in her life, and disappointment?

Well, suppose she was. People had to have some sorrow in their lives. Hadn't God sent her this friendship? She wasn't counting great things on this, just a nice pleasant—perhaps passing—friendliness. As free on the one side as on the other. No love making nor any foolishness. Why should she not enjoy it, why not be glad about it? She hadn't much else of earthly pleasure to enjoy. Even her college where she had a number of casual friends and acquaintances had been taken away from her. Had that been right? Ought she not to have fought to keep that college life till it was over? And yet Elaine had seemed so helpless, and it had been borne in upon her that for their father's sake she must stay here for awhile. Perhaps Elaine wasn't really sick. Perhaps she was perfectly able to work, to keep house and care for her children, to even get a job to support them. But it had seemed so heartless to charge her with that, and yet continually it came to her that her sister was acting a part, and wasn't really sick at all.

But sick or well she couldn't leave the house and all its sweet belongings to Elaine's heartless rule. There were things so inextricably connected with her mother that she could not bear to have them mishandled by her sister, who had never cared for any of the old family furniture, and she had no other place to store them if she tried to go away. Besides it would make endless complications. Elaine would probably sell half of her mother's things if there was any way to get money out of them. And if she tried to take them away, there again would be trouble. Also, this continual threat of a lawsuit was something that must be settled before she dared go away anywhere. She must be there near her friends. Judge Foster and Mr. Gordon had promised to help in case Elaine really carried out her threats, but they advised her to stay by the house and try to carry on in a sane and quiet way, as if nothing of the sort was proposed.

There had been a cessation of hostilities along these lines from Elaine for the past five or six weeks while Lexie had been studying so hard. But the real cause was that Bettinger Thomas was absent on a business trip and he had promised to get the evidence in shape while he was gone. So Elaine had relaxed and was waiting. She had written all the suggested sentences into the little book that the lawyer had selected for her, and which was a very good match in size, shape and color to the original book belonging to Lexie's mother. She had done her part and been highly commended for the delightful way in which she had imitated her stepmother's handwriting. She had produced several letters written to herself during the years by her stepmother, and these had been good examples of the script. The lawyer had had an expert's advice on the subject, or said he had. So Elaine felt she had done her part and had only to rest now and wait until her expert lawyer should arrive and produce results.

"Lexie, can you spare ten dollars for me?" she asked one afternoon when Lexie arrived home after her final examination, tired to death, and very much in doubt as to whether she had passed the test because the ways of the university were somewhat different from her college where she had spent the early years of her college life.

"Ten dollars?" said Lexie wearily lifting tired eyes to her sister's face. "I'm afraid not. I had to use the last ten I had for college fees and I'm just about cleaned out. I didn't know there were any big necessities ahead.

We have enough in the house to eat for the rest of the week. What is the matter, Elaine? Is it anything I can do for you?"

"No! Certainly not!" said Elaine. "I wouldn't have asked you for ten dollars if anything else would have done. I've *got* to have ten dollars, and if you don't fork it over I'll go upstairs and take some of your mother's old rattletraps and send for a secondhand man and *sell* them, for I just *must* have it!"

"Elaine! What is the matter?" asked Lexie, really alarmed, and trying to think what of her mother's precious relics would be pitched upon for this sacrifice. "Has something happened I don't know anything about? Some bill that has to be paid at once?"

"Don't be absurd!" sneered Elaine wearily. "Of course not. But my lawyer is coming back early next week and I've got to get a permanent and a wave and a manicure, and get myself in some shape so that I won't be a disgrace in court. Then I can sit up and feel some self-respect again. I thought I would send for a taxi and get them to take me into town and go to my old beauty parlor. They always turned me out looking like a million dollars!"

"I see!" said Lexie sadly. "Well, I'm sorry. I really haven't the ten dollars. You'll have to go to some of your other friends to borrow it, for I don't know how to get it."

"Oh, now, Lexie! Have a heart! You know I haven't any friends around here now, and you needn't pretend you haven't any money for I know you have. You see we are almost to the time, and you better get over your nonsense and come across. You can have your choice. Hand me over that ten dollars, or go up in the attic and bring down that quaint little writing desk of your mother's and take it down to Nerokian's. I sent for him last week and told him about it and he's very much interested in buying it. So you can run down to him with it and bring me back the ten dollars. If you can get any more out of him you can keep the extra for yourself. You see I'm quite generous."

Lexie stood still a moment looking at her sister, and

her lips began to tremble. Two tears formed in her eyes and she turned quickly away from her sister and walked out of the room her head up. Gently she closed the door into the dining room and turned toward the stairs. She hurried up to her own room and closed and locked the door, thankful that the children were still outside playing hopscotch on the sidewalk. She dropped on her knees beside the bed and turned her heart to her Lord. It was the only source of help she knew.

"Oh, my Heavenly Father! Show me what to do! Don't let me have to lose mother's dear lovely desk, the one her mother gave her when she was a girl. Please help me, dear Lord."

One moment she paused to get quiet and then it came to her what to do. She had no doubt but that the Lord had put the thought in her mind.

Quietly she got up, unlocked her door and went up to the attic. Far over in the corner under the eaves she had hidden the desk. Now she saw it had been pulled out and the contents spread over the floor. She had locked it when she put all the things away, and taken the key downstairs with her. But the lock had been broken, smashed in with a hatchet. The hatchet lay near at hand as if in defiance of decency.

Tenderly she picked up the desk, gathered up the papers and letters, put them safely inside, and then found an old straw suitcase, of the type that used to be called a "telescope," put the desk inside, covered it and fastened the leather strap firmly about it. Then she went down, stopping long enough at her room to get her hat and purse. As she passed through the kitchen she said in a low tone to Cinda:

"You need not say anything about where I've gone, not to anybody. I probably won't be back in time for supper, but it's all right. Can you carry on while I'm gone?"

"Sure thing, Miss Lexie! I'll carry on! She been putting the screws on you again? I thought so! Okay. You can depend on me."

So Lexie slipped out the back door and made her way down through the meadow and off to Mr. Gordon's house, first stopping to telephone and ask if he was at home and could see her.

Her cordial voice encouraged her, and helped to still her wildly beating heart as she hurried along to the bus that would take her within a couple of blocks of the Gordon city house.

She would much rather have asked this favor of Judge Foster but Judge Foster had been taken away to the mountains for a thorough change and rest before he returned to his duties at court, and she would not trouble his family. They probably knew nothing of her affairs. So she went with great temerity to explain, deciding on the way that she must tell him everything that happened since she last saw him. She must tell him of that Mr. Perrine, and find out if that complicated the situation, and whether she ought to go away for a time till this was over, or what she ought to do.

Of course if he said she ought to sell the little writing desk and give the money to Elaine she would do it, but she sincerely hoped he would not. It didn't seem as if even God would want her to do that. It seemed a desecration of her mother's property, and being a Christian didn't mean that one had to lie down on the floor and be a door mat for someone to walk over. Or did it? She was troubled about that. Of course if she was sure it was right she should give it up, if she thought God wanted her to do so, she would do it. But it did not seem the right thing to do.

It was a great relief to her to find Mr. Gordon at home ready to see her, and glad to take charge of her precious package. Moreover he told her absolutely not to give up her mother's treasures for any such foolish reason. Also he asked some very pertinent questions concerning the man whom Elaine said was going to testify about her mother's disposal of money that was falsely charged against her. He said he would investigate but he was almost certain a Harry Perrine had been involved before in false witnessing.

And when the interview was over—for Lexie had sense enough not to stay long—Mr. Gordon said:

"You'll be glad to learn, I know, that Judge Foster

is much better, and that a letter received from him to-day asked after you and made some suggestions concerning your affairs that may put a decided crimp in Bettinger Thomas' plans."

So Lexie went gravely back home, just as dark was coming down, and found Cinda had fed the family, put the children to bed, and happified Elaine with a new magazine. She was keeping Lexie's supper hot, and insisted on her eating it before she answered Elaine's imperative demand for her presence.

So Lexie ate a nice supper and then went quietly in to find her sister trying on some of her dresses, and deciding what alterations were necessary to bring them up to date.

"You wanted to see me, Elaine?" she asked, coming in quietly.

Elaine turned with a smirk on her face from the mirror, and held an artificial flower in her hair, as her eyes demanded admiration from the despised Lexie.

"Becoming, eh, don't you think, Lexie?"

"Very nice," said Lexie trying to keep her voice from being cold and disapproving. "You wanted to see me, Elaine?" she asked again.

For answer Elaine turned and slowly, amusedly surveyed her sister. When she spoke her voice was derisive.

"Well, naturally I did of course. What report have you to give me? You certainly took long enough. How much did you succeed in getting for that desk?"

"Desk?" said Lexie slowly. "Oh, I wouldn't care to sell the desk, it was very precious to mother, and is therefore precious to me."

Elaine shrugged her shoulders.

"As you please of course. I'm sure I don't see what good old outdated, wornout rattletraps are, if that's your idea, and you have other resources, hand over my ten dollars please. I want to use it in the morning. And while you're about it you better make it fifteen. There are one or two other items I forgot to mention."

"I'm sorry, Elaine. I told you I hadn't any money.

Was that all you wanted of me? If it is I think I'll go to bed. I'm rather tired. I had my last examination to-day, and it was a hard one."

"So silly and useless!" sneered Elaine, "but Lexie, I've simply *got* to have that money. You can get it whatever way you please, but I'll only give you till ten o'clock tomorrow morning, and then if you don't hand it over I'll take some of those precious treasures of yours in the attic and sell them myself. The desk will be the best bet because I really have a buyer for that."

Lexie was still for a minute and then she said sadly: "Good night, Elaine. It really seems useless for me to talk to you. Perhaps it would have been better for me to have stayed at college and the job I had. I don't seem to be of much use to you here."

"No, you don't!" said the older sister. "You certainly have changed. I used to think you were very kind and accommodating, but you have grown utterly selfish and insolent."

Then into the electric atmosphere of the house came Angelica's voice, sharply like her mother's, complaining:

"Aunt Lex, I wish you would come up to bed. Bluebell is crying herself sick for you. She says you are the only one who can tell bedtime stories and get her to sleep, and she keeps getting out of bed and coming over and pulling my hair and pinching me."

Lexie smiled.

"All right, I'll come, Angel. Tell her I'll be with her right away!"

"Yes, go! Steal the love of my children away from me too, with all the rest you are doing," sneered Elaine, "but you get that money for me in the morning or you'll wish you had."

But Lexie had escaped, and was rapidly preparing for bed, to nestle down beside Bluebell and comfort her baby sobs.

After a little the house quieted down, and even Cinda could stop sniffing and get a bit of rest. And in the still night watches Lexie's tired prayers arose. She and that soldier boy over on the other side of the world somewhere, were both praying to a God they knew, who was close beside them all the way, and as Lexie was dropping off to sleep she wondered if ever in the years ahead she would see that soldier again and they could talk over these things they had passed through? Well, anyway, perhaps in Heaven. Somehow there didn't seem to be much prospect of anything pleasant happening to her on this earth.

16

THE UNIVERSITY COMMENCEMENT was the next night and Lexie's dress which she had ordered at the other college with the girls of her class and which was to be forwarded in plenty of time, did not arrive until the morning of the day. Lexie had been wondering what she would do if it didn't come. Stay at home entirely, or go down in her old blue voile, which was the only dress-up garment she possessed that was at all in keeping with warm weather. And it was warm!

But that last morning the big pasteboard box arrived by parcel post, and eagerly Lexie carried it up to her room, thankful that Elaine was still asleep and wouldn't be demanding to see what had come.

But she reckoned without knowledge, for Elaine was not so soundly asleep that she had not heard the postman come, and she had been at the window looking out behind the curtain. Lexie scarcely had the box open before the stair door opened and Elaine called up the stairs, "Lexie, what was that package that came in the mail? Wasn't that for me?"

"No," said Lexie pleasantly. "It was just some things that I didn't bring from college."

"Oh! Things! So you have some more old togs, have you? I should have thought they wouldn't have bothered to send any more such worn out duds as you have."

Lexie made no reply and presently Elaine closed the door and went back into her room. But well did Lexie know that she hadn't heard the last of this yet.

However, she was presently engrossed in opening her new dress, and hanging it up where she could examine it.

It was white organdie, sheer and fine. Those girls who did the ordering for the class were wealthy girls and they knew how to select good material. Lexie's eyes reveled in the sheer lovely folds, the delicate lace with which the ruffles were edged, the lovely lines of the whole garment. And to think it was her very own! How nice it would have been if she might have graduated with the rest of her own class in the college where she had worked so hard, among those girls she had come to know so well, and some of them to love.

Then she began to put her fingers on the folds shyly, to smooth the skirt down softly as if it were a baby's skin. There were a few creases in it where it had been folded too sharply, in order to get the cover of the box on. Ought she to iron it, or would just hanging up in the air take the creases out? Perhaps that would be better.

She took one of her hangers and padded it carefully with cotton and covered it with white cloth, and then she hung the dress on it and placed the hanger where it would get the breeze from the window. The air was a little damp from the rain last night and that would surely take the mussings out!

So, with quiet step and careful hand she went out, closing her door. There was no point in locking it of course, for that would only arouse Elaine's suspicions and start her on the warpath again, asking uncomfortable questions.

Lexie hurried downstairs, and began dusting the living room, softly humming a happy little tune, till suddenly Elaine appeared in her bedroom doorway.

"Mercy!" she said scowling darkly, "do you have to *screech?* I can't imagine why. Stuck here in this horrid hole of a town, working hard to make both ends meet! But oh, I forgot, you are counting on the fortune you are saving till all suspicion blows over and you feel you dare come out in the open and flaunt your riches!"

Suddenly Lexie felt as if she simply couldn't bear another word.

"Oh, don't, Elaine, please don't talk that way! You know that isn't any of it true, and you are just saying those things to be hateful. Isn't it enough to make me glad and want to sing to think that after all the hindrances I've had I've really finished my college course and am getting my diploma tonight. That certainly is enough to make me feel lighthearted. But I'm sorry if I disturbed you. I didn't know you had gone to lie down again. I thought you were dressing."

"Oh, it's of no consequence of course. But dressing? What would I dress in? I need a new dress. I haven't a rag fit to put on my back, and today that noted financier is coming to talk with me. I'm sure I don't know what to do."

Lexie was silent. There really wasn't anything she could say to that harangue. And so Elaine was going to bring that other obnoxious man here to the house along with the disgusting lawyer! Well, perhaps she had better get out for a while. How would it be for her to run down to the store now, as soon as she had this living room dusted, and call up Mr. Gordon? He had asked to be told when either of those two came to the house, and promised if he found it out in time to do something to help her relieve the situation. Besides, he said he wanted to get a view of Perrine, and make sure he was the one they were after before he could do anything.

So Lexie hurried through her task, and started down to the store, but as she came down the stairs from her room, where she had lingered a moment to note that the air was taking the few wrinkles out of her new dress already, she heard Elaine calling.

"Yes?" she answered, opening the dining room door a crack.

"I wish you would scrub the front porch!" ordered the lady. "It looks as if the pigs lived here. I can't have gentlemen coming to see me with a porch like that!"

Lexie smothered a desire to tell her sister that the only pigs that lived there belonged to her, as her children had been eating bread and jam out there the night before and had smeared jam, and an overripe banana over everything. But she took a deep breath instead and endeavored to answer steadily.

"Sorry, Elaine, I can't do it just now. I have to go on an errand. Perhaps when I get back there may be time. I'm rather busy this morning." And then she went out and closed the door before Elaine could say any more, and was speeding down across the meadow before Elaine had roused to keep her from going.

A little talk with Mr. Gordon brought calm into her troubled soul. He thanked her for letting him know, and said he might come out himself during the morning if he decided that was a wise thing to do.

So Lexie went home a trifle relieved, and wondered if she really ought to go out and scrub that porch. Of course Cinda would eventually do it, but she wanted to make things as easy as possible for Cinda. She decided that if there was no limousine parked before the door she would see that at least the jam was washed off the chairback and porch. She didn't want even an obnoxious lawyer, nor a crook, to find things actually dirty.

So Lexie hurried into the house and was about to go in search of a pail and scrubbing brush and cloths, when she met Cinda coming in from the side door carrying them.

"I just been out to scrub her highness' porch," she said with a comical grimace. "I heard what the likes of her said, and I would not have lifted a finger to help, savin' I knowed you would do it when you got back, and I didn't want that to happen. So it's done."

"That was sweet of you, Cinda, but I think you have enough to do without that. Anyway, those two men she said were coming aren't worth any effort. But thank you for your thought of me," and Lexie went smiling into the house to make sure she hadn't left her dust cloth in the living room.

But when she opened the door she saw Elaine seated at the desk writing, and she was wearing a delicate white dress.

Lexie stared at her sister for an instant and then she recognized the fine lace on the edge of the ruffles, and it all came over her. That was her commencement dress! Elaine had gone up and got it and put it on! Oh, and she would muss it all up! Lexie was suddenly very angry, so angry she was petrified. She couldn't speak!

Then Elaine looked up from her writing; caught a glimpse of her sister's face and was startled. She hadn't

expected Lexie to return so soon, and she wasn't prepared for that look of utter anger and despair in
Lexie's eyes.

"Oh! So you *did* decide to come back in time to
scrub that porch! Well, you needn't have bothered. I
made Cinda do it. She's a lazy good-for-nothing anyway. She ought to do it without being told!"

But Lexie had no ears for anything about the porch
just then. She was struggling to regain her composure
and trying to speak in a pleasant compelling manner.

"Oh, Elaine! That's my commencement dress!" she
said in a cross between a wail and a protest. "Won't
you please go and take it off quick. And *please* be
careful. I've nothing else to wear tonight! You had no
right to go up and get my dress—!"

"Right? You talk of *right?* Why didn't I have a right
to do anything I wanted to do with what you claim as
yours, I'd like to know, when you have taken my
fortune and refuse to tell where it is?"

"Oh, Elaine, please, *please* stop talking like that.
You know I haven't any fortune. And won't you please
get up quick and take that off. Let me help you off with
it right away! Please be *careful!* Oh, if anything should
happen to it I don't know what I could do!"

"Get away from me, Lexie. Take your hands off my
shoulder! No, I will not take the dress off. I'm expecting callers any minute and this is a perfect negligee. It's
nothing extraordinary anyway. Just a white nightgown
affair. I have two old white dresses myself that will do
well enough for you to march on a platform with a
whole lot of other people. I intend to keep this on now,
I haven't time to change and you can rave all you
want to, but it won't do you a bit of good!"

Elaine waved her hand determinedly and her white
arm swept out across the desk and took the ink bottle
in its path, landing it directly in her own lap, where
it turned over and spilled a large wide path of blue-
black ink down the front of the cherished dress!

For an instant there was a dead silence in the room
as both girls were horrified at what had happened, and
then Elaine, gathering anger as she spoke, said:

"There! Now see what you have made me do?

Ruined my costume, and devastated your own dress! But that isn't all," as the enormity of what had happened came over her. "I had on my own best silk slip. The pink one that matches my only evening dress, and it's *ruined*. And that's *all your fault!* I know you can't buy real silk things any more and I never could match this again. Oh, what *shall* I do? Why don't you help me get this terrible dress off quick. Take the scissors and cut it off. You can't get it off any other way. There are the scissors over on the table. Cut it off quick before this vile ink gets all through my undergarments!"

True to her nature Lexie froze into composure with an emergency. She took charge of the frantic woman and made her obey just by the force of her own will.

"Stand up!" she said quietly, and took hold of her sister's arm firmly. "Wait! Don't stir! Let me get this waist unfastened."

No one noticed when Cinda came in, a basin of water in her hand, and several large clean rags which she laid down on the floor at hand. Then she went quietly over to the excited weeping Elaine.

"There, dearie," crooned Cinda in perfect acting form. "We'll fix ye all up in good shape before yer comp'ny comes. Just stand still and shut yer eyes. Hold out yer right arm. Yes, that's right. Pull it off gently there. And now the other. There, the waist is off! Now we're through the worst. Wait, suppose I take off yer pretty slippers. They're too nice to get spoiled. Stand very still!"

Lexie knew enough to keep her own mouth shut and let Cinda carry on. She knew that her voice would only excite Elaine. So she worked with careful quick, frightened fingers, unzipping and pulling off the skirt cautiously down over the slim angry hips, zealously guarding the back and sides of the skirt from all contact with the tainted front breadth until the skirt lay in a billowy circle about the feet of the distressed Elaine. Then suddenly Cinda arose and put her strong arms quickly about the slim waist of the young woman lifting her bodily out from the dress and setting her down fully two yards away from it. As she did so Lexie gathered the blackened front breadths closely in her hands and drew the whole skirt out of the room. It was deftly done, and perhaps no one who had not so much at stake could possibly have accomplished the feat, but there it was, out in the dining room, with sides and back unmarred. Now, what could be done next?

Lexie was quick and clever. She knew exactly the pattern of that dress, and even while she had been rescuing what part of it was still untouched by ink, she had been trying to contrive how she could yet wear it. So now as she laid it down on the floor for the moment, she knew just what she had to do. If only the ink did not reach too far, it might be possible to rip or cut out that marred front breadth and let out some of the gathering in the full skirt. But she must get rid first of that inky section or somehow it would contaminate the rest. The scissors were the quickest way.

She stepped to the kitchen and got the pair of shears that had always hung under the shelf by the dresser. Kneeling she cut swiftly, ruthlessly, through that beautiful garment that only an hour before had been such an object of delight to her tired worried young soul, the really prettiest dress she had ever had.

But she must not stop to think of that now. There was not a great deal of time in which to bring this garment into usefulness for her immediate need, and she must not waste a minute in useless repining. So with steady hand she cut from the hem, straight up to the belt, on each side of the stain, and then with a glance at her hands to make sure they had no ink on them, she gathered up what was left and carried it up to her room, laying it on the bed and locking the door to make sure no intruder arrived to hinder her.

A quick examination showed the shirring around the waist was very full indeed, and surely it would do no harm to take one small piece out of all that fullness!

So she went to work trying to steady her trembling hands, trying not to think of what her ruthless sister had done to her, as she carefully ripped the shirring loose from the belt, and then examined it again to calculate just how far she would need to rip out the shirring to make the skirt wide enough to go on the band again. How fortunate it was that the belt had not been touched by the ink!

And down in the living room Cinda had a problem all her own. The angry, bewildered woman who had been so precipitately lifted out of her borrowed garments, and placed trembling in the corner wearing a ruined pink slip with a great black stain down its front breadth, stood staring stupidly down at the devastation she had wrought, too bewildered to utter a word, which was a state to which she had seldom in her life been brought.

And just then, while Cinda wiped the small rivers of ink from the otherwise neat floor, they both heard that elegant limousine drive up to the door, and Elaine came sharply to her senses. Her callers had arrived, and she in a shocking pink slip with ink stains all down the front, and over one white arm, was standing unprotected in the opposite corner of the room from the door to her bedroom, and nothing between her and her callers but a worn old screen door!

Cinda was on her feet with the basin and rags in her hand. She gave a glance out the front door and saw the men getting out of the elegant car.

"Yer callers is here," she announced grimly. "Ye better beat it an' get some cloes on. I'll open the door for 'em," and she flung open the bedroom door. As Elaine scuttled across the room into her haven, Cinda went and stood guard before the screen door watching the two men come up the path.

But Lexie upstairs had no time to more than glance out the window, though she sensed what must be going on. Well, she had her work cut out for her, and she needn't take time to go down unless Mr. Gordon came, in which case Cinda would surely tell her. Thank the Lord for Cinda. What would she do without her?

Cinda, downstairs, let the two men in, scanned them thoroughly, classified them according to her wide knowledge and keen discernment, and then took her implements of service into the dining room where she took care to leave the door open a crack, and where she had beforehand carefully set her stage so that she could come and go and get on with her work, and hear all that went on without seeming to do so.

She lumbered up the stairs and touched Lexie's door with the tips of her fingers, giving a high sign, and Lexie softly unlocked the door and let her in.

"Them men is come!" she announced in a sepulchral whisper, "an' ef one cud look worse'n t'other, he *does*. Seem like I've seed him 'afore, too, but I wouldn't trust him with me dog's bone!"

Lexie managed a one-sided grin in the corner of her mouth that was now filled with pins.

"You'd oughtta seed *her*, scootin' acrost the room in her inky slip. It was a sight fer sore eyes! How ya gettin' on with the frock? Can ye do anythin' with it?"

"Yes, I think so, but it will take time. Don't call me down unless Mr. Gordon comes, though of course I'll listen for him."

"Okay! Well, is there any sewin' I kin do fer ye?"

"Not yet, I guess, Cinda. By and by I'll want you to see if it looks all right. I just took out a length in front and let out the shirring. That ought to look all right, don't you think?"

"Sure thing!" said Cinda. "It sure was a shame I didn't find out what that brat of a woman was doin' afore this happened, but I was tryin' ta get things in order early so you wouldn't do no work, an' here look at what come!"

"Never mind," said Lexie, "I guess I can wear it. There isn't but one little blot on the waist, and that's where I can cut the blot out and paste a bit of the organdie over it. I think I'll get by all right."

Lexie had run up the two seams of the skirt quickly, and adjusted the gathers about the waist line. She was just about to try it on when she heard a car drive down the street, and then another from the opposite direction, but when she looked out there was only one and it went on by and stopped across the street on the other side. Could that be Mr. Gordon's car?

She opened the door and listened. There seemed to be several voices downstairs, but she didn't hear Mr. Gordon's yet, and she did not want to go down till

Cinda called her. Elaine could make trouble enough without charging her with coming in where she was not wanted. So she closed her door and went back to her sewing, but she had an uneasy feeling that something was going on that she did not understand.

Then she went to her window again and looking out toward the side of the house she saw a man going like a shadow, silently, and disappearing out behind the kitchen. Quietly she opened her door again and slipped down the hall to the little window that opened out toward the back, and there she saw two men standing, looking toward the house, talking in very low tones, more as if they were whispering or using sign language. A horror came with the memory that the lawyer had suggested they might arrest *her*. How dreadful if they were really going to try that on her, and Elaine was going to let them do it, the very day she was to graduate! Would Elaine be as mean as that?

Then she heard Cinda coming up the stairs and she slipped back to her own room followed by Cinda, who came in after her and held the door closed while she whispered:

"That there Mr. Gordon you was lookin' for is in the kitchen. He says for you *not* to come down just yet till he sends you word. He's brung a lotta cops and got 'em all standin' around, an' he says tell you you was right, that's the man. An' it'll all be over in a few minutes, but you're to stay up here till I come after you."

Cinda vanished, and Lexie remained by her door listening.

She heard measured steps below the stairs, through the dining room three figures passed showing up sharply against the sunlight in the opposite dining room window. They were policemen! In uniform! What could it mean? And did Cinda say that Mr. Gordon was down there too? Or was he out in the kitchen? Oh, surely she ought to go down! But Cinda had been so sure that Mr. Gordon wanted her to stay upstairs till he called her. Then the door into the living room was swung open. She hadn't noticed before that it had been shut. But it swung so silently as if a deft hand had swung it, and she could hear low talk, then Elaine's rippling, apologetic laughter almost like a giggle. She did that when men were there, especially that outrageous lawyer of hers. And then—a sudden silence! A breathless silence it seemed, as if everyone in the room was suddenly suppressed, a frightened silence, though no one had made a sound since the talking ceased.

Then a strange voice spoke "Harry Perrine, alias Waddie Dager, alias Mike Gilkie, you are under arrest for forgery. I must beg your pardon, madam, for interrupting your conversation, but this man has been wanted by the state for more than a year and we can't take chances! Handcuff him, officer!"

Elaine gave a little childish scream. Lexie could almost vision how she would be shrugged down in her chair with her pretty slender manicured fingers pressing over her eyes.

Lexie could hear the other two men step forward to someone who sat in a chair just inside the living room door; and then a well-remembered voice that she had always disliked came tremblingly out:

"But, officer, you have made a mistake. I am not the man you are looking for. My name is not any of those names you spoke. I am James Bradwell, and I'm a respectable citizen. I have never been in any criminal trouble."

"No, Jimmy Brady, we haven't made any mistake. You can call yourself Bradwell, or Brady, or Tanzey Brown if you like, or any one of a dozen other aliases that I have on my list, but you're still the same old Harry Perrine you used to be when you got away with that big forgery game, and we're not running any chances."

"But I'm a respectable citizen," whined the culprit. "I can prove that I am innocent of any crime. These people are merely my friends and I was making a business call, offering them an investment that is worth its weight—"

"Oh, yes?" said the officer. "Your friends are fortunate that I met up with you before they signed any of your rotten papers. Come, Harry Perrine, let's get going. You arrived in a limousine but you will be going

away in a police car. You're sure none of the rest of you
feel you'd like to go with us?" Lexie could well imagine his glance at Lawyer Thomas as he said it.

But there was only an ominous silence, and then the
policemen marched away to their car with their reluctant prisoner in their midst.

Lexie remained at her door, wondering what would
happen next, wondering if the next thing would be a
call for herself to come down and see Mr. Gordon, but
after the police cars had gone she heard another car
going away, and stealing into her own room she saw
it was the car that had been parked across the road a
little while before. Yet she lingered, uneasily, and then
she heard Lawyer Thomas say:

"Well, Elaine, I guess that about finishes our interview for the morning. You can readily see that I've got
to go at once and see what can be done to release our
star witness."

"But I thought you were going to tell me this morning where that money is to be found. That is the point
I was so anxious about," wailed Elaine.

"Well, of course I was not anticipating any such
happening as has just occurred. I can't understand this.
Just who did you tell about this witness? You don't
suppose that sister of yours has found it out and told
the police, do you? You didn't tell her about this witness, did you?"

"Certainly *not!*" lied Elaine firmly. "And if I had
my sister wouldn't think of going to the police. She is
not that kind of a girl."

"Oh, isn't she?" queried the lawyer. "I understood
that you felt she would stoop to almost anything to
carry her point and keep this money. And besides, I'm
afraid you're going to have to let me have a little more
money right at once. It is going to cost quite a sum to
get this witness free, I'm afraid. And you know it is essential that we get him. If you could spare, say, fifty
dollars, right away I'll hurry down and see if I can
get him off. You know he is really the only one who
can tell you where that money is. If you'll get the
money I'll go at once and see if I can set him free."

"But I haven't any money. I couldn't possibly give you any today."

"What about that tight-wad of a sister of yours? Can't you work something on her?"

"Oh, no!" groaned Elaine. "I can't do a thing with her. Not now, especially. Oh, this has been an awful day!" and Elaine burst into loud weeping.

"Well, there, there! Don't cry. We'll manage somehow for a day or two, but I really must go at once. I shouldn't care to have these police get me mixed up in this sort of thing! Good by. I really must hurry!"

"This sort of thing?" screamed Elaine. "What do you mean? Are we mixed up in something terrible? Oh, I don't know what the neighbors are going to think with police coming here and taking a man away. This has always been a respectable neighborhood! Oh, you said you would take care of my affairs and I would have no trouble!"

"There, there, Elaine," soothed the hurried lawyer, "don't go getting excited. Just take it easy and everything will come out all right. Now good by for the present. I've got to go and see what I can do about that witness, you know."

With oily tones that were almost funny because he seemed so excited himself, he got himself out of the house and went plunging down the walk to his limousine, and away in a whirl around the corner and out of sight.

"Good riddance to him," breathed Cinda, coming softly up the stairs. "An' yer Mr. Gordon said he would be coming again some other day perhaps, but you had done good work, an' not to worry. He had to go away to some sort of a hearing in court, he said. An' I come to ast you could I do something about the dress, or would you want me to see the likes of her, an' get her quiet? But beggin' pardon, Miss Lexie, my advice is, to leave her be awhile till she comes to. She's had a good hard shake up, an' it'll be a while afore she gets her balance again. I'm hopin' it'll do her good."

"Thank you, Cinda, for all you've done, and I guess you're right about Elaine. Perhaps she won't be wanting to see either of us for a while. Suppose you come in and let me put on my dress and see if you think it will do at all, before I finish it up. I've got it on the belt, but I'm not sure it hangs just right. If I can get this so it's wearable I'll be able to think about other things."

So Lexie put the dress on and Cinda got down on her knees and measured the distance from floor to hem all around, and then held an old mirror off so that Lexie could get a view of herself. They finally decided they had done the best they could.

"And it's real pretty an' becomin', Miss Lexie. Maybe I ain't no judge, but I don't believe there'll be another dress as purty in the whole bunch. Now, Miss Lexie, you just don't worry another bit. You take that dress off an' hang it up an' I'll finish sewing them gethers fer ye, an' you go lay down an' rest. Goodness knows you've hed it hard enough this day, let alone gradooatin', an' you need ta get some rest."

Lexie gave a breathless little laugh and shook her head.

"No, Cinda, you've plenty to do, and I'll finish this myself. There isn't much more since you're sure it hangs all right. But I'd appreciate it if you would see if Elaine's all right. You know she's apt to get into one of her spells of hysterics after a time like this. And there'll be plenty of work for you today without sewing. And, by the way, isn't it almost time for the postman? I wonder if you couldn't head him off this once and get anything there may be for me. I've been getting notes from my former classmates, and I wouldn't like one of them to fall into my sister's hands in her present state. I'd never see it I'm sure, if it did."

"Okay!" said Cinda. "An' then agin there mought be some letter from foreign lands again, ye never can tell."

"Oh no," said Lexie. "Not so soon again. You know I just got one last week."

"Wal, we'll see!" said Cinda with a sly wink, and thumped heavily down the stairs. There were times when Cinda could walk feather-light, and again times when she defied the world with her stride. This was one of them. Her young lady had come through the fire and her graduating dress was still intact and quite wearable. So Cinda sailed downstairs, and peered cautiously into the living room, but there wasn't a sign of her ladyship in the room, and the door of her bedroom was wide open. A casual glance in there showed a dismal little silent heap on the bed, face buried in the pillow. Elaine was too stricken even for sobs. Besides, there wasn't any audience.

17

ELAINE'S COLLAPSE LASTED all through the day and into the next, which in a way was a relief to Lexie, because she had enough of her own concerns to attend to without trying to deal with her sister. And it was of no use whatever for Lexie to try and coax her out of her doldrums. It would only be a waste of time. So Elaine continued in her discouraged heap, woe-be-gone to the last extent. She refused anything to eat, even shook her head at the cup of coffee Cinda grimly offered. The whole collapse of her arrogant schemes was upon her and she could not creep out from under it even long enough to drink that cup of heartening coffee.

Perhaps, as the lonely day went on, and there were no sounds of more than light footsteps in the house, for the children had been invited across the way to lunch out-of-doors with their playmates, it may be that some sense of her own fault in all this disaster came upon her, though it is doubtful, for Elaine had never been one to see anything wrong with herself.

She was still arrayed in the street suit she had put on so hastily at the approach of her visitors. She hadn't troubled to take it off when in her despair she threw herself on the bed, and Cinda hadn't bothered to go and coax her into a bath robe. Cinda felt that this was Lexie's day, and whatever she did, beyond absolute necessity, must be done for Lexie. So Elaine had her room and her quiet entirely to herself, and whether she waked or whether she slept she was undisturbed. But it must have been brought home to her mind as the day wore on and there came no word from her lawyer, that she had got about to the end of her rope with him. He hadn't given her much hope when he left that if this arrested witness should fail

193

them, they had a chance to win a case. And Elaine was really a bright woman when she stopped thinking about herself long enough to exercise her brains. She was beginning to see that she was beaten. And if she couldn't get any money out of Lexie, what was she to do? Sit still and make Lexie support her? Maybe she might do that if she ever got up her ambition again. But how terrible. Lexie couldn't ever make enough to support her in the style she had lately been used to, and now that her husband was gone, who was there to care? And what was Lexie going to be like after that dress episode? Of course she could perhaps persuade her that the ink part was her own fault. That if she hadn't come in and startled her she never would have jumped and knocked over the ink bottle. But Elaine was at last so low in spirits that she couldn t even rouse to a lead like that.

If only Cinda would come in and say that Bettinger Thomas had sent a telegram or a message to say that his witness was free and everything was going to be all right, why then she could rouse up and even forgive Lexie for having been the cause of her ruining that lovely silk slip, the slip of the only really imported dress she ever owned. But as it was, perhaps she would say nothing more about that slip for the present.

So Lexie stayed in her room and put her dress in perfect order, and Elaine stayed in her room and finally slept, and at least there was peace in the house, if not harmony.

Cinda had brought up a tray for Lexie and on it was a note she said she found on the kitchen table. It was from Mr. Gordon.

Dear Miss Kendall:

Sorry not to have seen you, but later I hope to explain fully.

Meantime you have helped to do one of the neatest pieces of detective work I have seen in a long time, by making it possible to put into custody one of the slickest criminals in this part of the country. I am only thankful that we could get him before he put over any of his frauds on your family.

Let me know if there is any way I can be of immediate
service at any time, and I shall be seeing you again soon.
Sincerely,
A. R. Gordon

Lexie read the note over carefully and then after due
deliberation she tore it into small bits and put them
where they could never be read. She wondered as she
was doing it whether she would ever be able to trust
that sister of hers again, or would she have to go on
living in danger of perpetual annoyance?

Lexie went early to the city, for she had an uneasy
feeling that if she stayed in the house a moment beyond getting ready that something might happen to upset her plans and perhaps either spoil her dress again
or keep her at home. Elaine was perfectly capable of
staging a near-to-death scene if she thought that in
some way she could hurt Lexie. Lexie was running no
risks. She didn't even go out the front gate, for the
children, if they should spy her all dressed up, would
be altogether likely to rush across the street and make
an outcry that would bring the attention of the neighborhood, and they would probably embrace her with
sticky dirty hands, and ruin her dress once more. So,
gathering her dress up carefully, and getting Cinda to
help her over the fence, she went carefully down across
the meadow, the voluminous billows of her skirt gathered up on either side so that it would not come in
contact with grass and weeds, and at last she stepped
safely on the sidewalk of the highway, and could stand
in quietness and peace, waiting for the bus she knew
would be there very soon and bear her to the city.

So at last Lexie was started, and could get her breath
before the ordeal of the evening began, and just be
thankful that the various disasters of the day had not
been permitted to prevent her from coming to commencement. There in the quiet of the country road,
under a tall elm tree, as she waited for the bus, she
bowed her head and closed her eyes, and murmured
softly: "Dear Father, thank You for being with me all
day long. Please be with me tonight too, and keep me
when I get back home. Please look after all the rest,

and don't let Elaine make any more awful trouble for us."

Then the bus came and she was on her way.

There were few people on the bus, and she took a seat at the back where she could lean her arm on the window seat, put her head down on her hand and close her eyes. She suddenly realized that she was very tired. It had been a hard day, and it was almost done. What was it going to feel like to be through with college? Well, it didn't matter much now, since none of her friends could be with her, and her pleasant anticipations had all to be transferred to another institution, but at least she would be in a position to get a good job, even if Judge Foster wouldn't be well enough to need her. She still had much to be glad about.

The next thing on the docket to worry about was that lawsuit, which if Elaine carried out her plans might upset everything else she had hoped for. But she simply would not think of that tonight. God had taken care of her so far, and she could surely trust Him for the rest. How great that that awful Perrine was in custody. "Oh dear God, please keep him where he cannot do us harm by telling lies."

She was almost asleep when the bus reached the university and people were getting off all around her. Slowly she made her way out and entered the great gates that led from the street up to the auditorium. Somehow she couldn't seem to realize what she was about to do. Graduate? Yes, but why had it seemed so important? The nicest thing about it all was that she was away from her troubles for a little while and felt almost rested. She hadn't felt as rested since Elaine came back. And if she had only known it, she *looked* rested, and more than one passer on the street turned and looked at the pretty girl with the sweet eyes, who had such an expression of utter peace. Dewy-eyed she was from just those few minutes with her eyes closed.

When she entered the hall she found a great number of students in gala attire, and the graduating class in their white dresses. Her own dress was not *just* like theirs, but she felt happy and inconspicuous among them. And then, just at the last minute before the class would march up on the platform, one of the ushers hunted her up.

"There's a box of flowers here for you, Miss Kendall," he said and handed her a small box. "It says they are to be given to you *before* the exercises. You'd better open them here. They are probably for you to wear." He grinned as he went on his way.

"Oh, but nobody would send me flowers to wear," said Lexie to herself. "Even those crazy girls in my old college wouldn't think of it. I was really nothing to them, only a girl who worked hard and belonged to their class."

With trembling fingers she untied the knot, turned back the soft folds of green wax paper, and there nested three of the most gorgeous gardenias she had ever seen, fastened with silver ribbon, and all equipped with pearl headed pins to fasten them on.

"Oh, how lovely!" exclaimed one of the other graduates, smiling gaily at Lexie. "Gardenias! Aren't they spiffy! Here, let me help you fasten them."

"Oh, but I don't think I'm going to wear them," said Lexie shyly.

"Why sure you are. You wouldn't let such gorgeous gardenias as that go to waste. Sure! Put them on. We want all the honors in our class that are coming. Who is he anyway? Not your family?"

"Why, I haven't looked yet," said Lexie, her cheeks as rosy as if they were painted.

"Well, look quick, you simp! Here's the card. A soldier as I live! Benedict Barron! That's some name. Where is he?"

"He's overseas," said Lexie softly, her eyes starry with a new kind of joy. What a wonderful thing to come at the close of this awful day. Now, *now* she could go through the evening calmly!

It was not until the class was seated on the great platform with all the dignitaries and professors and speakers in their places that Lexie was able to get her thoughts in order, and begin to wonder how her soldier boy had gotten those flowers to her for this particular night. Yes, she had told him *when* her commencement came, but only a word or two to explain how busily she was working for her examinations. And here he had figured it out and somehow got word to a florist to send those wonderful blossoms to her in time for her to wear them. She held her sweet head up proudly, and looked down at the flowers nestling among her lace-edged ruffles. She laid her hands in her lap over the front seam at which she had worked so hard that morning, with never a thought for the ink stains that had almost ruined her dress. In fact the whole morning, obnoxious lawyer and lying witness, policemen, arrest, and Elaine's collapse had become a blank for the time. She was sitting here in this great throng, living through the thing she had dreamed about for years, the night that she and her mother used to talk about and plan for, and she had no thought for anything else, except the wonderful soldier friend who had sent her beautiful flowers for the crowning touch to her festive evening. It was all very wonderful, and she must not let other thoughts get tangled up with it, for she wanted to remember everything just as it happened. It would be the shining evening of her young life. Other girls might be looking forward to going into society, and then marriage, but so far as she could see now there would be only plain days of work for herself. And grateful enough she would be for even that if she could be free from such incidents as "suits" for money she never had, and contact with unholy, dishonest lawyers. At least she had a God who was protecting her! Look how He had spared that dress so she could wear it, in spite of her sister's ruthless unkindness. Look how He had sent those policemen to arrest that criminal witness! Look how the lawyer had been frightened away! Might not God always frighten away her enemies who were trying to plot for her downfall? Oh, she would be willing to work hard all her life if she might just have peace, and now and then a little pleasantness. And this assurance she now had of God's caring for her was wonderful.

But the exercises of the evening were beginning, and her interest was caught away from the troubles of the day. Music and speeches and well dressed young people made a pleasant combination, and how pretty some of the girls looked! Lexie did not know that she herself was as pretty a girl as any on that platform. But she was not thinking of herself except as she was thrilled by being a part of this great pageant.

For a little time she was lost in the program, as if it were a ship on which she had embarked, sailing down the evening. Then the sweet breath of the flowers on her shoulder would speak to her, mingle with her consciousness, make themselves apparent, and a thrill would come over her. She was like other girls. She had a friend. She was wearing flowers, flowers a man had been thoughtful enough to send her! Oh, of course there was nothing lover-like about it. He was just a friend. A friend "of the years," that was it. That sounded well, if Elaine should ask her. For she would have to wear the flowers home. She couldn't just lose them, even to save Elaine from desecrating them by her sneers and questions. She must make them last as long as possible. Her first flowers from a young man! Suppose the sender of them was half-a-world away from her, it was nice that he should have thought to do it.

She tried to think it through. She had only told him about that commencement in her last letter. He must have cabled for the flowers to get them here so soon.

Then she bethought herself of the card she was clasping tightly in eager fingers. She hadn't read it yet. But of course he could only cable the words. They would not be in his handwriting. Her eyes sought the card. It said:

"With best wishes to Lexie for a happy commencement. Wish I could be with you.

Benedict Barron

It seemed to Lexie as if she had never been so happy as now, when she sat there with that card in her hand and those gardenias on her shoulder. At least not since her mother died. And how she longed just then to be able to tell her mother all about it.

"But then perhaps she knows. Perhaps she sees the flowers, and is glad for me," she thought to herself.

So in a daze of joy she sat through the evening.

Then at last came the diploma for which she had worked so long. Brimming over, that evening was, just *brimming* over with nice things, even enough to off-set the awful morning that had passed.

And then as if that were not enough there were more flowers, afterwards, different personal gifts to the graduates from friends. That was something of course in which she would not share because she was a stranger among them, she thought, but lo, they brought her three! First a great basket of lilies and blue delphini-ums, from her class at the dear old college, and the inscription, "For our dear Lexie from her own old class," and all their names signed. How lovely of them to do it! She hadn't thought they cared about her. Then there were beautiful pink roses from Judge and Mrs. Foster, and an exquisite purple and white orchid from Mr. Gordon. How kind they all were!

And by this time Lexie was so tired that the tears were very near the surface of her starry eyes. What a lovely wonderful evening it had been, to have come after all that troubled morning!

She looked down at her pretty white dress, and saw it was as crisp and trim as when she started away from home.

And then suddenly it was time to catch the bus and go back to all that there was to call home. But the joy and the thrill lasted all the way home, and she didn't let herself worry about what Elaine would say, or whether she would try to tell her about her flowers, or what would be coming the next day. She just sat quiet-ly and enjoyed her evening over again. There might not be any more such lovely times coming to her ever again through her life. This might be the last one, but she would therefore cherish it, and sometimes go back to it in memory and enjoy it all over again.

She found Cinda waiting for her at the corner when she got off the bus, and they walked slowly back to the house, Cinda carrying the basket of lilies and the box of roses and the orchid, Cinda gazing at her young lady an' reveling in her sweetness in the dim moonlight. Cinda rejoicing that the gardenias had come from the soldier boy, and that people who had good taste and judgment had sent her flowers of distinction.

It was Cinda who unfastened the gardenias and arranged and sprinkled them in their box for safe keeping over night, and Cinda who saw that the other flowers were sprinkled and cared for. It was Cinda who insisted that Lexie get to bed right away, and then lingered to look at the wonderful diploma and talk some more.

She answered Lexie's anxious questions.

No, Elaine hadn't eaten any supper, just drank a cup of strong tea. No, no lawyer had come that evening, but a telegram had arrived from Lawyer Thomas, and Elaine had made her read it to her, because her own eyes were so swollen from weeping she couldn't see. It said: "Impossible to contact witness at present time. I advise calling a halt in proceedings for the present. Am suddenly called away to West Coast for an indefinite period, and cannot do anything more for you at present," signed B. Thomas.

Lexie looked at her in wonder.

"Oh!" she said, and "Oh, *isn't* God *wonderful!*"

"Okay, Miss Lexie, only I don't just follow you."

"Never mind, Cinda. I was just thinking aloud," said Lexie smiling. "But how did Elaine take this?"

"Well, I can't say she took it so good. First off I thought she was fainted dead away, an' then she bust right out cryin' somethin' fierce. But after whiles she got calmer, an' now I think she's asleep. I guess she was just plain exhausterated from all her carryin's on. But now, Miss Lexie, you *must* get to bed."

So Lexie went to bed. She thought she was too happy to sleep, which wasn't so at all, for she was soon sound asleep and dreaming of a land where the fragrance of gardenias was all about her, and a dark eyed soldier was smiling at her across a great distance.

Cinda was up early next morning. She had arranged it so that Bluebell had a little bed by herself near Angelica, and Lexie had her own room to herself. In the morning she adroitly suppressed the noisy children by promising to make cherry tarts for them if they would be good and quiet. So when she had got them off for their morning play she went to Elaine, cherrily tidied up her room, and herself, and talked affably just as if the grumpy lady was all interest, though she wasn't, but she heard the elaborate account of the evening in silence, and never spoke except to say *"Gardenias?* Of course you don't mean gardenias, Cinda. Nobody would send Lexie gardenias. They must have been snapdragons!"

"No ma'am, they was gardenias. Great thick white leaves like white kid, an' the most heavenly smell you ever smelled! It filled the whole room when she come in. I'll go get the box an' let you see 'em. An' then there was a great wonderful basket of lilies an' blue delphimium, that was from her old college classmates back in New England. An' then some pink roses, an' a funny-looking orchid from two other folks, I don't rightly know their names yet. But they was swell flowers all right."

Elaine lay and listened hungrily, jealously, unable to believe that her little sister whom she chose to consider "plain" had been received with so much attention, and she finally retired into more tears and spent hours in vain regrets.

But it was a gloomy-eyed sister that Lexie met the next morning when she took her breakfast tray in to her, and Elaine vouchsafed no reply to her pleasant good morning, except a fresh burst of tears. So for several days this went on, Elaine eating almost nothing, drinking strong coffee, refusing to talk, until Lexie began to feel that her sister was really ill now, and ventured to suggest that she send for a doctor. But Elaine only shook her head and wept again.

So Lexie turned her attention to the children and began to coax them to stay at home. She taught them pleasant games, and some that were also useful, resulting in swept sidewalks, and little garden plots. She offered prizes for picking up crumbs dropped, and keeping the rooms in order. Sometimes the prizes were privileges, sometimes stories, and sometimes little home-made articles that she had contrived herself for them out of scraps of bright cloth from the attic.

Little by little Elaine came out of her shell and transferred herself from the bedroom to the living room, lay silently on the couch watching what went on, seldom smiling, seldom speaking, a great gloom over her face. She seemed like an utterly cowed, disheartened dictator who had come to an end of his machinations and couldn't seem to get hold of life any more. She had made money a sort of god, or rather what money would buy, and she could not seem to bring herself to take an interest in a life that was not full of luxury.

But after a little she began to watch Lexie, to see her kindly forgiveness, her utter lack of resentment for all she had tried to do to her, her happy expression, her willingness to serve whenever she could, and somehow her own life and ways began to stand out in sharp contrast. It wasn't apparent that this was happening, of course.

Lexie was praying for her sister now. Half-heartedly at first perhaps, but as the days went on, with more faith, And this had much to do with the way Lexie lived her faith. Elaine couldn't make it out, and more and more her selfish soul was condemned.

Then one morning there came a special delivery letter from Judge Foster's office, saying that he was back at work again, and he had a job for Lexie if she was still free. Would she call at the office as soon as convenient?

So Lexie went flying across the meadow to the bus line quite early the next morning, neatly and simply attired, and was at the office almost as soon as Judge Foster arrived. When she came back late in the afternoon her face was shining with contentment. She told her sister that she had a job now and things would be a little easier for them all.

18

THERE WAS ONE thing that troubled Lexie, as the days went on and she was continually happy in her work at the office, and the resultant money in hand, and that was that although she had written the day after commencement to thank her soldier boy for the wonderful flowers, she had not received any more letters from him. Was he done with her, and had those gardenias been a lovely gesture for good by?

Well, if that was it at least she was glad that she had had those gardenias and his delightful letters.

And then a new thought came to trouble her. Was he worse again, unable to write? Perhaps near death's door?

But when her heart trembled at that thought she carried it to her Lord. He was in her Lord's care. He loved him. He would take care of him! And so she was able to throw that care away.

Of course, too, there might be another explanation for his silence. He might have been sent into action again. He had hinted in his letters that there was such a possibility, and that he would like to go back, even if it meant being under fire again.

The thought made her catch her breath, and then she remembered that God would be with him, even if he went under fire again. God had brought him through before. Surely He would not desert him now. She could rest on that. But even if he should be wounded or die, and she never have the privilege of seeing him again on earth, there was something comforting in the thought that he was God's own child and that she would surely meet him in Heaven. And they could talk all this over sometime. That would be nice. Only there was a great wistfulness in her heart, for she did so want to see him now, on earth. She did want to be able to tell him with her own lips how happy he had made her by sending her those gardenias, and how his letters were being treasured by her. And sometimes at night, after she had read her Bible, she would get out his letters and read them over. It seemed to help her to feel she had some Christian fellowship with someone. Of course if she never had anything else of this sort in her life, she at least had had this knowledge of a Christian friendship.

Lexie went to church as often as she felt she could be spared from difficulties at home, and sometimes she could coax some one or the other of the children to go with her. But they were not churchly-minded children, and Elaine utterly refused to allow them to go to Sunday School because she had not the money to dress them in what she considered "suitable" clothes.

But the church in their little suburb was a rather coldhearted place, more interested in church suppers and social affairs, or, at best, war work, than in getting near to God, and so there was not much real spiritual comfort to be found there, except as all real Christians can feel they are worshiping God when they come to His house. But Lexie felt very much alone, except when she was in the office where the mere nearness of Judge Foster comforted her. She knew he was a good man, a Christian man, and her father's friend.

The rest of her fellow-workers in the office were very pleasant, and Lexie felt that the lines had fallen to her in pleasant places as far as her work was concerned. Sometimes she remembered how distressed she had been to give up the job she had been promised in the college town, and now here this work in the judge's office was so much more desirable, and much better pay, besides being among such congenial people. It was wonderful what God can do for one when He decides to change the background of one's life, and takes away cherished hopes and plans, He always seems to be able to give His yielded ones something better when the right time comes. Something like that idea floated through Lexie's mind occasionally as she voiced her daily prayers of thanksgiving.

And yet, there were fires to endure at home, even

now. Elaine had so far roused from her stupor of gloom to be quite insistent about certain little things, and could fly into a rage as easily as ever, and fill the house with more gloom. She could still incite her young children to open rebellion against simple household rules made for the comfort of all of them, and she could still sneer coldly, angrily, when Lexie told her firmly how much money she could afford to spend on the household, and utterly refused to lend her money for beauty parlors and new dresses, or to write any letters for her to Bettinger Thomas asking when he was coming home.

But fortunately these flares on the part of Elaine were not now *daily* occurrences, or nobody could have survived it. And Lexie could see that each time they happened her sister was more and more discouraged about any suit she had been going to bring for non-existent money. Less often she spoke of any such possibility as there having been money intended for her, and now and then she even said something pleasant about her stepmother. Nothing important. Just little sentences that gave Lexie a happier feeling toward her sister. Sentences like, "Your mother always had such good taste in dress, Lexie," or "Nobody could make such nice desserts as your mother. She had a hand with her cooking."

But such little breaks of sunlight in the mental attitude were of course few and far between, and the daily routine was often like going through fire, with no hope of let-up ahead.

Then one day, after Lexie had about given up hope of ever hearing from her soldier boy again, a letter arrived. It was very much battered up as to envelope, and had evidently been missent, or held up, and the envelope was full of different directions. The wonder was that it ever reached her at all. She opened it almost in fear, like a message from a dead friend it seemed.

The letter itself was brief.

Dear Lexie:

I am suddenly being taken away from this location, perhaps on furlough, or else to return to the front. It will be

as God wills. I have no time to write, the order is imperative, and I do not yet know my destination. Will let you
know as soon as I have opportunity,

I hope you had a happy commencement, and that my
flowers got there in time.

They have come for me and I must go. May God be
with you to bless and help.

With my love,
Ben

The letter was dated a long time ago. It must have
been written around the time of her commencement,
but apparently he had not yet received her own letter
of thanks. And where was he now? Oh, there were so
many terrible possibilities. He might have been on one
of those transports that had been sunk, or in that
clipper plane they said was missing, or, his body might
be lying at the bottom of the sea, or he might have
been captured by the enemy and be even now in an
internment camp somewhere, or have been shot, or—

"Stop!" ordered her conscience. "Haven't you and
he a God? Didn't your God promise to be with you
both? Hasn't He done it before? And won't He do it
again? What right have you to anticipate horrors that
may never be in God's plan for either of you? Let God
work it out. Just trust. That's what he said he was going to do. You must not fall down on your job and
go around looking glum. God does not forget, and He
knows what He has planned for your good! When He
has tried you He has promised that you shall come
forth as gold."

Lexie was learning a great deal from her Bible in
these days, and she was growing closer to her Lord
through prayer than she had ever been before. Somehow the things at home that used to seem like the
hottest fire to her shrinking soul, did not seem so important now. They were merely experiences through
which to pass. And she must pass through them brave-
ly.

But day after day Lexie kept looking for another
letter. And still the days went on and none arrived.

Morning after morning Lexie scanned the newspapers, noting the disasters reported to transport ships, and other modes of soldier travel, a mail plane crashed and burned, all other possibilities, and then breathed a prayer that her soldier boy might not be involved. But though she scanned the lists of names of killed and wounded whenever there were any, still she found no Benedict Barron. But what had become of him?

Of course there were ways of searching out what had happened to missing soldiers, and perhaps she could write somewhere in Washington and find out—perhaps, but had she, a young stranger, practically, and not a relative, nor even a friend of long standing, a *right* to go to headquarters asking for his whereabouts? Perhaps he was tired of his correspondence with her, and had taken this way to vanish out of her life entirely. Well, perhaps—but certainly she would not feel justified in going to any government headquarters to trace out knowledge of him. Just an acquaintance was all she could possibly claim. There was just one place, one all-powerful Person to Whom she might go, and that was her God, and his God, and she would have to let it rest with that. After all it was God who was managing this whole thing, and He knew what He was doing.

There came a bright beautiful Sunday morning after a day of heavy rain, with a cool crispness in the air so heartening after the heat of the week that was just past.

Lexie was wearing a new dress, just a cheap little blue dimity she had seen when she went to the store to get a few things for the children, and her preference now was always for *blue* dresses, because she felt that it brought her back to the days when she used to swing on the gate, and the soldier boy had noticed that her dress was like her eyes. It was silly of course, and she often reproved this tendency in herself to buy blue things, but still they seemed to draw her irresistibly. And now she was wearing the dress for the first time.

The children had been invited to go to some kind of a children's Sunday School celebration with their play-

mates across the road, and they had cried to go, so
Lexie had brought home some simple garments for
them bought at a sale. Their mother had rather contemptuously allowed them to wear them and go.

So it was very still around the little white house.
Only the sweet notes of some wood thrushes could
be heard now and then, and the mountains in the distance had on their smiling holy look as if the night's
rain had brought them comfort and serenity. The
neighborhood was quiet, for they had all gone with
their children to see the exercises in which some of
their little ones were to have a part. The day seemed
perfect.

Elaine had retired to her room to weep, after she
had watched her children in their new cheap garments trip happily away. Lexie sat down on the porch
with her Bible, gazing off at the mountains, and taking
in the sweetness of the flowers that were blooming
along the little front walk down to the white gate. And
then she heard footsteps, brisk footsteps, coming up
the street. Turning, she saw it was a soldier, tall, good
looking, well set up, his uniform gleaming with its
touches of gold emblems and brass buttons.

Of course she watched him. Soldiers were always interesting to everybody now, during war time, and
especially to her, for there was one soldier that she
longed very much to see. She made no excuses to herself about that now. He was her own soldier. She cared
a very great deal about him. But of course, she probably
never would see him again.

The soldier came on, walking straight toward the
white house as if he knew the way, had been there
before, and had an aim in coming. He paused by the
little white gate and looked at her with a nice smile.
A smile she remembered from long ago.

She started to her feet, and dropped her Bible on the
chair. It was her soldier boy! It was Benedict Barron in
the flesh, looking just like that picture she had of him
up in her room. Smiling and looking as if he might ask
her what her name was. And then he called it, and his
voice was just as she remembered.

"Lexie!" he said. He didn't put a question mark after it, as if he wasn't certain about her. There was assurance in his tone.

"Yes?" she said and flew down that path to the gate straight as a bird to its nest.

When she reached the gate she stood there looking radiantly up into his face, and he looking down into her eyes, with a deep sweet searching gaze, as if he wanted to make sure it was really the girl he knew. Then he put his hands out and laid them on her slender shoulders, looked down deeper into her eyes, and said: "May I kiss you, Lexie?" He stooped and laid his lips upon hers and it seemed to her as if all Heaven looked down and held its breath in joy, as their two souls came together at last.

"You're just the same," he said at last, lifting his head and looking down at her. "My little Lexie! I'd have known you anywhere. The same eyes, the same smile. Oh, my dear! To think I'm here again at last! And it's *really you!*"

Her eyes went up to his, full of delight.

"And you're the same, too," she said softly, letting her eyes caress his face. "Oh, I'm so glad you've come! I thought I never would see you again. I was afraid something had happened to you!"

He smiled gravely.

"Something did, my Lexie! Our transport was torpedoed, and a couple of us floated for days before we were picked up and carried all around the globe till we got where we could contact the right parties. But that's a long story and I haven't so much time just now. I've got to get back to Washington this afternoon. The army trucks are passing the highway at exactly four o'clock this afternoon, and I've got to be waiting for them, for they haven't time to wait for me. But I'll be back later, in a week or two, or maybe sooner if I can find out what the plans for me are, and then we can tell the whole story. In the meantime, let's make the most of this little time. Where were you going this morning before you saw me? I see your hat up there on the porch, and you must have been going somewhere."

"Oh, I was just going to church, but it isn't necessary this morning. I want to hear all about you."

He smiled appreciatively.

"I'd like to go to church with you," he said tenderly, "is it time?"

"No, not for an hour yet," she said.

"Then there's time to take a walk first," he said, "or, was somebody going with you?"

"Oh, no," she said with a laugh. "I usually go everywhere alone."

He looked down at her tenderly.

"Not any more," he said, "not when I get home to stay! Then come, let's go. Do you have to tell anyone you're going?"

"Why, no," said Lexie, "only, you'll have time to come back to dinner won't you? I ought to tell Cinda, though she's liable to have seen you and have something ready."

"Don't let's bother with dinner today, we haven't time," he said. "I'll come again later. Get your hat and Bible and we'll take our walk and find a church before we get back."

So she got her hat and Bible from the chair, and was back at his side. He drew her hand within his arm and they walked off together, she with her hat in her hand and he with her Bible under his arm.

"There used to be a woods up this way. Is it still there, or have they cut it down yet?"

"It's still there!" said Lexie.

"Then we'll go there," he said. And side by side they walked away to the woods, while Elaine stood peering out of her bedroom window watching them eagerly, taking in every item of his uniform, noting a decoration or two, noting his smile, and the way he walked, and everything about him.

And out of her kitchen window that looked toward the woods Cinda was watching.

"That'll be him," she said delightedly to herself. "An' ain't he the soldier man! He'll do fer my bairnie. He has it written all over him. Good an' brave, an' a looker besides! Wonder what I oughtta do about dinner? Well, there's fried chicken enough. I don't needta save any fer meself. It'll be all right. An' that cherry pie turned out real good ef I do say so as shouldn't.'"

But the two who were sitting under a great tree in the woods, with their feet resting on a bed of velvet moss, and the songs of the thrushes overhead, were not thinking of what they would have for dinner, nor even intending to come back for dinner, not today. They were getting acquainted, and looking into the years of eternity ahead of them. Two people who had met God, and trusted Him utterly, because He had been with them through fire and flood and circumstance.

Eventually they went to church, but before they left the woods they sat hand in hand and read a few of their precious verses from the Bible, and then bowed their heads together and prayed a few words. Shy words, they were. Neither of them used to formal prayer before others.

"But you see I love you," said Ben Barron as he lifted his head with that grave sweet smile on his face, "and we had to have some sort of a ceremony or dedication or something to mark it. We belong to each other, now, in God's eyes, don't we?" and he searched her face.

"Oh, yes," said Lexie drawing a deep breath of joy. "I am so glad! Now I won't ever have to worry again, thinking you don't care, I was so afraid if anything should happen to you I would never find out if you cared at all."

"You dear!" he said stooping to kiss her again, and gathering her in his arms, holding her close. "But I don't see how you cared when you didn't really know me. When you hadn't seen me but once."

"Oh, but I *did,*" said Lexie. "I grew into loving you before I knew I was doing it, and I was so worried lest I had no right."

"Precious child!" said Ben. "But you were only a child."

"Yes, I was only a child!—but—you say *you* loved me!" she gave him an endearing look.

"Well, yes, of course I wasn't conscious of it when I first saw you, for I wasn't grown up either you know, but something caught in my heart, and came back to me in the fire that night, and I guess God had this planned for us all the time."

So they talked, and they very nearly didn't get to church on time, if Ben hadn't been a soldier, used to timing himself, they wouldn't have.

But they walked into church just as the first hymn was being sung and were given a hymn book and stood and sang together:

> Mine eyes and my desire
> Are ever to the Lord;
> I love to plead His promises,
> And rest upon His word.

and their eyes as they met told a story of love and trust that the watching eager church-goers read and interpreted.

"My don't they make a swell couple!" said one envious girl as she watched them go down the aisle together at the close of church.

"Yes, and did you get on to the way they sang, as if they really *meant* it!" said another.

"Oh, *that!*" said a third girl. "Their looks were for each other, not for the words they were singing."

"No," said another girl, "they *meant* it, I *know* they did. You can't fake *real* things. Not like that!"

"Oh, piffle! There *aren't* any real things any more!" said the first girl whose lad had gone off to war without saying the word that counted.

But the two who were walking in Heavenly ways, went happily on with their brief short day, treasuring every second of it for sweet memory.

They took a brief lunch at a little place along the way they walked, for they could not take time out for formalities, and Lexie went with her soldier over to the highway, where they sat under a tree together to wait for the army truck to come. And then quietly, just before he had to get on, Lexie started up the lane that led home to the little white gate, and when she got to the turn of the lane, where a tall tree arched over her, she stood, a slender figure in a soft blue frock, and a big white hat, waving a small handkerchief toward the great dark army truck that was moving down the highway toward Washington. He was gone, but he was *hers!* Her heart thrilled with the thought. And she was wearing his ring! A sweet dear ring, its bright clear diamond sparkling on her finger, filling her with continual joy. To think that she should be wearing his ring! And she had a tender thought for the first owner of that ring, Ben's mother. She must have been a wonderful woman. And Ben had worn that ring on a slender chain around his neck ever since she died. He had worn it all through that awful experience in the fire. It was almost like having something that was a part of himself.

She walked slowly home in the quiet of the late Sunday afternoon, and thought what wonderful things God had been preparing for her all these years when she had thought things were so very hard and never would be any different. And now Heaven seemed to have opened before her and all around her.

And then she got home, and there was Elaine out on the porch looking fretful and impatient!

19

"WELL, SO YOU'VE got home at last! Where on earth have you been all day Sunday? This is something new for you!"

Lexie looked up and smiled with that dreamy smile that shows one has been far away in a heaven of one's own, and for some reason it made her sister angry and jealous.

"Oh, have you needed me?" said Lexie. "I'm sorry. But I've been having a wonderful time. We went to church, and then we took a walk."

"Oh, you took a walk, did you? All this time? You couldn't have come home and told what you were going to do, could you?"

"Why, no, I couldn't very well," said Lexie, the sweet-memories look in her eyes.

"Well, who was the man? Someone you picked up on the road? I didn't think you were that kind. Your mother certainly wouldn't have approved of that."

Lexie laughed.

"No, I didn't pick him up. I've known him a long time."

"Oh, you *have?* And why did he never turn up before?"

"Why, he's been overseas," said Lexie. "We've been corresponding for a long time. He's just home on leave, and he doesn't know but he may soon be ordered off again. He thinks though that he can come back at least for a few hours before he has to go anywhere."

"Oh!" said Elaine, "so he's coming back!"

"Yes, he'll be back," said Lexie joyously.

Elaine gave her a sharp look and then she said:

"Whose ring is that you're wearing? I never saw you have that on before. Is it a real diamond, or just paste?"

"Why, it's my ring," said Lexie, lifting her hand proudly. "It was his mother's and he's worn it next his heart all through his war experience. And oh, yes, the diamond is real. His father bought it at Tiffany's in New York when he and Ben's mother were engaged."

"It's not very large," said Elaine sharply. "They can't be very rich."

"I don't know," said Lexie. "I never asked anything about that. I really didn't care."

"No, you *wouldn't!*" said Elaine contemptuously. "Well, I hope you're happy. I thought I was once, but it didn't last."

"But this will," said Lexie with a grave sweet smile, "because we both love the Lord Jesus, and whatever comes we are both His."

"Oh, *religious,* is he? Well, that *would* be the kind you'd pick. Well, I'm sure I wish you well."

"Thank you Elaine," said Lexie brightly, and she went over and kissed her sister on the forehead which was the only part of Elaine's anatomy that she presented for the salute.

Then Lexie went in the house, and out to the kitchen to find Cinda and show her her ring.

But Elaine sat still on the porch into the deep gloaming of the evening, and let the slow tears course down her cheeks unchecked.

The days that followed brought great joy to Lexie. Ben came back within the week to tell her that he had been put in charge of an important training camp for a while, because they felt he must not go back to fighting for the present till he was in better shape physically. And besides, they felt his experience would be more worthwhile in training others just now to fight as he had done, than in going back again to fight. Incidentally he was wearing a decoration of honor for his valorous deeds under fire, and several times he was called to speak on the radio, giving a little sketch of the experiences of soldiers fighting fire. It was all very wonderful to Lexie, and she took great pride in him in her shy sweet soul. Especially when she saw the honor Judge Foster and Mr. Gordon gave him, and heard their words of commendation.

And all this had a great deal of influence with Elaine. She treated Ben with the utmost deference, and actually changed in her habitual manner toward her sister, when he was present, till Lexie almost cried with joy at the sweet way she spoke to her.

It happened a few days after all this that a letter came to Elaine from the war department, stating that her husband was still alive. It was found that he had been taken prisoner, placed in an internment camp by the enemy, and had been there so long that his health was greatly undermined. But he had at last managed to make an escape, and after various thrilling experiences in which he almost lost his life and more than once his freedom, he had managed to reach this country and get into contact with the proper authorities. They had placed him in a hospital in Washington, for he had not been fit to travel farther, and now he wanted his wife. Could she come to Washington at once to see him? He was in a very weak condition and his life was hanging by a thread, but the doctor thought that his wife's presence might materially aid in a possible recovery. Could she come at once? Cinda sniffed when she heard this.

But it was a new Elaine that came in excitement to Lexie with her letter, and asked most humbly if there was anyway she could lend her a little money to go. She was no longer weak and helpless. She was alert and eager, and ready to start at once, without going to a beauty parlor or purchasing any new clothes.

"But, are you *able* to go?" asked Lexie, looking at her in surprise.

"Able!" she said sharply. "Of *course* I'm able. Don't you understand it is my *husband* who needs me, and he may be dying! It is my husband *whom I love!* The only man I ever really loved. I *must* go, and I must take the *first train*. Will you find out how I can quickest get there?"

"Of course!" said Lexie, and went to work.

It was Lexie who arranged it all, who took her sister in a taxi to the station, asked her if she didn't want her to go with her, gave her all the money she would need, told her to let her know if she needed more, and then promised to look after the children while she was gone. As they waited for the train to be open Elaine suddenly spoke:

"Lexie, I've been a fool. I may as well tell you before I go because something might happen I never could. I knew better than to torment you the way I did. I practically knew I was chasing a fool's hope when I tried to get money out of you. But I met that Thomas lawyer and he was telling how he found a fortune for one woman, and I began to tell him about my father and how he once said he wanted to leave a small fortune to each one of his girls. Then he got me all worked up to think that perhaps this was really so. He's an old robber himself, for he got an awful lot of money out of me at one time or another while that was going on, and he promised me that it would be no trouble to make you and me both rich. But I was a fool to believe him. And I owe you a great apology. I hope you'll forgive me!"

"Oh, that's all right," said Lexie with a sigh of relief. "I'm so glad you know at last that I was telling the truth."

"Oh, of *course* I knew you were telling the truth all the time, but he kept telling me if I worked it that way you would let fall something and I could get a part of some of my father's old holdings out of people who owed him. But I was a fool."

There were sounds about now that the train was ready to go, and Elaine picked up her suitcase, and then lingered an instant.

"And Lexie," she said in a low hurried tone, "I want you to know that I think you're wonderful. If there ever was a Christian, you're that! The way you've stood all I've put upon you was something great. If they gave decorations for things like that I'd vote for one for you, and some day, maybe I can be your kind of a Christian too. I never wanted to be one before, till I watched you under fire."

Then she gave Lexie a quick kiss and hurried onto the train, and Lexie went back home with happy tears in her eyes.

She went and told Cinda about what Elaine had said, and Cinda, listened, and sniffed unbelievingly.

"Humph! Pretty Christian *she'd* make! Wull, I 'spose God *ken* do *any*thin' He *loikes,* but I shouldn't advoise His wasting His toime on such poor material. Well, it may be so, but I'll believe it when I see it!"

But a few days later when Ben Barron came down to talk over plans for their wedding in the near future, she told him of Elaine's words, and he listened gravely.

"The Lord knows how to work, doesn't He, and bring glory out of shame. My dear, there are going to be many surprises in Heaven when the decorations of honor are handed out to the quiet saints who have been under fire for years without complaint. I was reading in Timothy this morning: 'Therefore endure hardness, as a good soldier of Jesus Christ. No man that warreth entangleth himself with the affairs of this life; that he *may please Him* who hath *chosen* him to be a soldier.' I guess my dear we're going to find that all the fires we have to go through are worthwhile when we come to stand before His presence."

Novels of Enduring Romance and Inspiration by

GRACE LIVINGSTON HILL